FIVE MINUTE FANTASIES
VOLUME TWO

A collection of twenty erotic stories

Edited by Cathryn Cooper

Published by Accent Press Ltd – 2007
ISBN 190517070X / 9781905170708

Printed and bound in the UK by
Creative Print and Design

Cover Design by
Red Dot Design

Contents

Lucy And The Way That It Is
by Ralph Greco Jr

Part 1 – The Red-Haired Lady Emerges From A Long Sleep

Lucy had the kind of ass you could sink your teeth into and forget all your problems…which is exactly what I was being offered when the lady sashayed across my worn brown carpet and begged me to take her case. She smiled in that crooked way she had, reminding me as it always did of an eight ball teetering at a side pocket: all taunting potential. The fact that we hadn't seen each other in five years and this lady was now married (and not to me) didn't stop the broad from bending across the pitted top of my oak desk, lifting her tight dress and exposing snapping-tight garters, stockings and perfect silk white panties.

'Consider this a small advance,' she said, looking to her side, the smile still playing across her pale features. Lucy's husband made good money and she could afford high-class unmentionables so I figured the least I could do was take a moment to admire them. Last time I saw something that round and bright I was standing on the Catalina coastline at sunset.

As the dull grey L.A. morning slashed through my blinds like a rummy sliding off a bar stool, I knelt to eat the lady's fine alabaster ass.

'Ben...Ben. There's so much...Ben...' Lucy tried as I pressed my face up into that lovely scented smell, nuzzling into the crack of her ass while moving the side of soft panty enough so I could get my stubble chin deep between my ex's vertical smile.

Much as I remembered them, Lucy's alabaster fleshy cheeks were still oh-so-perfectly curved. There may have been a bit more to them since I had last been south of this particular lady's border, but my ex still sported one of the best derrières I had ever seen...or tasted. I quickly found Lucy's puckered pink starfish and stuck my tongue in to say hello.

From her reaction I'd say Lucy was happy to be paying in advance.

Part 2 – Two Good Friends Discuss Old Habits

The way things happened in this town, or more precisely my life, why would I be surprised that my ex looked me up, and let me 'look her up' all so I could find out if the man she had left me for five years ago was cheating on her?

Running into *Musso and Frank's* for my usual lunch libation I called Rudy over to join me in my reserved red plush booth; like any of a number of sandwich and steak runners in this eternally hungry town, Rudy could be trusted. The two of us first came to the land of lemon groves and lights in '39. The lanky guy with the runny right eye and I had gone our separate paths career-wise but nothing could hinder our friendship. As Rudy had moved up to maitre d' in the past three years, I made my bucks tracking down cheating husbands, spying on business partners and finding the hophead starlet or two. Rudy knew Lucy well, had been around to see first-hand how twisted our history had been written and was more then surprised the dame was back in my life to write another chapter.

As he slid in I regaled him with as much as I could given client-private dick privilege.

'So whatever this job is, you gonna take it?' he asked, sipping his rock and rye as I sat there next to him doing the same.

'Yeah, got to, she needs my help,' I agreed, sipping hard.

Musso and Frank's is about as dark as I keep my office. I hoped to get out to my Packard with my hat pulled low enough so I might never have to see the grey sunshine of this day.

'Old habits die ha...' Rudy began to offer, but was cut short by a loud conversation at the bar.

We both looked up and recognized the arguing couple; *he:* our congressman embroiled in what was brewing to be a very messy parting of opinion with a *she* who could be young enough to be the man's daughter...but certainly wasn't. You don't grow into Rudy's position without knowing when to put a quick stop to an escalating fury, even in the light lunchtime crowd such as *M&F's* support.

Of course Rudy downed his drink before leaving the table.

I didn't regard Lucy as a habit, but I guess in a way she was. I had long ago forgiven the leggy redhead for leaving me; she had simply weighed her options and rationalized that her new man (the very guy she now suspected of cheating on her) could provide her with a life her current man (me) could never hope to achieve. Some place deep down in my too-tight suit, under that cigarette case she had given me our second year together, my heart flipped a few extra beats knowing the lady was back in my life. And I knew damn well that gettin' back into bed (or across a desk) with Lucy would do us both more harm than good, but what could I do? There hadn't been another dame even come close to the redhead these past years and, while it might

3

sound romantic to be married to your work, it had left me a little too friendly with the sauce.

But, *habit*, I wasn't sure was the right word. More like ache, need, slap-across-your-face rushing fever when we were in each other's presence; that was what Lucy and I had had and it seemed, if the events of the morning were any indication, still had to some degree. Of course the lady could be trying some revenge while she hired yours truly to get on the hunt, but I never asked those big questions of my clients. The way I see it motivations, rhythms and reasons are for the people who hire me. I just took the pictures, stuck on the tail and collected my fee.

I gulped my drink and avoided the muted sunshine coming up Hollywood as I left *Musso and Frank's* without the usual house-specialty potpie warming my belly. I determined straight off to give ol' Mr B.J. Ralstone an honest-to-goodness, old-fashioned tail; that's if I could find him in the crawl that was Los Angeles afternoon traffic. I had my camera, my notebook and I had Mr R's schedule (as best Lucy knew it) so I was ready to stay on the man's hide like a Chinaman doing his books.

I made one of those wide U-turns my car executes so well and the earth spun off its axis as I turned the car around.

Part 3 – The Lady On Her Own Turf

I have been to most places in L.A., but I had to admit my jalopy had never spit and sputtered its way up this particular twisty canyon road. Early the next morning, after not finding Mr R at any of the spots Lucy recommended he'd be, I got a call from the missus to meet her at her home; she reckoned she had more facts for me. Shower, shave and dress and I was steering my wheezing car up this tight road

4

to a hillside encampment called, for reasons not apparent until I learned the lineage of the house, 'Amton Faire'.

As the butler (Sydney was his name) walked me under the impossibly high wooden ceiling of the front hallway, he informed me that this particular house had been built by silent film studio executive Russ Amton, back in '21. I have to say I was impressed as the man led me through the kitchen, complete with a smiling brown-skinned cook and then to the back porch with lime green shades, wood moulding and wicker chairs.

I knew Lucy had done well for herself, but I never thought her 'trading-up' had taken her this far. The house was big, even by Hollywood standards. What was it Lucy had said her husband did?

'A happy marriage has nothing to do with trappings, Ben,' the lady said, as if reading my mind, which in my case is akin to breezing through the funny papers.

Lucy had come through the door I had just walked through. She closed it behind her...then locked it.

'Hello,' I said, trying my best to look anywhere else except at the vision standing before me.

Where yesterday it had been all tight business dress, combed-up hair and neat heels, Lucy joined me as I stood to greet her in nothing more then a long silk bathrobe. She was barefoot, her red hair cascading loose to her shoulders.

'Thanks for coming at such short notice.'

'I am your employee,' I quipped.

A quick kiss on the cheek and a smile and the lady of the house walked around to the other side of the low glass table.

'Tea?' she asked, already well into pouring me a glass.

'It *is* quite the house though,' I said, tipping my glass to clink with hers as we settled in. Sitting back, the slightly resistant rocker let me go, and I winced at the ten extra pounds I had given myself for an early Christmas present. I was still under one-eighty and Lucy hadn't mentioned anything, so I figured I looked OK.

'Anything yet?' she asked, not hiding the fact that she was bare underneath the robe. As she sat back she let the front folds open enough to reveal an alabaster coastline view of her creamy white thighs almost all the way up to her forbidden red sea.

'Your husband was nowhere you told me he'd be,' I offered through another sip.

'He hardly ever is,' Lucy said and spread her legs as she sipped her tea through a smile. I spread mine and opened my jacket even wider.

In this pretty quiet porch in this high-class hilly neighbourhood, I knew all manner of encounters happened, as twisty and dangerous as the curvy canyon roads leading up here. Dupes like me – who didn't belong here, unable to afford a pass even for an afternoon's recreation – we got it the worse. I had seen plenty of men and women spend their youth being the attachment on some studio exec's arm or some Hollywood grand dame's 'gardener', only to get thrown away or weeded under, without so much as a monogrammed toothbrush for the trip down. And though I was a guy who had a few angles covered, and liked what was being offered (if indeed it was being offered) I would damn well step lightly in Lucy's neighbourhood.

'Where we goin' with this, Lucy?' I asked. Straight ahead like a swimmin' shark, that's my motto. 'You know this can't lead to anything good.'

'Good's got nothing to do with where I want to go,' the lady quipped as I tried not to look at her upper milky thighs winking hello. I caught just a whisper of Lucy's fiery red bush as she wiggled her rump hard into her chair.

I reached down, eased down my fly and opened my pants.

'My marriage doesn't mean much more to me these days than the money I will see when we can prove he's seeing somebody else,' she explained, running her free hand down the front of the robe to open it all the way. Her little red nipples were rock hard arrowhead points on her tiny round breasts, her tuft of hair glistening as she spread even more.

'That's true love for you,' I quipped, easing my cock up over and free.

If Sydney walked in what would he think of this very peculiar afternoon tea?

'I didn't really care about his money at first...' she started to explain, reaching to finally place her ice-tea down on the table between us. '...well maybe I did a bit more than I wanted to admit.'

'Well shit, Lucy...' I said, pulling out to cup my balls. '...my ego never allowed me any other possibility as to why you left.'

'It seems such a long time ago, Ben,' the lady sighed, snaking both hands down and in between her legs. 'We all do what we can.'

'We do at that,' I said, taking myself in hand as she inserted a finger.

'You should have come to me sooner,' I added, starting to pump hard into my fist.

'I *am* a married woman,' Lucy squealed, as if that admission made her even more determined. One hand pressed to her downy belly, the other in her lap, the lady definitely was inserting now.

She sighed. 'I needed a good reason, although I've wanted to see you for so many, many years.'

With this the lady suddenly sat forward, spearing herself. She bit her ample lower lip and began to shake. I did the same.

'Lucy,' I growled as I fucked my fist and the lady across from me ground her hips hard against the chair…and her hand. 'Lucy.'

'Yesss,' she said, looking straight across at me, her beady blue eyes burrowing into mine.

'Ben!' my ex screamed, as she lifted herself from the chair then sat back down with a shudder and a quick orgasm.

'Lucy,' I sighed, still stroking as a minute later the woman smiled, poured herself down and out of her chair.

'Lucy,' I whispered as the mistress of the house got on her knees, scooted across the cool porch tiles and put my cock between her lips.

I lasted a boys scout's ten seconds before I lost myself in Lucy's generous mouth.

Part 4 – The Tail And The Talk

Mutual masturbation, eating ass, coming down Lucy's throat; I must say this private eye stuff was proving pretty damn interesting! But I knew if I really wanted to 'earn' what Lucy was 'paying' I'd have to get to work finding her husband in a compromising position. Thing was, even as I limped like a soaked lime from the averted eyes of Lucy's household staff, I really had no idea if Mr B.J. Ralstone would be anywhere Lucy said he was. A cheating husband doesn't make himself visible and though it was my job to catch the guy, Lucy had reiterated, as I cleaned and zipped up, that her husband's schedule was hazy at best.

But down I went into the sunshine, through the traffic and to where the lady said she 'thought' I might find her husband on a Tuesday afternoon in springtime L.A.

I made what I call the full circle. All the way down Sunset, cruised by where she said he might be at the beach, even parked and took a walk under *Tony*'s awning, but

Lucy's husband hadn't taken a late lunch. Then it was down the interstate for a while and then the loop back into the city proper. What I was hoping for was to catch the guy on his way to or away from his mistress; I knew he'd never be so stupid as to jet around town with a floozy in the front seat!

Lucy had the *Bel Air* listed as well so I took a spin there, paid Frank the valet a quick fin to keep my car close and decided on the bar for a little look-see.

It was the usual early afternoon array: wannabes, has-beens and will-never-get-close-to-ever-bes. You stay here long enough, these faces all wash past your eye. I mean you notice the Lana Turner look-alikes, some even looking more like ol' Lana then the lady herself, and occasionally I'd get a look from one of those guys I knew from the studio who had used me for whatever so far back I'd be hard pressed to swear to it in court. But mostly I made my way, put my hat on the end of the bar, and saw a bartender I knew only by face.

'The problem is, I really do love her,' I heard a low voice say as I turned to face Mr B.J. Ralstone!

So much for wondering if he was here.

'Am I being followed?' I asked.

'I know who you are.'

'OK,' I said

'To save you and me both a lot of time, I'll say it again, I *do* love her,' he said leaning in so close I could smell his cologne.

The guy was my height, but he had ten years on me at least. Lean, dark eyes, high cheekbones, I could see why any woman would turn her head to look at Mr Ralstone. Given the guy's wealth (what the hell did he do? I still didn't know) and his obvious guts I could see this guy was the whole package.

'Well I guess that makes two of us.'

'Oh I didn't mean, Lucy, I mean Ann,' Ralstone replied leaning back then to sip the drink he had on the bar.

'Ann?'

'Lucy is a great gal, really. But it's been over between us for years. I am only sorry to say I had to push you two to this point.'

'I'm not sure I foll…'

'…you know Lucy,' he continued. 'She needs to feel she is doing things for the right reasons. She's always loved you Ben…I can call you Ben ?'

I nodded without falling off the stool and he continued.

'She married me more or less for my money. I married her for her looks and the fact that she was rather passionate in bed.' Here he stopped, sipped again and actually winked at me!

'But all that fades in time, you know that. Ann, well Ann and I are everything Lucy and I will never be.'

'So why am I am tailing you, sounds like you want the marriage over too.'

'I needed to get Lucy to come to you for a reason other than that she loves you.'

Part 5 – The Lady And The End

I wanted to meet Lucy where this all started: my office. On my desk I had papers from her husband, drawn up months ago, papers that only needed Lucy's signature.

Ralstone was a straight shooter. He had set up a trust fund for Lucy, she'd have nothing to worry about for the rest of her days and she could have her pick of houses, either Amton Faire or a quiet and spacious little bungalow at the beach. (Her husband had assured me that Lucy, being ever practical, would want the beach property as she had always complained the house was too big for her.)

I opened the door on her first knock, bade Lucy into my office and walked her to my desk. I indicated the papers on my desktop, not that I wanted to see her bent across it.

'I don't…'

'…I'd sign it if I were you.'

'But…'

'…we'll never catch him Lucy and believe me, I am good.' I said. 'Besides he wants what's best for you. This attends to that.'

'I don't understand. You found him but you didn't find him?'

'It doesn't matter,' I said, leaned in and kissed her.

The broad literally melted into my arms. Of all the strange intimate moments this lady and I had shared these past forty-eight hours, this one simple movement, a quick kiss on the lips meant more to both of us then anything we had yet managed.

As she took the chair opposite my desk, I told Lucy all I had learned the afternoon before.

'It's true,' she admitted. 'I guess I did need a reason to come to you, something to justify to myself the love I've never been able to shake.'

'Well, now you got the money…and me,' I said.

Though that realization stung me somehow, I wasn't about to let it stop all this. I've lived with worse realizations.

But Lucy reached across me and ripped-up the divorce papers!

'Tomorrow get me something simple drawn up, OK?' she said, her blue eyes full of tears. 'No money, no house. Just out so I can be 'in', here.'

Lucy was up in arms and we were down on the desk.

It's hard to surprise me. What with all I've seen it takes a bit more than my horse winning at the track or gettin' a little extra bourbon poured in my glass to have me raising my thick eyebrow. It has never ever been my experience that someone doesn't go for the fast buck when they can. But this broad was putting a spin on my week, and, I dared to dream, the rest of my life.

A Little Bit Of Luxury
by Kitti Bernetti

There's something about things being brand new which really does it for me. Always has. I don't know why. Even when I was a child there was that sheer joy of opening a new packet. The cellophane would crack in the silence as I ripped the sticky label off. I'd take the item out carefully and lay it on the table. Even something mundane like a new school shirt would bring me total satisfaction. With all the reverence of performing a Japanese tea ceremony, I would unfold it, take out the pins and the cardboard collar and hold it to my body, all stiff with starch and that clean smell of cotton newness. It was like no one else had ever touched it. I was going to be the privileged one. Be the first to defile it. I'm the same now. Except I've set my sights a lot higher.

I like luxury. That's why I'm here this morning in this recently built penthouse flat. The block's just opened. It's the ultimate in expensive living. Everything bright spanking new. I can't wait to indulge myself. Thinking about it sends shivers juddering up my spine. I'm such a lucky girl.

There is nothing like the feel of a fresh bedroom before any other person has slept in it. Rick said I should phone him as soon as I got into the flat. But I'm going to put down my handbag and the keys and breathe in that new-paint smell. I want to savour my moment alone just a bit longer.

My heels sink into the white carpet as I make my way to the window. New sheer stockings swish against the lining of my black silk dress bought earlier today. The skirt's tight and constricting, just the way I like it. Everything I have on today is new, as a homage to this flat. I wanted it to be perfect for the first time in here. I'm so wound up, so excited. I don't know whether to take in the view first or to turn and look back at the whiteness of the smooth walls. I take off my neat black jacket. My mobile rings out in the silence. Damn.

'You couldn't wait, could you?'

My impatience at the interruption is momentary. He can tell I'm smiling now.

'Are you in?'

'Of course I'm in.'

'Congratulations, darling.'

'Thank you.'

'Is it fabulous?'

'Totally and utterly. I've always wanted a flat like this.'

'I've always wanted a woman like you. And now I've got her.'

'You're sweet. Thank you.'

'Okay. So tell me about the apartment. Talk me through it. What can you see?'

I keep on smiling. Trust Rick to say 'apartment'. He watches too much American television. But then he's as excited as I am about this morning and the new flat. And preparing himself for our little game. I can tell. I can hear him settle down, invisible on the other end of the phone, I can see him clearly in my mind's eye. He'll be sitting at his desk, legs up, one ankle folded over the other. His hand lying in his lap, ready.

'I can see the view. London looks so fabulous at dawn from up here. I feel like I'm on top of the world.'

'Okay, enough. You're not selling it to me. Let's get down to business. Have you been in the bedroom yet?' Rick doesn't hang around. I always have to slow him down.

I'm holding the phone close to my lips, glossy with pillar-box red lipstick, as I walk slowly over. 'I'm going there now. Do you want to know what I'm wearing?'

'Yeah, yeah I do.' I hear him breathe in slowly and imagine his hand resting now against his crotch.

'I've got a new black dress on. The skirt is very, very tight. So tight I can hardly breathe. But it has a slit up the back so that I can walk. The slit is quite high, almost as high as my bottom.'

'Um.' Rick likes to let me know he is still there. Still connected. At times like this he's a man of few words. He likes me to talk.

'I'm in the bedroom now. It's absolutely gorgeous, just like we've always talked about. The walls are a mink brown. There's a massive bed in the centre of the room with a fur cover. Nothing else. It's clean and totally unused. I'm going to be the first to use it Rick. Do you want me to get on the bed?'

'I do. I want you to.'

'Not yet, I'm going to tease you a bit first. Guess what's on the wall, I'm looking at it now.'

His voice becomes thick. 'A mirror.'

'That's right, a huge great wall to ceiling mirror.'

'Are you still standing?'

'Yes.'

'Undo your dress.'

I reach up and pull the zip slowly down imagining Rick listening to the sound of it like a cat's purr. The material peels away. 'I'm taking it off my shoulders now.' The dress drips to the floor.

'Step out.' A moment's silence then he remembers something. 'What shoes are you wearing?'

'Which do you think?'

'The red ones.'

'Uh huh. Red and high with fuck me heels.'

'Keep them on.'

'Say please. You bad bad boy.'

'No way.'

'Then this is where I stop and the dress goes back on.'

'No way. Please, pleeease.'

He knows I'm only joking about getting dressed. I'd die of frustration if I stopped now. I can feel my heart pounding. It always does when I get down to my underwear. Yes, you've guessed it, new on today. I could take prizes in shopping. Shame it isn't an Olympic sport.

'Where's your hand? Resting by your cock, I hope.'

'You guess right. Top marks to the lady in high heels and stockings.'

'How did you guess I was wearing stockings and not tights?'

'My favourite. I knew I was in for a treat. After all, it's Saturday and I'm having to work.'

'Poor baby. If it's nice and quiet there, why don't you undo your trousers and get that cock right out.' I move my legs apart till I'm standing in a straddling position. A scent, my animal scent, reaches my nose as I detect a moist creaminess soiling the lacy gusset of my nice new knickers. I feel very relaxed. Very in control.

'Thank you ma'am. That's the best offer I've had all day.'

I imagine him undoing each button of his flies, one by one, trembling a little. He always tries to undo the buttons too quickly when I'm not there. Like a little boy dipping into the sweetie jar, he can't wait.

'Now just picture me standing here in front of the mirror. Red shoes, black stockings. I'm feeling sooooo warm. My new knickers were very very expensive. Coffee brown lace with a sheer net panel over my little bush. Do you know, I just can't wait any longer. I know it's bad, very very bad, but I can't resist stroking that little beaver. She's waited so long and been so good. Mmmm I wish you were here. If you were, you know what I'd do?'

'What?' I hear Rick swallow. I stroke myself through the sheer fabric and feel my own warm liquid seeping out, dirtying the lace.

'Are you holding your cock?'

'Yes.'

'Tight?'

'Yes.'

'I'm afraid I'd just have to get down on my knees in front of you.' I paused. My lips were dry and I ran a wet tongue over them.

'And –?'

'And I'd have to take that lovely big lollipop of a cock in my hands and run my tongue all down the side and then back up again to the tip.'

'Mmmm.' He moaned and I knew he'd started pulling his hand up and down the shaft of a gorgeously erect penis.

'Rick?'

'What?'

'Just checking you're listening. I hope you're good and hard.'

'Rock hard.' He breathed deeply and I felt my throat constrict, reacting to his mounting excitement.

'If I were kneeling in front of you, I'd take the tip of your cock in my mouth and suck it with little licks. Tasting you on my lips I'd rub you over my face and in my hair.'

'I want you to sit on the bed,' he said urgently.

17

'I'm sitting.'

'Lie back.'

I felt the fur warm and slidey on my near naked skin. My suspender belt constricted me like a rope. I liked the feeling of it tightly wrapped around my waist, straining over my ample buttocks.

'Lick your finger.' He commanded and I obeyed. I let him hear the sound of my tongue lubricating my finger and I knew what he was going to ask me to do.

'Put your finger in your knickers.'

I breathed a huge sigh of relief. I'd been wanting to do that so badly. Wanting to feel the relief of something, anything, to probe my warm pussy. She needed desperately to be stroked. She'd been needing it ever since I got in here. All night I had thought of this moment, longed for it to come and now, here it was. Rick breathed at the other end of the phone, working himself up in time with my stroking movements. Completely detached, we were completely together. In our own little worlds and in each others' heads.

The lace of my knickers was totally sodden now as I drew them aside. They rode up the cheeks of my arse, cutting me, but I didn't care. I wished I had time to take them off but time was running out. I knew I had to get a move on.

My voice sounded low and croaky and my eyes looking back at me from the mirror were half closed and dreamy as I said, 'I'm looking at my clit in the mirror now, all pink and swollen. I wish you were here.'

'So do I, darling, but you can imagine me. Just listen to what I tell you. Put your finger in your honey pot, get it really sweet and moist and then whisk gently round and round. Imagine it's my tongue on the tip of that juicy little cherry, lapping you up.' As he spoke and I moved my finger over my soft warm flesh I could hear him furiously working away at his tool. I could hear his own moisture lapping up over the head of his cock as I imagined him pumping up and down, the muscles in his arm standing out as he gripped and pulled with tightly wrapped fingers.

I closed my eyes and listened to his words growling instructions at me insistently.

'Work that finger harder, harder, press against yourself. Imagine it's me sucking and drinking your juices, imagine my face buried in your sweet little pussy, breathing you in...'

I groaned, I moaned and, like standing under a shower of rain, I felt my skin tingle and the hairs over my body stand on end as I came, arching my back into a shuddering mind-blowing orgasm. As I came to, I listened down the phone to Rick's guttural breathing. I listened with a smile as I heard him grunt, the way I had heard him grunt with satisfaction so many times before.

'Does that feel better?' I asked.

'Mmm,' he murmured. 'Though you're going to have to get this uniform cleaned again, love. Can't have a security guard with a mucky uniform now can we?'

The door bell of the flat went and I looked at my watch. Nine o'clock. Bang on time. 'Got to go, sweetheart. See you later,' I said, shoving the mobile in my bag and fishing my clipboard out at the same time. I ran my fingers quickly through my hair, slipped back into my dress and pulled my business jacket hastily over my shoulders. The bell rang again as I opened the door.

'Mr and Mrs Allen?' I beamed my best estate agent's smile. 'Thank you for coming so early, this is going to be a popular flat. I've got ten people booked in for viewings today. Come through to the bedroom first,' I gushed. 'It's truly spectacular.' I just managed to smooth the fur cover on

19

the bed, my hand brushing over a small traitorous wet patch, before they followed me in.

Dancing For Women
by Stephen Albrow

Dancing for women is different, thought Lucy, as she stood in the car park of the Kitten Club awaiting her cue. It was her first time performing for an all-girl audience. She'd done strip routines and kissagrams for hundreds of middle-aged men in the past, but she'd never even *been* in a lesbian bar before, let alone stripped naked and danced in one. She felt her body shivering, partly due to nervousness but mainly due to the icy breeze that was shooting up her navy-blue miniskirt and cooling the bare flesh above her stocking tops. The birthday girl was a member of the police force, so she'd been asked to wear her saucy WPC outfit. It looked fantastic, but the tiny skirt and revealing blouse were hardly suited to the cold March weather.

Lucy hugged her arms across her chest, rubbing away the goose bumps on her breasts. Her blouse was unbuttoned to below bra level, exposing her cleavage to the cold night air. Her nipples had frozen into rigid bullets, almost sharp enough to rip through her white lace bra cups. *The girls are gonna love that*, she thought, her nervousness beginning to fade. Her desire to get out of the cold was now far greater than her fear of dancing for a room full of lesbians. She muttered 'come on' underneath her breath. She seemed to have been standing around for ages, but then, at last, her music started!

Here goes, thought Lucy, opening the door of the Kitten Club. It opened straight out on to the main bar, where the birthday girl and her friends were partying. The music went silent, like it always did at that point in Lucy's routine, allowing her to point to the birthday girl and shout 'You're under arrest!' Instantly, everyone in the place turned and looked straight at the sexy WPC. There was a moment's pause, while everyone figured out what was happening, then suddenly the wolf-whistling started, closely followed by the dirty chants.

'Get your tits out for the girls,' sang the revellers, as Lucy marched towards the birthday girl, Jenna. *Perhaps dancing for women won't be any different, after all*, thought Lucy, as she saw how raucous the crowd had become, not to mention the way the women were ogling her body. Lucy took confidence from that – she knew that if everyone was bedazzled by her tits and arse, then it was guaranteed that she could dominate the room. The music started up again, just as Lucy reached for Jenna's hand. She dragged the pretty young cop out in front of her friends, then sat her down on a plastic chair.

Jenna looked even more nervous than Lucy felt, but Lucy was used to dealing with nervous customers. Part of her act involved getting the customer to lick chocolate sauce off her cleavage. But most men seemed to be terrified of going anywhere near her bosoms, especially if their wives were in the audience. In fact, most men were terrified throughout her act, in case they embarrassed themselves in front of their friends. They were scared of not looking at ease with a gorgeous woman, or of getting an erection and looking like a sleaze, or of *not* getting an erection and appearing gay!

With Jenna, most of these worries were irrelevant, so Lucy hoped her nerves would quickly fade. Her friends began clapping along in time with the music, as Lucy went into her dance routine. She circled Jenna's body a couple of times, before sitting down in the WPC's lap. Their lips almost touched in a teasing kiss, but as Jenna leaned forward to accept the kiss, Lucy jumped up again and span around.

Lucy leant down and touched her toes, making her skirt ride high above her stocking tops. As the audience cheered, she reached for her belt and unhooked one of her props, a plastic truncheon. Playfully, she took aim at her buttocks and then struck herself a couple of blows. She then turned around and pointed at Jenna. Next, she looked back out at the audience, as if to ask them the question – should I spank her?

Eager cries of approval greeted Lucy's suggestion, so she made the birthday girl stand up. Suddenly, Jenna couldn't stop giggling, so Lucy knew that she was up for some fun. She lifted up the WPC's skirt, sending the audience into raptures by exposing the between-cheeks strap of her purple thong. Lucy gave Jenna's buttocks a mischievous grope, then she took a step back and went to work with the truncheon.

In perfect rhythm with the music, Lucy delivered five quick blows to Jenna's behind. Each one was greeted by a holler from the audience. There were yells of 'spank her' and cries of 'harder'. One woman even shouted 'Me next, officer!' Everyone one in the room was really getting into it, and that brought out the best in Lucy. Every aspect of her performance grew in self-assurance. Her sexy gyrations became even sexier. Her dirty dancing grew even dirtier!

As for the moment when the strip-tease started, Lucy completely brought the house down. She made Jenna undo the remaining buttons on her blouse, then even before the blouse was off, she pulled at the Velcro fastening at the front of her bra. The cups sprang aside, uncovering her bosoms, the nipples still rock-hard and pointed from the cold. In the very same movement, Lucy did a twirl, then sent her miniskirt plummeting to the floor. Next, she bent down, scooped up the skirt and chucked it into the grateful audience.

'How do I look?' Lucy asked the birthday girl, as she led her back across to the chair.

'Beautiful,' said Jenna, sitting down like she was told to, then allowing Lucy to straddle her body. Lucy liked Jenna's answer. She'd never looked at another woman before and seen such an obvious look of lust in her eyes. Every man she danced for wanted her body, but she'd never expected Jenna to feel the same way.

'Your friends will love it if you touch me,' said Lucy, the professional guiding the amateur through the performance.

'Gladly,' said Jenna, then she grinned at her pals, before grabbing hold of Lucy's arse cheeks. As the WPC's fingers spread out across her buttocks, Lucy reached in the pocket of her gaping blouse. She removed a toy gun, which was filled with chocolate sauce. Lucy leaned back and pushed out her tits, then shot a dollop of sauce on one of her nipples.

Jenna didn't need any more guidance; her mouth was on Lucy's nipple in an instant. She swallowed it whole and licked up the chocolate, then gleefully gobbled up even more jug. The audience went crazy, shouting 'Get a room!' and calling the performers 'Lesbo sluts!' The atmosphere was truly electric, but Lucy still felt able to take it higher.

Lucy squirted some chocolate on her other nipple, then watched as Jenna's tongue went in hot pursuit. She lapped up every last drop of the delicious sauce, then continued sucking even after the syrup had vanished. Sweet sensations erupted in Lucy's body, as the lesbian WPC titillated her teats in a way that surprised and even shocked her. The birthday girl's nerves had completely vanished, to be replaced with an overwhelming confidence. Taking courage from the joyful reaction of her friends, she ran her hands all over Lucy's body, groping the kissagram's stockings and suspenders, while flicking her tongue all over her breasts.

Lucy had never lost control of a performance before, but Jenna seemed to be taking charge. Most men get shy when confronted by a beautiful, naked woman in a crowded room, but Jenna was thriving; pretty Jenna was having the time of her life. She grabbed the toy gun from Lucy and squirted some chocolate sauce on Lucy's lips, then all of a sudden the two girls were kissing. Jenna kissed the chocolate off Lucy's mouth, then her tongue pressed deep between her lips.

The noise in the room reached fever pitch, as the real WPC kissed the saucy one. Lucy had never known a customer to react so boldly before, and there was nothing she could do to stop herself melting in the young woman's arms. There was something in the way that Jenna had sucked her nipples that excited Lucy beyond all measure. The chocolate routine was usually so clumsy, so awkward, with some petrified man licking gingerly at her teats and just wanting the whole thing over as fast as possible. But playful, passionate, adventurous Jenna didn't seem to want the routine ever to end. And she hadn't just gobbled up the chocolate sauce; she'd kissed, licked and sucked Lucy's swollen nipples as if the two of them were long-term lovers making out in a private room.

Lucy could still feel her nipples tingling, even now that Jenna was kissing her lips. She'd lost it for a moment, but she had to reassert control. She was meant to be the professional performer and she couldn't allow herself to be overawed just because she was dancing for a woman, not a man. Her act normally climaxed with a split-second flash of pussy, so she extricated herself from Jenna's embrace and tried to get things back on track. She placed a hand on the front of her knickers and thrust her crotch into Jenna's face. On the final beat of music, she would rip off the silk. But something distracted her – her knickers were wet!

For the first time ever, Lucy missed her cue, tugging off her knickers a second too late. The Velcro strips came apart as planned, but the scent of cuntjuice rising from her gash wasn't something she'd expected at all. Neither was Jenna's cheeky reaction. Instinctively, the WPC squirted a dollop of chocolate sauce between Lucy's thighs.

'You are a bad girl,' Lucy said, as the audience roared its approval.

'I know,' said Jenna, already leaning forward. She stuck out her tongue and touched the sauce on Lucy's clit. Lucy heard herself gasp, as a clitoral spasm sent a feel-good sensation coursing through her veins. Jenna had licked her so softly, so gently, giving promise of something, intriguing her, arousing her.

Normally Lucy couldn't wait for her act to end, but for once she was sad to hear the music stop and the ovation start. As she and Jenna took their bows before the delirious audience, Lucy sensed that this had been a missed opportunity. Dancing for women had been special for her. Her nipples had been licked many times before, both onstage and off, but not even her favourite boyfriends had shown such a delicate, sensuous oral touch as Jenna. Gazing out at the crowd of cheering lesbians, she suddenly realised why. Of course, only another woman could ever really know how to satisfy a female erogenous zone. After all, she'd sucked many cocks in her life, but she'd never had a cock, so she could only guess what would feel nice. But Lucy knew what she liked having done to her pussy, so she'd know how to pleasure another girl, just as Jenna would know how to pleasure her.

'Happy birthday!' Lucy told Jenna, giving her a final kiss on the cheek. Both girls were still buzzing from the thrill of the performance, and from the delighted reaction of the crowd, which seemed to show no sign of abating. Everyone seemed to want the moment to last for ever, as if they all knew it was the high-point of the evening, and the rest would be just an anti-climax. And no one felt that more than Lucy. As she hurried off to the ladies to change, she felt an overwhelming sadness that she'd not been able to finish what she'd started.

A wistful Lucy could still hear the cheering, as she stood before the mirror re-doing her make up. She felt pleased that she'd shown everybody such a good time, but it was Jenna's surprise reappearance that really lifted her spirits. The WPC came bursting into the ladies, lifting off her dress, as she walked over to Lucy. She led the kissagram into a vacant cubicle, then dropped straight down on to her knees.

'I think I might have missed some chocolate sauce,' said Jenna, pressing her face between Lucy's thighs. Her lips formed a circle around Lucy's clit, then her tongue started stimulating the sensitive nub. Lucy gazed down at the gorgeous woman kneeling down before her, happy and relieved to have her back again. She placed her hands on top of Jenna's head, holding her face against her cunt. This time she wasn't going to let the birthday girl escape so easily. This time Jenna was going to keep on licking until Lucy had experienced the orgasm she so desperately craved.

'Make me come,' Lucy whispered, then she bucked her pelvis forward. Jenna's mouth slid through folds of soft pink skin, till her lips were circling the kissagram's orifice. She

27

thrust her tongue forward, entering the sticky hole, then slapped her hands against Lucy's buttocks. As her fingers dug into the toned, tanned cheeks, Jenna began to pump her tongue back and forward.

Jenna's clitoral licks had been soft and tender, but the taste of Lucy's pussy seemed to bring out the beast in her. Lucy's orifice was tight, but Jenna wouldn't be beaten. She jammed her tongue through the tensed up muscles, her forceful licks making Lucy squeal. Again and again, she pushed her tongue back and forward, desperate to feel the first orgasmic pulsation rippling through Lucy's muscles. She could already smell and taste the sex-juice, as well as hear the squeals, so she knew Lucy's orgasm was fast approaching. All that was missing was the first big pulse, so she drove her tongue forward as hard as she could.

Lucy let out a high-pitched moan, as her cunt muscles parted to receive Jenna's tongue. She felt her knees start to buckle, so she released her grip on Jenna's head. She pressed her hands against the sides of the toilet cubicle, steadying herself against the wooden walls. A huge wave of sexual pressure was pulsing through her pussy muscles, causing her insides to spasm around Jenna's tongue, which was two-inches deep inside her hole. A massive orgasm was welling up inside her, ready to burst out at any moment. She wanted it to happen, but her body was demanding further stimulation. Like a sneeze that continually wrinkles the nose but doesn't quite come, her orgasm left her standing on the precipice.

Jenna pulled her tongue out of Lucy's pussy and looked up into the kissagram's face. She could see the frenzied sexual tension in her eyes; the about-to-burst feeling in her flushed pink features. Sliding her hands up Lucy's body, she reached her pert, curvaceous jugs. Her fingers tightened around Lucy's nipples, then her tongue sprang back into action. It slid over Lucy's orifice, en route to her clit, where just one lick was enough to make it happen.

Lucy beat her hands against the cubicle walls, as a clitoral spasm re-ignited the wild pulsations between her legs. Another wave of tension went shooting through her pussy muscles. Another quickly followed, accompanied by a sudden outpouring of syrupy juice. Lucy started screaming, just as Jenna started licking. Suddenly, her tongue was everywhere, lapping up the streams of come with obvious enjoyment. Jenna's passionate licks served to heighten what was already the biggest orgasm of the kissagram's life. She stared down at the WPC, unable to believe that another woman was capable of making her feel so good.

'Kiss me now,' said Lucy, helping the WPC back up to her feet. Their lips came together, but not for long, because Lucy wanted to return the favour. She leaned down and started kissing Jenna's breasts, but Jenna just pushed her down to her knees. Her purple thong was wet with juice. Lucy tugged it aside, then licked Jenna's cunt.

'Now *you* make *me* come,' Jenna said, as Lucy zeroed in on her clit. She planted six wet kisses on the sticky-out stub, then opened wide and licked it hard. The WPC started groaning immediately, like she was almost ready to climax. *She must have really loved the taste of my fanny*, thought Lucy, as she placed a hand on Jenna's gash. Her finger pushed between two moist lips, then carefully slotted deep inside.

Jenna's sex was full of tension; Lucy could feel it straight away. The muscles were gripping skin-tight to her finger, which she pushed back and forward, while licking Jenna's clit. Lucy smiled as she detected the first real hard convulsion, reminding her of her recent climax. Wanting to feel that same intensity again, she jumped back to her feet and parted her thighs.

Lucy kept her finger in Jenna's pussy, and the WPC responded in kind. Their bodies pressed together, their breasts and mouths meeting, as they finger-fucked each other's cunts. After a matter of seconds, Lucy felt her earlier orgasm coming back to the boil, but it was Jenna who pulled her lips away from Lucy's and was first to yell with orgasmic delight. She spasmed hard around Lucy's finger, her juices gushing into the palm of the kissagram's hand. Lucy's response was instant – just feeling Jenna's climax was enough to bring her back to the glorious orgasmic heights of moments ago.

The two women yelled the sexual tension out of their bodies, then with the screaming over, they could kiss once more. Their lips tasted of pussy, a familiar taste to Jenna, but a new one to Lucy, and one that she'd quickly learned to like. Dancing for women had been different for her, and so had making love to one – different, exciting and wholly fulfilling. There'd be many more men for her to dance for in the future, but Lucy hoped, in fact, she couldn't wait, to dance for women again.

Plain Jane
by J. Carron

I laid the advert on my knees and looked around at my
fellow guinea pigs. Piggie we all were one way and another.
Right little hogs. I'd never been a beauty, not like my sister.
I had the brains. She had the cute stuff – long legs, button
nose and pert breasts.

Of the girls in this room, there wasn't a button nose
among us. Plain. A rotten word to describe a poor
defenceless female. Plain I was though, and I knew it.
Cruelly, this waiting room had a whacking great mirror in it.
It wasn't one of those discreet 'just-checking-my-lipstick'
mirrors. It was flipping huge. More of a look-at-your-ugly-
mug mirror. I'd never had need of the lipstick mirrors
because I'd never worn the stuff. Just like I couldn't
remember the last time I'd been to a hairdresser. I realised a
long time ago that painting and preening my sad features
was time wasted. What I was born with I was stuck with.
Acceptance was my mantra, not camouflage. Until now, that
is.

I looked at the advert again. 'Women Wanted for Clinical
Trial.' The payment was good and the letter I'd received
inviting me to this first session was intriguing. *Are you
attractive to men?* It asked. I scratched an inky black cross

in the 'no' box there. Do you have difficulty finding a partner? Yes sirree, you betcha. A couple of sad fumblings at university parties summed up my adventures with men. As soon as they saw me outside in the light, any half good-looking ones suddenly found urgent reasons to get home. And they must have lost the telephone number I pressed desperately in their palms because none of them phoned. Only twice had I ever been taken back to a fellow student's bedroom. One was so drunk I practically had to carry him. The resulting coupling (yes, there was one) was like life. Nasty, brutish and short.

'Can you all please come in now?' The nurse in the white coat swished open the door to a small lecture theatre and twenty unlovely women took their seats. I won't bore you with the science because pheromones aren't my thing. But basically the drug we would be testing, if we decided to go ahead, worked on the principle of butterfly lust. Sorry, have I lost you? Well, they lost me at one point but I did grasp from the cartoon diagrams that butterflies exude some sort of scent which drives the opposite sex to distraction. Yes thanks. I was twenty-nine and I'd like some of that. Correction. Lots of it.

The next stage was each of us entering a cubicle with a doc who questioned us on everything from how many sexual partners we'd had to our diet and lifestyle. Mine checked out as Miss Lonely. Work, more work and nights at home with a packet of Doritos. The doctor then checked through the blood and other samples we had provided weeks ago. At the end, he gave a triumphant smile and told me I was just the sort of saddo they were looking for. It was then he handed me the magic bottle. Blue pills. I was to take one a day, before breakfast, and record on the datasheet my experiences. Then I must report back to this office at the date he marked on the front. Maybe I imagined it, but I thought he gave me a wink as he wished me luck and assured me I'd notice an upturn in my 'activities'.

It was well after breakfast, but I had nothing to lose. I've never been a conformist, so I broke the rules and shoved in one of those little blue beauties straight away. As I went to bed at the end of the day I felt extraordinarily rested, more relaxed than I had for some time. The next morning, curious to see whether anything had changed, I went into town and had my second pill washed down with a cup of cappuccino sitting on a squishy leather sofa in the high street coffee shop. I sat by the window and watched men passing. Wouldn't it be heaven to have any one I wanted? Like a skinny woman in a patisserie I became choosy. If this experiment worked, I wouldn't have to take any old specimen sporting a limp dick and a weak chat line. I'd be the one choosing.

As I watched geeks, ghouls and I-*love*-myself-in-these-jeans specimens of the male gender mooching past, I crossed them scornfully off my mental list. Then I clocked, standing with a clipboard, one of those guys who try to get you interested in giving to charity. I sat up. Here was a dream come true. All those guys are out of work actors or models, that's what makes them happy to approach strangers and chat them up just to extract cash. It also happens to put them tops on the gorgeous guy scale.

Here was a top-drawer testosterone dispenser in seriously stylish packaging. A head above the other men on the street, his face was squarish, framed with understated sideburns and peppered with stubble. Streaky blonde hair, dishevelled and not unclean, made him look as if he had just got up from a night's torrid lovemaking. In repose, he looked slightly snooty as if he was above all this. But when he made his choice of victim and zeroed in on (I noted) a pretty girl, his blue grey eyes lit up and the dimple on his chin dispersed in a widening smile. It may have been something to do with taking that pill, but as I absently spooned bitter cappuccino foam into my mouth I began to feel disgustingly horny.

I knew it was ridiculous to think it would work that quickly, but paracetamols did, why not this? I wished I could have checked my pasty face in a handbag mirror but I didn't possess one. Still, this was more a recce than a fully armoured assault with combat gear. Downing my coffee, and gathering my handbag, I paid, hearing the comforting rattle of those little blue pills. Once outside on the street, I wondered where those pheromones would appear. Would I breathe them out or would they exude from my skin like scented oil?

I watched my prey as he combed his fingers through a mop of hair, nonchalantly collapsing it back onto his forehead while he listened to the girl and scribbled on his clipboard. I imagined his hands cupping the back of my head, and a feeling shot through my stomach like I was going down in a fast lift. Then, horrors, he looked up and our pupils locked. Instead of turning away embarrassed as I would have done in the past when I thought I had no chance, I found myself staring back. Then, most unlike the old me, my brazen lips edged upwards into a smile. Mr Cool responded with a raised eyebrow. My heart tap danced. Then, after pausing longingly, he turned and reluctantly went back to his interviewee.

I let out the breath I had been holding. This was power. I had experienced it at work. But never, ever with men. I turned and drifted thoughtfully off through the shoppers. Remember that old song about walking down this street before but the pavement always staying beneath your feet until... Well this was my moment of revelation. I was suddenly jet propelled with new hope. Observing in a way I had never done before, I looked at men and women as they floated past. The attractive ones had a sex-filled swagger. It came in their walk, the way they held their heads up, the way they tossed their hair. They believed in themselves. They had it in spadefuls and I couldn't even muster a teaspoonful.

Then I caught my reflection in a shop window. That word plain came back, slapping me across my insignificant face. My outlined faded into the background. Black trousers, brown jumper, safe duffle coat. I was the colour of the street, grey, unchallenging. I turned to look at the clothes on the mannequins. Bright, in-your-face reds, upstart black and white checks, cinched in waists, hip-hugging lycra. The sort of clothes I wouldn't even try on. They could never have my name on, could they?

I went in. It was a shop I knew was too expensive. The sort of shop where they serve you, where clothes aren't jam-packed on the rails like a jumble sale but where they hang in stately splendour, to be admired and savoured. I told the salesgirl I wanted to try on every one of the items on the mannequins. Eagerly she rushed off then stood outside the changing room ready to hand me more as I slipped in and out of the luxurious materials. Pure new wool, soft leather, textured silk. I wasn't fat, never had been. In fact I'd forgotten what my body looked like. I spent my time, day or night, in a self-imposed uniform of loose fitting shift-dresses with round necked jumpers designed to disguise, not enhance.

As I completed one outfit exactly as it had been in the window I gingerly stepped out wanting to see the effect in a large mirror. With my new pheromones working overtime, the mirror had become friend, not foe. 'Wow,' said my salesgirl. 'I'd never have believed you were the same woman.' I gave her a sideways look. 'No, honestly, I'm not just saying that. You've got a fantastic figure. You just need, if you don't mind…' she advanced towards my hips, I felt her hands over my waist and then smoothing the cashmere jumper over my stomach. Then she paused at my waist, tightening the leather belt, instantly granting me an hourglass shape. It wasn't an unpleasant feeling, somewhat like being frisked at an airport, only more sensuous. 'Mmm,' she swooned, 'that's wonderful perfume you're wearing.' Nil points my friend. I wasn't wearing any. Never have. I looked at her tight arse and small breasts. What was happening to me, for heaven's sake? I was fancying girls! 'There, that's better. If you've got a tiny waist and a full bust, why hide it?' She stepped back and looked at me admiringly, with a longing in her wide mouse eyes. These pheromones were gold dust. I wasn't just becoming attractive to the male sex but to everyone. A perfectly hetero sales girl was developing a crush on me.

'You look gorgeous,' she sighed. Was it true? There were certainly curves there, curves I'd given up on. 'If you don't mind my saying though, you ought to get yourself a decent bra. Support is vital.'

I was persuaded. I bought two of the complete outfits, one of which I chose to wear immediately, and also some madly expensive underwear, a designer perfume and a pair of kid leather boots costing a month's wages. Sod it. A months' wages had bought me a million-dollar thrill. As I sashayed out with my bags, the girl pressed her card on me. I watched her lip-glossed mouth as she said, 'I do personal shopping sessions. Feel free to phone me any time.' She held my arm a fraction longer than was decent. I smiled and left. I was the one doing the choosing now. Maybe I'd phone her. Maybe not.

But now, like a room that's newly painted makes the curtains look shabby, I was aware of my nothing hairdo and porridge-coloured winter face. I looked over the road and there was one of London's premier hairdressers. They didn't have an instant appointment, but could do me in an hour. Just enough time for me to wander into the nearest department store and submit to one of those make-up girls.

Half an hour of being gently caressed, painted with brushes and moulded with expensive cosmetics made me feel like a princess. The sensation of the make-up girl's lithe body pressed warmly against me, her breath drifting across my skin, sent my head reeling. At fever pitch I prayed to God the pills were going to work in the way I hoped. If not my pussy would surely self-destruct with frustration.

As I looked at my made-up self in the mirror, I felt as if I were wearing a magic mask. My ordinary features were transformed into a vibrant terrain of shadows and light. Turning my face to the warm lights, I discovered I had cheekbones. Could those really be *my* luscious claret red lips and eyelashes to die for? As she admired her work, making adjustments here and there, the girl said, 'I love doing faces like yours. If you don't mind my saying, scrubbed clean your face looks quite ordinary. But it's very symmetrical, like lots of models. So it's easy to transform. Your skin hasn't got a blemish. It's the perfect sort of face for going to town on. These smouldery, smoky colours really suit you. I love them. Don't you?' I could have kissed her, partly with gratitude and partly because she was extraordinarily cute. I bought every potion, lotion, powder, gloss and sparkly, sprinkly pot of witchery and sorcery she had on offer. 'Come back again,' she wrinkled her nose. 'I'll do you for free any time.'

The hairdresser pouted and lifted up a skein of listless hair. He looked as if he was fingering a rodent that had expired messily on the front step of the salon.

'Well, we have our work cut out here, haven't we?' He yanked a comb through my offensive hair and let it sag.

'Who cut this for you last time? Or have you never had it cut? It's very long.'

'Me,' I confessed.

'No surprise there then.' I gave him a look which I hoped said, 'okay, smartarse, I'm paying through the nose for this, just do your job'.

'Still,' he mused, redeeming himself, 'the raw material's good. You're lucky your hair's thick and because it's had no colouring it's in good order. Pierre,' he clicked his fingers, 'shampoo my lady now.' I lay back and let the shampoo boy massage my scalp. I could really feel those pheromones kicking in with a vengeance as he worked on me. Deep down inside my sex, the rhythmic massaging made me swell, feeling the ebb and flow of my senses dipping into my depths. He pushed his fingers into the indents at the back of my skull and I felt my meridians clearing, the blood surging through my body. As he wrapped the towel around my head he almost had to help me to the stylist's chair, I felt so relaxed.

Like a sculptor practising his art, the hairdresser crimped his way, snipping a sprig here, teasing a curl there. Once he'd cut he started with the hairdryer, running his fingers through now bouncy, flouncy, frankly fantastic hair. All superciliousness had evaporated as he walked behind me revealing his handiwork to me with a hand-mirror. I had obviously proved to be his most remarkable transition. Like a lion with a mane of curls I hardly recognised myself. Handing over the plastic, I'd have happily paid double for this feeling and tipped him an obscene amount just to prove who was boss.

Bags swinging, looking and feeling like a Hollywood starlet, I made my way back to the scene of my earlier conquest. Tousle-haired Romeo was still there, and I stood on the pavement admiring his simply staggering beauty. I wanted him more than anything I had ever wanted. And for once in my life I believed I really could have a guy like that. As he talked to his current victim, I saw his eyes zero in on me, and do the most perfect double take. He drank me up like a man in the Mojave Desert cracking open a freezing can of beer. He finished and dismissed the person he was with. I stood and watched, challenge in my every fibre, as he placed one leg in front of the other to ease his way over to me. He got the clipboard out. 'Ma'am, could you spare a few minutes to answer some questions.'

'Certainly,' I pouted crimson lips at him.

His voice entered my ears and shot straight to the top of my legs. What the hell he was saying I couldn't register. None of it mattered until the last bit where he snapped shut his clipboard and said. 'Look, I've finished for the day and what I really wanted to ask is whether you'll come for a drink with me.'

'Maybe,' I said. 'On one condition?'

'What's that?'

'Champagne's my favourite drink. Could you run to that?'

'As a poor charity worker, I'll have to take up robbing banks. But for you, it'd be worth it.'

Looks, brains and a sense of humour. The man was a triple whammy.

We drank a bottle together, starting off in a dimly lit bar and finishing it on the carpet of his bachelor flat. Fully clothed, he said, 'would you like to come to bed now?'

'I thought you'd never ask.'

He lifted me as if I was a single white rose, cradling me in his arms and enfolding me onto the leather armchair in his bedroom. I watched from my ringside seat, heart pounding as he walked with the pace of a tiger. He paused by scented candles standing in the fireplace and lit every

39

one. The candlelight was kind. Where I once would have been creased with embarrassment, with this man, in this half light, I held my body straight and proud as he knelt before me and ran practised fingers over my tingling skin. I breathed in jasmine scent emanating from the candles and held my arms up. I allowed him to ease off my top, and heard his hungry gasp as my breasts in their new lilac bra bounced into his face. He kissed every inch of skin between my neck and my thighs, pausing to breathe deep where those sassy old pheromones were gathering in my warmest places. Have you ever had a man who so desired you, that he breathed the natural scent in the pit of your arm as if it were a newly gathered bunch of white lilies? No? Well try it sometime. Forget every aphrodisiac known to man. That level of devotion to the art of sex sends a girl weak-kneed begging for completion.

I lay back on the coolness of Egyptian cotton sheets and felt his warm hard eager body cover my own as I shook with desire. I felt the roughness of his jeans against the nakedness of my skin. I could almost feel the pheromones collecting on my sweating body as I looked wide-eyed while he brazenly peeled off his clothes. Then he presented me with the finest gift any woman in a high state of arousal can have – the glowing torso of a man fired with passion. He lay back on the bed and straddled me over his stubbled chin. He unhooked my bra and kneaded my breasts as I rested my sex over his half-open mouth. Gently I sank on to his waiting lips, landing my pussy onto the warmth of his tongue. As I gripped the leather bed head, my head swam while he sucked and blew, his fingers digging into my thighs. Never before had I wanted to come so urgently.

But, like the expert he was, he didn't let me. Instead, he pushed me down over him positioning my thighs either side of his. I teased myself with his moist erection, my mane of shampoo-fresh hair falling onto his face. He placed me expertly, teasing my opening with one glorious erect cock. I sensed him watching me, studying my face as I chose exactly which moment was right, bucked up and then down, pinioning myself on his superb hardness. I sank into him as he grasped my hips and lifted me up and down, causing his breath to issue ragged and urgent.

When he put his thumb in his mouth and sucked leaving it slippery and warm, and pressed it against the top of my clitoris I thought I might faint. My eyes closed, I leant back at the knees, swimming in the feeling of his gentle rubbing, filled with his erection. He could tell I was climbing the mountain, upwards and upwards until with a sensational burst of release, I shuddered to a climax, gripping his ankles for support. As I lay my head, sated and exhausted, on his chest I heard him murmur, 'you're the most beautiful woman I've ever seen.' It wasn't true, I knew it wasn't true, but for that one ticking second I found myself believing and held him so tight I thought he'd cry out, when all he did was smile and hold me tighter.

It was with feet heavy with trepidation that I headed back to the clinic to hear the results of the trial. Oh, I had a tale to tell them. A tale of making love every single day since I had been popping those little blue pills. A tale that would fill them with joy for the efficacy of their preparation but which filled me with blinding horror. Because when the trial was over, the supply would stop. It would have to. What about the other ugly girls' successes or failures? If their development hadn't been so spectacular as mine, maybe the wonder drug, the drug that had transformed my life would never be manufactured, would never come on sale, would fade into obscurity. And I would fade with it. My enthusiastic lover, the lover of my sleeping and waking dreams would sense a change. He would go off me. He would look at me through creased eyes and wonder what on earth he had seen in such a lumpy, dumpy specimen. My life would return to its greyness and I would live alone and unloved.

I eased myself in my tight black pencil skirt into the chair opposite the doctor, crossed my stockinged legs and told him of my great adventure. I waited, listening under the strip lights to his breathing as he wrote my results down. 'So,' I asked with a catch in my throat. 'Was the trial a success?'

'Totally and utterly.' The doctor sat back closing his notebook. 'You and the others were a resounding success.'

I trembled, hope escalating, 'has the drug finished its trials, will it be on sale soon? Where can I buy it?'

The doctor steepled his hands and looked me over, shaking his head gently from side to side. 'There is no drug,' he stated.

'Well, no, I don't have any now. I finished them all off yesterday. I just wanted to know when and where I can get some more.'

'There is no drug. There never was a drug.'

'What are you talking about? Then what have I been taking?'

'Just a sugar coated pill. A placebo.'

'That can't be,' I stuttered, painted finger nails holding the empty box up at him as if he were an idiot. I ran a shaking hand through my soft wild curls. 'I've been transformed. You gave me pills and I was transformed.'

'Yes, I gave you pills. Little blue tablets of confidence. You transformed yourself. You believed and so it came to pass. You are beautiful because you believe yourself to be beautiful.'

'And the trial?'

'A psychological trial into the mysteries of the human mind. You weren't the only one. All the women responded in a similar fashion. You all had it in you all along. You just needed those little blue smarties to make it happen.'

I shook his hand and walked down the street, back to my gorgeous lover, the little pill box, moving silent and empty and unnecessary, in my handbag.

Half Measures
by Jeremy Edwards

I never did learn exactly why Millicent showed up at my place with no pants on at 1:30 in the morning. I had a general idea, of course, of the type of evening out that might have resulted in this scenario. But I still don't know any of the specific details. I'm delighted to report that Millicent and I see each other quite often. But by the time it crosses my mind that she still owes me the rundown on this incident (among others), we're always too busy living in the moment for me to interrupt with sentimental reminiscences and pump her for back stories. Not that there isn't usually some pumping going on – but that's different.

It had been a quiet Saturday night at home for me, and I was looking forward to hitting the sack and perhaps indulging the autoeroticism habit before nodding off. First choice for me under the covers is always to be part of a dynamic duo; but I don't mind admitting that I like masturbation, too. And anyway, it happened to be the best proposition I'd had that night.

I wasn't particularly surprised to hear the knock on the door. I live near the strip of groovy bars, and my friends – some of whom are a little wild – know that I am usually a congenial host, even to spontaneous, inebriated guests, and that if I really don't want to be bothered, I won't answer. I had learned, though, to ascertain who it was before opening up. There are some people whom I consider friends by daylight but do not wish to entertain in the wee hours of the morning.

'Hi. Who is it?' I asked in my most noncommittal, to-host-or-not-to-host tone.

'It's Millicent,' a voice hissed back in a courteous, don't-disturb-the-neighbours sort of whisper.

Millicent! This was the best thing that had happened in weeks.

'Can I come in? I don't have any pants on.' And then she laughed, just loud enough for me to hear.

I laughed, too. 'Now Millicent, you know you don't have to pretend to be half-undressed to gain entry to any apartment of mine. You're always welcome, even fully clothed.'

'I'm not kidding, Stewart.'

'*What?* No pants?'

'No pants.' She laughed again. 'Why don't you open the door and see for yourself?'

Millicent and I were the kind of pair who could turn almost anything into a game. 'You can't fool me so easily,' I reasoned. 'You're wearing a skirt, of course.'

'Nope.' More giggles. Millicent was obviously enjoying this as much as I was, so I decided to drag it out.

'A dress?'

'No.'

'Shorts?'

'Nuh-uh.'

'A swimsuit? A skirt? Culottes?' My guesses were getting more far-fetched. I wasn't even sure what culottes *were*.

45

'None of the above,' she tittered. Her laughter was as beautiful as it was contagious. She didn't even sound drunk.

'Commencement robes? A sari? A paisley dressing-gown?'

'No, no, and no again.'

'A kilt? A leotard? One of those big ol' Native American blankets?'

Now she was laughing too hard to say 'No,' but it was clear that I was still flunking out.

'Car-repair coveralls? Scuba gear?'

'*No*, Stewart. I'm completely bare-assed.'

'Oh! Well, why didn't you say so.' I opened the door, beaming at her. Millicent scurried in, naked from the waist down and elfin from the neck up, and gave me a quick peck on the cheek.

She stood next to me for an instant, catching her breath after all the laughing. Then, without standing on ceremony, she zipped past me and headed down the hall that led to my bathroom. I noticed how well her long-sleeved coral-pink blouse hugged the petite, elegant contours of her back. Its smoothness led my eyes down to Millicent's waist, where the silk signed off and creamy, bare flesh took over. I watched the neat little globes of her bottom jiggle purposefully as she receded. Too soon, the dreamy ass wished me *au revoir* as its owner took a sharp right turn into the john.

One muffled flush later, Millicent re-appeared. On this return trip, I was able to relish a view of her dark, fuzzy nexus, where her sleek legs dovetailed so perfectly. Soon she was with me again.

'That was a fun guessing-game,' Millicent said, touching my elbow lightly.

'I enjoyed it, too.' I paused before continuing. 'I also enjoyed watching you move down that hallway. You have a very nice ass, my dear.'

Millicent smiled a mixture of gratitude and mischief. 'Likewise, I presume.' She pivoted her head from side to side, as if trying to get a peek around at the back of my jeans.

'But even better than admiring your bottom as it travels down my hallway is having you back at this end of the corridor,' I admitted, taking her hand. 'I guess I've been a little lonely tonight.' It was funny – I hadn't realized I'd been lonely until I felt the contrast of being with her.

'I feel lonely, too, in a way, being the only one who's half-undressed around here,' she noted.

I had hoped things might go in this direction.

'No problem,' I said eagerly. 'I can take my pants and underwear off, if you like. In fact, based on past experience, I think I can even get completely naked without too much trouble.'

'Let's try just naked from the waist down, for now,' she replied. 'My friends and family *are* always complaining that I like to do things by half-measures, after all.' I had heard this complaint, and I knew that dear Millicent's life was indeed a landscape of semi-abandoned initiatives. She was the first to admit it, and I admired her for being able to poke fun at herself.

'Whatever you wish,' I said gallantly, very glad to be assuming the role of host for this particular late-night guest. 'But before I shed half my clothes, Little Miss Half-Measures, can I get you half a glass of wine perhaps, or half a cup of coffee?'

'Yes to the wine,' she said. 'I'll have *two* half-glasses. But why don't you take the jeans and shorts off first. I might get bored watching you mess around with the corkscrew, unless I have something else to look at.'

So there we stood in the kitchen a minute later, my dick flapping for Millicent's entertainment while I wrestled with the wine bottle. She was laughing at the spectacle I provided, but in a manner that flattered me. I could tell I was making her horny. When she stood up to claim her double-half-glass of wine, she gave me a lewd little slap on the butt, and I noticed a minor wet spot on the chair she'd been occupying.

By the time we'd made our way to the living room couch, I had matched Millicent's wet spot with a classic Saturday-night hard-on. We sat side by side and knee to knee, and I could smell her arousal over the bouquet of the merlot. I reached around and under to fondle her backside. When she moaned appealingly, I decided to leave my hand there. This allowed me to punctuate our chatter and giggles with light, sensuous squeezes, and to send the occasional, lascivious finger into her hind crack.

In a little while, Millicent took my wine glass from me and set it on the table. She then directed my free hand straight into her crotch and carefully guided it into the caresses she craved. All my fingers were now occupied on Millicent's person – squeezing ass cheeks, tickling butt-crack, tracing paths of pleasure upon and within moist pussy-lips – and my cock began to twitch for attention. Millicent responded promptly, abandoning her own wine and initiating the tenderest strokes my member had ever felt. I rewarded her with my best manly moans.

'You know,' she breathed, 'I'd kind of like to feel you all the way inside me, right now.'

'Kind of?' I asked.

'Okay, not 'kind of',' Millicent confessed. 'Absolutely and totally and completely.'

And with that, she hopped up, turned her coral-lovely back to me, and let her sweet ass hover briefly over my lap. Then she reached backward, grabbed my thighs for support, and gently lowered herself onto the waiting, throbbing pleasure-stick. My, she was juicy. It was hard to avoid coming immediately as she slid down, letting her soft cunt ingest me as far as I could go. And when I could go no further, she began pounding my upper thighs with her bottom cheeks, dancing wildly to the beat of her inner joys.

I reached around to stroke her breasts, teasing the nipples that poked at me through the silk. I nibbled soft kisses onto the back of her neck as we bounced. I felt my loins and hers melt into a churning, boiling mother-lode of ecstasy. The roaring bliss engulfed us both until we pulsated as one and gave in to the seething sensations that rushed over, around and through my buried member and the dripping, sensuous cunt that clasped it. It was quite possibly the best orgasm I'd ever had. And, judging from Millicent's urgent, lyrical cries, it must have been a pretty special moment for her as well.

Ripple after ripple of pleasure tickled through us as we held the pose. Finally, our conjoined organs were still, and we rested gently in a motionless hug. 'So much for half-measures, darling,' I murmured into Millicent's fragrant hair.

In The Liquor Store
by Gwen Masters

The old wooden floor creaked and shifted under our feet as we made our way down the narrow aisles. Bottles of every size and fashion stood at attention, their colourful labels touting the brand of the liquor within. A low and sultry guitar rang out through the ancient radio on the counter.

Daniel hummed quietly along with the melody as he lifted a bottle from a rack and examined it. He gently replaced it with the tiny clink of glass on glass. I looked up at the ceiling of the old liquor store, taking in the rough exposed beams from which hung all sorts of artefacts: guitars, fiddles, ancient bottles, even a voodoo doll here and there.

The place smelled of old wood and even older wine. This was a liquor store that had been in business for decades, and it showed in the vintage bottles on the highest shelves. There was a wine cellar in the basement, or so the sign said – it promised to hold only the best wines. Daniel turned a corner at the back of the store and I followed slowly, exploring everything around me but the liquor. The store was a mesmerizing kaleidoscope of history and I was duly fascinated.

'Honey, come look at this,' Daniel said. His voice came from the far corner of the store. I made my way around a freezer full of tall bottles of dark, rich lager.

Daniel stood in the back of a darkened aisle. Here the bottles were dusty and old. There was a stepladder to one side. This must be where they kept the overstock merchandise. Even the freezer was dark, but I could hear the motor quietly humming away.

'Did you notice that no one is here?' Daniel asked quietly.

I looked up at the counter. There had been an older man there when we came in, but he had tipped his hat toward me and excused himself to take care of a shipment. There was a little truck outside, and he headed for it with an air of purpose. It appeared that he hadn't returned.

I smiled up into Daniel's face. His dark hair looked almost black in the dim light. His eyes were no longer their placid shade of brown – they looked just as black as his hair. I shivered, remembering the voodoo doll hanging from the rafters.

Daniel's eyes searched mine for a moment before he bent his head to kiss me. His hips came up against mine. Something hard stirred against my belly and I giggled into his mouth as his tongue traced my lips.

'Daniel,' I lightly scolded.

'No one is around,' he whispered back, his lips trailing up my jaw. 'You know, I've been in this liquor store a million times, but I've never once fucked in it.'

'Daniel, for shame!' I laughed, and he looked around, his eyes on the front door of the old liquor store.

'No one is here. Just a quickie, honey, come on. Let's do it,' he whispered urgently.

I was already getting caught up in the spirit and thrill of possibly being caught. I was always the kind who fantasized about a public kind of encounter, but never had the guts to go through with it. This, though – it wasn't entirely public, was it? And even if we got caught, what would the punishment be? A scolding, a fury in the eyes, or a barring from the store, perhaps – but what more than that? What did I have to lose, really?

My hand slid down Daniel's shirt to the brown slacks he wore. I pressed my fingers against his erection. He grew even harder under my hand. I was already wet. My pussy practically hummed with the anticipation.

'It has to be fast,' I whispered into his mouth. I found his belt buckle and quickly opened it. Daniel moved back just enough to give me room. I unbuttoned his slacks, then pulled the zipper down.

'Here on the stepladder,' he ordered.

'But it's old – and rickety…'

'Where is your sense of adventure?' Daniel hissed.

I laughed quietly as he picked me up and set me on the old wooden stepladder. He nibbled on my neck. His hands found my long skirt and clenched into the fabric, pulling it up inch by inch as I pushed his slacks open and pulled him free of his boxers. He was long and hard and ready to go. Daniel moaned softly as he throbbed in my hand.

'Fuck me,' I whispered.

Daniel yanked my dress up to my waist. Underneath it he found the tiny pair of red satin underwear that covered what he wanted. Daniel curled his fingers around the fabric and with no hesitation he ripped it from me. The seams held for a valiant moment, then gave way. The tatters fell to the dusty concrete floor.

I twined my legs around his hips and thrust upward as he pushed against me. His cock sank into my tight passage with one almost vicious thrust. I tightened my legs and pressed my heels into his ass, pushing him harder into me. I dug my nails into his shoulders, little stabs of pain that I knew would urge him on – he loved it when I did that. I whispered into his ear as he began to fuck me.

'You naughty bastard,' I growled.

I rose up to meet every thrust of his body into mine. Daniel was hard and solid inside me, every vein and ridge of his cock throbbing in time with his racing heart. Daniel pulled my legs tighter around his hips as he drove deeper.

We heard a noise from the front of the store. I froze but Daniel kept going. He whispered into my ear. 'What would you do if he came back here and saw you, huh? Would you like it if he saw my dick sliding into you? You look just like a fucking slut, don't you?'

'Yes,' I whispered back. I was suddenly wetter at the thought, and Daniel definitely noticed. He grinned wickedly at me in the dim light. I bit my lip to stifle a moan.

His teeth settled on my earlobe and he bit down, his breath short and fast. His hips sped up, pumping into me with the sole purpose of making us both orgasm, quickly and hard. He moved closer to me and angled his body so that his shaft brushed over my hard clit with every motion of his hips. He knew my body well – he knew what would work. His lips made their way down my throat, and he nipped at the rise of my cleavage above the low neckline of my blouse.

The orgasm was building quickly inside me, driven higher by the danger of being caught. My hands went to his hair. I pulled his head back so that I could look into his eyes while he fucked me. Daniel rammed me harder. The pleasure threatened to turn to pain, but I wasn't about to tell him to stop – I was too close to even *think* about stopping.

'Come on me,' he hissed, then his hand found my hair and he yanked once, hard. 'Come like a fucking slut,' he taunted, loud enough that someone might hear.

Even though I didn't make a sound, Daniel covered my mouth with his hand as I came. My body squeezed tight around him. The throbbing was hard and deep, and seemed to go on forever. My nails dug into his shoulders and Daniel sucked in a quick breath at the pain. I bucked hard against him until the tremors in my body faded. I was suddenly light-headed.

'Breathe,' Daniel ordered, and I took a great gasp of air. The world swam back into focus. I had been holding my breath as the orgasm ripped through me.

Daniel watched me with eyes that had gone dark with passion. He kept up a steady rhythm, moving in that certain way that always makes him come. I moved in counterpoint to his thrusts. I squeezed down hard on him, and the remnants of my orgasm made me moan. The throbbing was still there, amazingly enough, just quieter now. Daniel felt it and shuddered. He was close, ready to topple over the edge with just the right touch, the right word. I raked my hands through his hair, then kissed the hollow of his neck and licked back to his ear.

'Your turn, Daniel,' I cooed. 'Come now, baby. Come for your woman. Come inside me.'

Daniel gasped and groaned as he exploded within me. I was flooded with heat. It seemed to catch fire between my legs and spread all through me. My skin tingled with it. Wetness slid out of me and down one trembling thigh. Daniel's whole body jerked, then he held very still while the last of his orgasm faded.

He finally collapsed against me, sending us both rocking a little on the rickety old stepladder.

'Wow, that was fast,' he gasped, trying to catch his breath. I buried my nose in his thick dark hair, breathing deeply of the shampoo and sweat. His heart beat hard and fast. He tightened his arms around me and buried his face into my cleavage. I squeezed him one more time with my secret inner muscles and he groaned. Then he began to laugh. The sound moved his belly up and down against me.

'God, that was great,' he sighed. He glanced around, then quickly dropped to his knees. His tongue found the centre of me. He spread my legs wide and licked up and down, tasting both of us. I twined my fingers through his hair and the fire started again, down low where it really counted. If anyone had come around the corner then, they would have seen quite the show.

When I started to buck up against him, Daniel stopped. He stood up with a sly grin that said he knew exactly what he was doing. He wanted me hot and ready when we got home.

'Go get cleaned up,' he whispered in my ear. He pulled me down from the stepladder and handed me the tattered remnants of my panties. He bestowed a little slap on my rump as I walked away on shaky legs. I found the bathroom and cleaned up, wiping away the wetness that made its way down my thighs. I looked in the mirror at a woman whose face was attractively flushed, hair in disarray, eyes filled with passion. We wouldn't be hiding anything – anyone who took a good look at me would be able to tell I had been thoroughly fucked.

I stepped out of the bathroom and Daniel was in the aisle, waiting for me. In one of his hands was a bottle of Jack Daniels and in the other a bottle of Bacardi Rum.

'One for you and one for me,' he said.

'You recovered almost instantly,' I said, still breathless. He might have himself under control, but I definitely noticed the flush on his face. It was so red, it looked like sunburn. I winked at him.

'I recover quickly when I have to,' he smiled, then cocked his head. The man was back behind the counter and

55

was looking at us with knowing eyes. He didn't look angry or uncomfortable – if anything, he looked curious. I smiled at him and then quickly looked away. I knew the blush was rising from my chest all the way up. My ears burned like fire.

Daniel bent to kiss me. He held out the bottles. 'I think you should pay for these.'

My eyes snapped to his. 'No way.'

He pushed the bottles against my fingers until I had to take them. He pushed the twenty into my cleavage. I knew I could get out of it with just a little more force to my protests, but surprisingly, I was enjoying the idea. Daniel walked with me to the counter, and I faced the man behind it.

The man looked me up and down. I set the bottles on the counter. He grinned and reached forward. I stood very still as he slowly pulled the twenty out from between the rise of my breasts. He rang up the sale and raised one eyebrow as he held out the change. I took it with a shaking hand.

'You come back anytime,' he said, and his grin turned into a full-fledged, wicked smile.

'*Anytime.*'

I smiled back, even though my ears were burning with heat.

'We will,' I said.

Call Girl
by Landon Dixon

I'm a supervisor at a call centre. You know, one of those
boiler rooms crammed full of cubicles and minimum-wagers
who phone you up at dinnertime urging you to buy some
product or subscribe to some credit card, or who you
sometimes phone for customer support. It's not the most
glamorous job in the world, but it pays the bills, and it
hasn't been relocated to India or the Philippines, yet.

One benefit of supervising a low-paid, transient
workforce is that I get to see plenty of pretty young girls;
girls still in high school and working part-time, or girls just
graduated or expelled from high school and working full-
time. And even though I'm on the shady side of thirty-
something, it's the young ones I still like, and love – tight,
hot, teen flesh; small, pliable titties and juicy, baby-faced
cunnies; girls with bright eyes and innocent faces, eager to
learn all they can from a horny, experienced gent like
myself.

So, when I hired cute, little raven-haired Vicky – who'd
only recently turned eighteen – I immediately put her on the
midnight to eight a.m. shift, where I could make my patent-
pending moves under the cover of darkness, with fewer
prying eyes around. And I didn't wait long to put out some

feelers, so to speak. On the young girl's second shift, around four in the morning, with most of the lights in the huge, open office turned off, and with me turned on, I slipped into Vicky's cubicle to give her some real hands-on training.

She was chattering away into her telephone headset, fingering her keyboard, and I surprised her by putting my hands on her bare, buff shoulders, and starting rubbing. She glanced back at me, startled, then smiled nervously and covered her mouthpiece and asked, 'Can I, uh, help you, Mr Morgan?'

'Just trying to keep my employees loose,' I replied, smiling down at the delightful teen, my cock hardening into steel inside my pants as I continued rubbing her warm, sun-kissed shoulders, gently probed her long, slender neck with my fingers. Then I bent down and nuzzled the side of her soft neck, gently kissed and licked her smooth, clear, scented skin.

She giggled uncertainly, tried to shrug me off, but you don't get far in this business by being easily discouraged. I ran my tongue up and down the side of her neck, shifted her shiny, black curtain of hair to one side, and sent my tongue in behind her ear.

The charming little teenager didn't cry 'Mommy!' or anything, instead she moaned softly when my wet tongue licked at the back of her delicately shaped ear. Then she turned her head and looked at me with her wide, baby-blue eyes, her face burning red. 'Whatcha doin', Mr Morgan?' she asked in a little-girl voice.

'Helping you deal with the stress, sweetheart,' I whispered, before replacing words with action and swirling my tongue around inside her rose petal of an ear.

'Mmmm,' she murmured. 'No, no, sir, I didn't say anything,' she hastily spoke into the headset, to the customer dangling on the end of the line. 'I was just, uh, you know, thinkin' about what you said. Please, go on.'

I took that last part as being directed at the both of us, and as the customer droned on about his computer problem, or some such nonsense, I batted Vicky's earlobe around with my tongue, then caught it between my lips and tugged on it. I pushed the straps of her Hilary Duff tank-top off her shoulders and caressed the honey-coloured flesh of her arms and chest, slid my big, sweaty hands beneath the thin fabric of her girlish top and openly fondled her boobs, skin-on-skin.

'Yeah...' she whimpered, the guy on the phone thinking, no doubt, that she was agreeing with what he said.

I cupped and squeezed her firm, high, handful titties, played with her rubbery nipples, her buds flowering rapidly to fullness as I rolled and lightly pinched them. I kissed her neck more urgently, biting into her delectable flesh, inhaling her young girl essence as I felt up her titties.

'Don't stop,' she breathed, her head lolling back on her shoulders, basking in the erotic sensations that my loving hands and lips were eliciting. She tilted the receiver up, away from her mouth, her hand shaking, her entire slim body quivering slightly under my fingers and tongue.

I spun the chair around so that she was facing me, and she stared into my eyes and bit her lip, realizing, quick study that she was, that I meant to have her cunny – meant to make her come right then and there, while she handled a customer on the phone, as a reward for her one-and-a-half nights of labour.

One of my greatest pleasures in life is tasting come-of-age coochie, digging my probing tongue into a ripe, juicy, barely-legal pussy and swirling it around, lapping at a teenaged babe's soaking wet box until she squirts girlie-juice into my mouth, all over my face. I love the taste of cunny-honey in the evening. And there's no better way to begin a, hopefully, long-term relationship with a sweet young thing than to eat out her conch, demonstrate to her that you're as interested in her pleasure as your own.

Vicky nodded her head.

I plucked the headset control box off the elasticized waist of her tiny white shorts and set it on the desk, then pulled her top all the way down, leaving her chest bare and heaving. She was tanned all over from what must have been countless hours spent lying under a grateful sun on the beach, except for a couple of small, white triangles on her pointed boobs where her bikini top normally covered her up. Her cherry-red nipples jutted out at me, yearning for my hands and mouth, the exclamation points on our mutual want.

I dropped to my knees in front of her, gripped her titties, and without further ado, began teasing her blossomed buds with my tongue. 'Ohmigod!' she yelped, leaning forward so that I could make better mouth-contact with her teen queen jugs.

'Huh!? No...I'm, uh, all right, sir,' she mumbled into the phone, flipping the receiver back down to her mouth. She took a deep breath and ran her trembling fingers through her long, shimmering, jet-black tresses, as I flicked my tongue underneath first one swollen nipple and then the other, swirled it all around and over her rigid nubbies.

The customer babbled on, little realizing that his teenaged service rep was getting some servicing of her own. I latched my lips onto one of Vicky's wickedly engorged buds and sucked on it, pulled on it, before swallowing up as much of her succulent titty as I could. She thrust her chest out, urging me to devour her tender titties, and I disgorged her left boob and went to work on her right, clutching and squeezing the sopping flesh of one breast while I nursed on

60

the other. She closed her eyes and moaned, her burnished upper body gently undulating as I fed on her tits and nips, felt up her boobs.

Then I pulled my head back, gave her glistening titties a final playful squeeze, her nipples a pinch, and slipped my fingers under the waistband of her shorts. Her eyes popped open and she vaguely shook her head. I nodded slowly and surely, and she grinned mischievously and brought her slender, bronze legs together and arched her body off the chair, so that I could slide her shorts down. I took my time, the backs of my fingers rubbing her slim, supple legs all the way down.

I pulled her shorts off her dainty, bare feet – it's pretty casual at our workplace – and threw them aside, gazed with satisfaction at her moistened cunny. Her mound was as bare as a baby's bottom, except for an inverted triangle of downy, black fur that crowned her slit. Her quim glistened under the fluorescent lights, her puffy, rosy-red lips crying out to me to tongue and taste them, fuck her sexhole with my tongue, lick and suck her clit.

She spread her legs as wide as the chair would allow, and I picked them up and placed them on my shoulders, then leaned forward and brought my face to within an inch of her slickened cunny. 'Do it, Mr Morgan!' she hissed, prompting another agitated inquiry from her phone-bound client.

I gazed at her luscious poon for a good, long moment, licked my lips, inhaled the musky scent of her aroused girlhood. Then I ran my tongue down the side of one of her thighs, bit into the vulnerable flesh right next to her pussy. I repeated the process with her other thigh. She gasped, her legs quivering as I stroked her inner thighs with my tongue, painted her hot skin with my spit.

She covered the receiver with her hand and yelled, 'Eat me, Mr Morgan!' her blue-fire angel eyes blazing.

I took firm hold of her fleshy thighs, dipped my head down, and plunged my hardened tongue directly into her cunny. Her body jumped as I parted her shiny lips with my tongue, but I held on tight, driving my pink sticker deep into her sexual core. Then I started rhythmically fucking the young beauty with my tongue.

'Yeah!' she shrieked, frantically gripping her jugs and squeezing them.

I pistoned my head back and forth, pumping my cock-hard tongue in and out of the girl's soaking snatch, totally immersing myself in the erotic taste and smell of her cunny. I spread her slick folds with my fingers, exposing an even deeper pinkness, and excitedly tongue-fucked her for a while longer, before dragging my slimy pleasure tool in long, hard, slow strokes from her butthole to her clitty, over and over.

Vicky held onto her pert titties for dear life, her pretty face a grim mask of sexual agony. But, top-notch employee that she'd already become, she still managed to squeak into her headset, 'And, uh, have you been... experiencing any other problems, sir?' which, of course, he had.

I lapped at my young colleague's cunny, savouring the slick feel and tart taste of her teenaged coochie. Then I gave her puss one final long lick, smacked my lips with satisfaction, and exposed her clit with my fingers. I quickly covered her pink button with my mouth, sucked hard on her inflamed clitoris, desperate now to bring the eager-to-be-pleased youngster to shattering orgasm and drown myself in her sticky juices.

Vicky stared fixedly down at me, her teeth clenched, her hands kneading her swollen boobies, her fingers pulling on her stiffened nipples. I unmouthed her engorged clitty only long enough to slap it with my tongue a few times, and then I went right back to sucking on it, sucking her off.

'Y-yeah, r-right,' she gulped into the phone, then squealed with joy when I shoved two fingers into her greasy slit.

That did it. Her body went rigid, her muscles locking and standing out in stark relief on her bowed, brown body, and then she was jolted by orgasm. I desperately ploughed my fingers in and out of her cunny, sucked and tongued her clitty, as her sweat-dappled body jerked around like her nerves had been short-circuited, shocked by ecstasy again and again and again. How she managed not to give her customer a blistering earful of genuine hardcore phone sex, I have no idea. But she did. She rode out her orally-induced orgasms in stunning, flaming silence, her bucking body and gushing cunny speaking volumes.

The following afternoon, when I was wallowing in paperwork, I had an unexpected visitor to my office.

'Heya, Mr M,' Vicky said, suddenly appearing in the doorway, even though her shift didn't start for another ten hours.

'H-hi,' I stammered, my eyes widening and mouth watering as I took in the outfit that the young hottie was wearing.

She was barely-clothed in a tight, tiny candy-apple-red tube-top that struggled to contain her twin peaks, flashed her warm, brown cleavage, fully revealed her flat stomach and metal-studded bellybutton, and a midnight black, form-fitting mini-skirt that highlighted her tight, round bottom and lithe, dancer's legs. Her hair was braided into twin ponytails, and she had a black choker around her neck, red, ankle-high boots with stiletto heels on her feet, a pile of silver and gold bracelets around her wrists and up her arms, and enough make-up on her face to make a painted whore blush with pride.

I swallowed hard and said, 'Uh, what's up, Vicky?'

'I need you ... like, right now,' she replied, her glossy, crimson lips breaking into a smile.

I stood up, ran around my desk, and hustled the young cock-tease inside my office, slammed the door shut before any more of our co-workers could get an eyeful. 'I'm kind of backed up with paperwork right now,' I began, before the telephone rang, cutting me off. I walked past Vicky, through a cloud of perfume, and scooped the phone up off my desk. It was Takkinen from head office; he wanted to discuss, in detail, the latest monthly incoming-call report. I gave Vicky a tight smile and gestured for her to sit down.

She didn't. The tarted-up teen flipped the lock on the door and twisted shut all the venetian blinds on the windows that looked out on to the cubicle farm, her taut butt cheeks twitching suggestively under her incredibly brief, clingy skirt. And then, while Takkinen nattered away about the two percent increase in call-connection times over year-to-date average, Vicky nonchalantly pulled up her top and down her skirt. She stood there in front of me, in my office, completely and jarringly naked except for her boots, jewellery, and slut-paint.

'Time for some payback, Mr Morgan,' she stated, grinning evilly.

I eyed her nubile body, my eyes lingering hazardously on her perky titties, her erect nipples, her shiny slit. I tried to make sense out of what Takkinen was yammering on about, but my brain had gone all warm and mushy. Vicky puckered her lips and blew me a kiss, cupped her boobs and spread her legs wider apart. She squeezed and kneaded her tits, rolled her jutting nipples between her fingers, her trim lower body swaying from side to side. Then she turned around and bent at the waist and pointed her heart-shaped, oh-so-grabbable ass at me, awkwardly but effectively.

'Yeah, baby,' I mumbled, rubbing the hard outline of my cock through my pants.

'What'd ya call me?' Takkinen asked.

'Huh? Sorry, nothing. Just agreeing with you, is all. Keep talking.'

Vicky nodded, straightened up and faced me again, her scorching teen body searing my eyes as Takkinen talked shop in my ear. She strutted, stumbled over to me, until we were mere inches apart, and then she brushed my hand away from my swollen cock and replaced it with hers.

'I'm gonna suck your big, hard prick till you come buckets – right in my mouth,' she breathed in my face, her breath hot and humid and smelling of bubble gum.

I nodded excitedly when Takkinen asked if there was someone in the office with me. 'N-no, no,' I muttered. Then I held my breath as Vicky fumbled my zipper open and pulled out my cock, grasped the hard, pink power-tool in her hot little brown hand and squeezed it, her spangle-tipped fingers barely fitting all the way around my throbbing member. She started gliding her hand up and down my swollen pecker, and I gulped down my excitement and croaked into the phone, 'What's, um, up with that new call-tracking software, anyway? I-I bet you want to talk about that, huh?'

Takkinen cooperated, went off on a long-winded monologue as Vicky squatted down in front of me, stuck out her kitten-pink tongue and licked at my bloated cocktop. I groaned, barely able to maintain my composure. She tickled my dickhead with her darting, devilish tongue, her hand swirling all over my prick, and then she sucked my purple hood into her mouth and tugged on it.

I leaned back against the desk, Takkinen's voice rattling on in the distance, Vicky sucking on my cockhead, stroking my shaft, juggling my balls around with her fingers. I stared down into her child-like eyes, watched anxiously as she sucked and tongued my hood a while longer, hand-polished my pecker, and then ran her tongue all the way up from my tightened balls to my mushroomed dicktip, bathing my shaft in hot saliva. She gripped me at the base and licked my pulsating schlong like she was determinedly tonguing a popsicle before it melted all over her hand.

'Fuck, yeah, baby,' I growled, my voice a strangled whisper, my balls boiling with semen, as I watched that young innocent hungrily attack my meat with her mouth.

'It'll lower operating costs in the long run…' Takkinen continued, not suspecting for a moment that I was getting a truly wicked blowjob from a pretty little workmate, while he was blowing wind on the phone.

Vicky tilted my rigid cock downwards and engulfed my dickhead with her warm, wet mouth again, sucked vigorously on my cocktop, her cheeks billowing, her tongue buffing the sensitive underside of my hood. She started bobbed her head up and down, taking more and more of my jacked-up dong into her mouth each time.

I cradled the phone receiver between my head and shoulder and grabbed on to the anxious young girl's ponytails, trying to guide her head, her mouth, back and forth on my straining cock. She scraped me with her teeth a couple of times, but I hardly noticed, and the talented teen got a good, sucking rhythm going, her lips sliding easily up and down my raging prick. She wet-vacced more and more of me into her mouth, rapidly driving me to the slippery edge of all-out orgasm.

I doubt if she could've gobbled up all of my prong, but I was in no condition to find out for sure. The whole dangerous liaison had fired me up so much that I lost control even quicker than usual, such that when she'd devoured a good three-quarters of my cock, I threw back my head, grunted with joyful abandon, and rocketed spicy, sizzling jizz deep into her dirty mouth, down her throat. I clung to her ponytails, crushed the phone between my ear and shoulder, my body spasming uncontrollably with each and every cum-blast.

Vicky, naughty girl that she was, didn't even try to peel her jism-slick lips off my rupturing cock. Instead, the sexy wild-child stared up at me with a happy expression on her flushed face, her throat working as she earnestly chugged my spurting sperm. Takkinen went on and on, but, unfortunately, I wasn't so lucky; my dick was soon convulsing on empty, drained of an incredible heated load by my eager-beaver co-worker.

Vicky yanked my dripping cock out of her mouth and squeezed a final few drops of goo from my slit, tongued them up and gulped them down. Then she shook my hands out of her hair, climbed to her feet, and kissed me sloppily on the lips, before quickly re-clothing herself.

'See ya tonight, big guy!' she yelled over her shoulder, as she slipped out the door, giggling.

'You get what I'm saying?' Takkinen inquired on the other end of the line.

'Sure...sure,' I replied exhaustedly, zipping myself back up with a shaky hand. 'You've been a real help.'

A Rank Outsider
by Phoebe Grafton

Sometimes I used to wonder what Janet saw in me. She was my best friend, was Janet. We had known each other since school. We just didn't seem to have a lot in common. While she was out being chased by all the boys, I was in being pencil monitor.

Physically, there was no similarity at all. We were like two pieces of a jigsaw. Where she stuck out, I caved in. Where she caved in, I stayed the same.

Some unkind soul christened us Beauty and the Beast. Janet, vivacious, hour-glass figure, blonde. No prize for guessing which one I was supposed to be. The relationship had mutual benefits when we left school and tackled the world of commerce. Janet and I shared a flat.

Any persistent guy that managed to get past the front door felt his ardour cooling rapidly when he found me there.

Particularly when we explained that it was a one bedroomed flat.

It wasn't really, but that usually worked. Of course when Janet encouraged a persistent guy, that was a different ball game altogether. Groans, grunts and sighs would flood through the thin bedroom wall.

It was like television without the picture. Meanwhile I'd be munching my way through a chair leg in sheer frustration.

The breakfast which followed such nights were awful. The guy would strut the kitchen in his jockey shorts, all limp macho and stale sexuality.

He'd get the last egg…I'd settle for the wholemeal crust. Janet would get a pat on the bottom. I'd get a pat on the head.

For all that, Janet didn't seem really ready for a permanent relationship. That's why we decided on a holiday together.

We kicked several ideas around. Like the words of the song – we'd been everywhere man. After much discussion, a quick argument and a sulk or two we settled on an Aegean cruise. Neither of us had been to sea before, so at least it would be a new experience. You only had to look at our baggage to realise that.

Janet and I had a council of war about the accommodation.

'After all,' she explained. 'If one of us hits the jackpot, it's going to be awkward if we are sharing a cabin.'

I got her drift. She didn't want me cramping her style. Yet I might get lucky, I reasoned to myself in the tall bathroom mirror. Then I took another look. I should live so long.

The negative mood didn't sustain. This was holiday time. Anything could happen. I was determined to enjoy myself even if I had to ambush a short-sighted, rich, old Greek pensioner.

It was nice to find that many of the passengers aboard were of a similar age, and single. Perhaps this would be the turning point. Even if I did get the worst of a pair in a foursome, it was too far to swim ashore.

Luck seemed to favour us on our first night at sea. We were coupled in a social get-together with two very presentable young men. Janet got Mark, a bank manager. She would. I got…well I got…a man. OK, so my escort was cross-eyed most of the evening trying to keep his eyes off Janet.

It was fun. We drank and danced the evening away.

Perhaps we drank a little more than we should, but it was our first night afloat, so what the hell.

We left the men to return to our separate cabins alone. There was always another night.

Was it an hour later? I'm not sure. I was dozing peacefully when I heard a gentle tap. Half in a daze I opened the cabin door.

My daze soon turned to excited expectancy as I recognised the silhouette. It was Mark's friend, my companion of the evening. If he was expecting a protest he didn't wait too long for it. He pushed into the cabin and took me in his arms.

Kicking the door shut behind him, he kissed me with an urgency that brooked little delay. I could feel his hunger in the darkness as he diligently explored my lightly clad body.

I was excited beyond belief. Was it Christmas already? Easing back from me, I heard him remove his jacket and drop it on the floor. This was swiftly followed by the unzipping of his trousers, as he sought to disrobe with all speed.

My own frustrations were almost at boiling point. At last, at last I cried to myself in the darkness. I switched on the bedside lamp to assist my would-be lover.

The light caused him to blink and stare for a moment.

'I'm sorry.' He said awkwardly. He suddenly looked quite ridiculous with his trousers around his ankles, stuttering apologies.

He hurriedly pulled his trousers up. 'I thought,' he began, 'I mean…I didn't mean to.' Snatching up his jacket he fled, leaving me frustrated and angry.

Through the long night I tried to calm my raging thoughts. At least I'd been fondled. For a short space I had been desired. Such compensating thoughts had no lasting effect.

In the morning the ship berthed at Istanbul. There was an arranged trip to the Blue Mosque with the afternoon free. Janet, Mark and friend wanted me along. Mark's friend had passed apologetic glances in my direction all morning. I ignored them. My mood was not sociable enough to fit the gaiety of my companions.

I left them to their explorations, while I went off alone to sulk in a souk. Certainly you cannot be alone in a souk. The jostling crowds, the persistent traders, all serve to lend an atmosphere which is unequalled.

In the subdued light I made my way along the narrow passage, stopping here and there to examine silks, leathers and gold on display. Such pauses were necessarily short to escape the traders whose only failure in English was in not understanding *No!*

I was attracted by a shop which displayed an interesting pair of sandals. While I was bargaining with the young trader, he was joined by an older man whom I took to be his father.

The older man, having established my nationality, smiled a welcome. Then he held out his hand.

'Come with me, English missy. I have a surprise for you in my shop'.

'No thanks' I told him.

71

'Come, come,' he insisted. 'You no be afraid of Yousef. Yousef, honest trader.'

He flashed a row of white teeth. What the hell, I thought. The last man that showed this much interest in me apologised afterwards.

The rear of Yousef's shop was like an Aladdin's cave. With the room stacked full of Persian rugs, and Yousef dressed in his nightshirt, it was like a scene from the Arabian Nights.

He went to a safe in the corner and took out a small bracelet. Not very attractive. It looked copper with some green and opal stones inset.

'This is a very ancient bracelet from the Land of the Pharaohs, passed down through the ages' he said solemnly.

I groaned inwardly. Oh God! Not another ancient Egyptian bracelet. Everywhere you went, somebody tried to flog you an ancient Egyptian bracelet. They must breed like mice. Even Woolworths had them.

'No thanks,' I began.

He quickly interrupted me. 'Please,' he said eagerly, 'for you special price...you try on.'

I took it and tried it on. It was quite ugly...and yet...and yet. I began to feel good. Not just about the bracelet, but about me, about everything.

In that back room I noted something different. Yousef was beginning to breathe heavily.

'You are very beautiful, English missy,' he said in a thick voice.

His hands moved about me. His eyes lustfully bore into my own. Without preliminaries his hand vanished beneath my dress to grind and massage those places which, up until now, had remained largely unexplored. I didn't scream. I was grateful.

So grateful, in fact, that when his hands started to pull my knickers down, I struggled not one little bit.

So it was that I saw on Yousef's face a look of pure Turkish delight.

The real Yousef was a little difficult to reveal at the outset. He had more petticoats than a Victorian nanny. Once he removed them though, his resemblance to a Victorian nanny instantly vanished.

Not that I'm experienced, as I explained, but Yousef did seem generously endowed. Such contemplation was short lived as he turned me and bent me over a large pile of rugs. It afforded me a close up view of the rug pattern, as well as a brief moment of further contemplation. I'd only come for a pair of sandals.

Spreading my thighs, he grunted with satisfaction as his searching fingers found my moist entrance. A man of few words was Yousef.

Expertly parting the lips of my vagina he guided the head of his shaft inside. I was right. He was big. Grasping me firmly by the hips he thrust inwards and upwards.

I felt the huge, rampant cock of Yousef filling me, stretching me. It was a rapid confusion of pain, wonder and desire as he plunged into me again and again.

Desire won, for as the rhythm intensified I became aware that I was thrusting back to meet his pulsing rod

My loins felt on fire as I matched him in ecstatic convulsions. Inside, I felt his thick penis swell as I sensed Yousef was near completion. Without warning he almost completely withdrew from me to instantly ram in his pumping manhood.

Moaning, as this new experience overtook me, I thrust back upon him fiercely, milking his tool, as the encompassing joy of my first climax overwhelmed me.

Just as with the lack of foreplay, so with his completion. Yousef's next thought was to get about his business.

Making all sorts of excuses about his wife he ushered me from his shop. For Yousef it hadn't altogether been a bad day. It wasn't until I'd left the souk and was on my way back to the ship that I realised. I'd lost my knickers and six hundred lira. Furthermore... I still didn't get my sandals.

Back on board I sat on my bed gathering my thoughts. I'd been fucked by a Turk. The memory of it was not in the least bit displeasing. All I had to show for it though, was a grotty bracelet, which cost an arm and a leg. So what? I shrugged.

This English missy had enjoyed herself.

I took the bracelet off and was about to put it in the drawer when I hesitated.

It was the only memento of a lusty interlude that I was likely to get for some time. I decided, provided my arm didn't go green, that I'd wear it for social occasions

So I wore the bracelet that evening. Once again when I put it on I felt that wholesome feeling, a strange completeness, as if there was nothing but good in store for me.

My general appearance must have improved. Janet asked me if I'd been stuffing my bra. She noted my change in appearance almost, I fancy, with a sniff of disapproval.

She finally dismissed my emphasised frontage by saying that probably for the first time I was holding my back up straight. Who needs a mother when you have a friend like Janet?

I stole another look in the full length mirror before dinner. Yes, no doubt about it, I certainly looked more attractive. Was it a glow from my recent experience? Perhaps the bracelet did possess powers beyond normal comprehension. Whatever the explanation, I felt justified in the knowledge that I'd already spent far too long in the shadow of the attractive Janet.

Mark obviously liked what he saw. We danced together quite a bit. Janet was relegated to the second division with Mark's friend, my midnight non-event.

Once again we drank and danced until way past the witching hour. Mark and Janet finished the evening with the last dance, before we once more retired to our respective cabins.

The tap on my door a little later was not totally unexpected. Nor was I surprised to find it was Mark. This time I took no chances. My cabin light was on.

'You looked quite stunning tonight,' he said.

'Are you sure you have the right cabin? Janet is three doors down.'

'Janet who?' he queried, eyes sparkling full of mischief and desire.

I helped him off with his jacket. It wasn't fair on Janet, of course. Yet I'd spent too long in my friend's footsteps to be troubled by conscience.

Was it true? Desired by two men in one day. An earlier thought came flooding back. I was right. It was Christmas already! Mark brushed such thoughts away.

We lay together in the narrow bed. Mark's lovemaking was an orchestrated, yet measured, interlude of fulfilment. My resultant climax, a feast after so many years of fasting, filled me with pleasure.

I snuggled close to Mark. My experience was very limited indeed.

Yet in that quiet cabin I decided, as far as lovers go, I preferred British bank managers to Turkish tradesman.

There was a quiet tap on the door. I slipped from Mark's protective arms.

'Who is it?'

'It's Janet…I can't sleep. Mark didn't come.'

I didn't share her complaint.

'Perhaps he had a headache' I offered sympathetically through the closed door.

'Can I come in?' she whispered.

'Not at the moment,' I answered urgently.

'Oh…right,' she hesitated. 'Got it. See you in the morning.'

Next morning proved to be a laser display of stolen glances. Janet looked at Mark's friend knowingly…Mark looked at me gratefully…Janet looked at Mark quizzically.

It didn't last. The penny, for Janet, finally dropped. The warm Eastern Mediterranean sun turned, suddenly, decidedly cool.

For the next few days everybody avoided everybody else. Well, not everybody. Mark continued his nocturnal meandering which always managed to end up at my door. No complaints from me. I had a lot of catching up to do.

This brief respite, in an otherwise hectic programme, gave me time for serious contemplation. My whole world had been turned topsy-turvy. Sceptical as I was, I had to admit that the bracelet seemed to be at the core of this transformation in my life.

To be turned from nondescript, non-desired woman, to one that men couldn't wait to get at, called for a little readjustment. One thing was for certain. The bracelet would stay as my most treasured possession even if Mark did complain that it scratched in bed.

Before the general thaw set in between Janet and me the cruise was over. Then we were back to the flat and normality once more. Until Tom, that is.

Tom was one of Janet's regular boy friends. He was dishy alright, even if he was the one that always got the last breakfast egg.

Previously he hadn't paid a great deal of attention to me. So I didn't think anything of it when he arrived one mid morning.

I was slobbing about in my old dressing gown. Janet was out.

It was time for the usual coffee and small talk. I was making the coffee when I sensed rather than saw Tom behind me.

'There's something different about you,' he said.

'Oh really,'…I began,

That's as far as I got, because he slipped one hand inside the top of my dressing gown and began playing wicked games with my breasts.

Did I tell him to stop? I honestly can't remember. I know I should have done. Anyway, cupping first one breast, he teased the nipple to firmness. I leaned against him, coffee forgotten.

He slipped loose the belt of my dressing gown. The only thing underneath was me. As he stood behind, his hands played sweet music over my unresisting body.

Touching here, there, probing gently, he sent hot desire coursing through me. Ceasing for a moment I heard the now familiar sound of a zip behind me. Seconds later his hand guided mine to grasp his rampant shaft.

We abandoned the idea of coffee altogether as he led me into the lounge. Sitting on the settee I pulled his pulsing weapon free. I bent to tease.

Holding it firm I allowed my tongue to wander lightly over the purple head. I took it in my mouth, sliding my lips wetly up and down its length. He liked that. I felt Tom begin to respond to my rhythm.

Then Janet walked in.

The relationship between Janet and me went down hill rapidly after that.

That was always her trouble – no sense of humour.

All was not lost. Janet and I still ring each other occasionally. I moved out, of course, Tom came with me. He stayed…right up until this morning.

It was this way. I was in the bath this morning when Tom came in. Even as he started to soap me in his usual, sensual way I could see his obvious interest.

'I think I'll join you,' he said.

'Man, you're insatiable,' I teased.

'Are you complaining?'

'No way…hurry up the water's getting cold.'

'Why do you have to wear this old bracelet?' he queried. 'You'll do somebody a nasty injury one day.'

So saying he slipped the bracelet off my soapy arm and left the bathroom, putting it on the dresser as he went. I could hear him singing, and seconds later he returned, clad only in a towel. He stopped singing abruptly. He stood staring at me for a moment, nonplussed, confused. Finally he spoke, panic words tumbling out.

'I've just remembered,' he stammered. 'I've got an early appointment…can't stop.'

He rushed out. I could hear him clattering about for a while. I called out, but he didn't answer. Very soon I heard the front door open and close with a bang. Then there was nothing but silence in the flat.

I sank back into the soapy water. Really I should have been quite upset at Tom's hasty departure. I wasn't. On the contrary, I felt quite contented, so much so that before long I began to hum to myself.

As I lay luxuriating in my foamy bath I could look across at my bracelet on the dresser.

Tom had gone. So what? I shrugged and allowed myself a secret smile. I hadn't done too badly for a pencil monitor.

Tom would be back tomorrow. If not, then there would always be another Tom tomorrow...or another...or another...or another.

A Sculptor's Touch
by Roger Frank Selby

'Hello, I'm calling about the job. Is it still vacant?'

She sounded very nice, young and positive. 'I'm still interviewing. Have you done any modelling work before?'

'Yes... Well, just a little at Art College.'

'You realise of course that I'll require you to pose in the nude?'

There was a very slight hesitation. 'Well, of course.'

'You don't have a problem with that?'

'Hardly. It's what I did at college.'

Maybe she did, but he detected a note of anxiety. 'And you were quite comfortable with that?'

'To tell the truth, I was always a little embarrassed showing my figure in front of all those students...'

'Well, it's only me, and you'll have no need to be embarrassed, as you will see. Would you like to come for an interview, er...?'

'Angela.'

He called Bess over, tickled her behind the ears – which she loved – and patted the side of her chest. He was rewarded with a lick. 'Good girl! Well, that one seemed okay. I wonder what she'll be like in the flesh?'

She arrived at the substantial house and noted the new Mercedes in the drive. He opened the door. He was quite tall. 'Come though to the studio, Angel.'

Angel. She liked the sound of that. He led the way. He was younger than she'd thought from his voice and manner. The only thing that worried her was that he never seemed to look directly at her. But he never looked at her breasts either. Most men never seemed to take their eyes off them.

'You have a *lovely* house!'

'Thank you. I have been lucky with my work. It sells all over the world. Here we are.'

She looked around the studio. Large Venetian blinds over the huge window blocked out most of the light.

'I suppose you have to have those screens to stop the neighbours peeking in?'

'Oh, are they still closed?' He walked over and pulled the cord. Light flooded in. There were no neighbours to be seen, just a vast private garden, then miles of open countryside.

'It's beautiful! You're not overlooked at all. I'm going to enjoy working here.'

'You're getting a bit ahead of yourself, aren't you? We haven't even started the interview.'

'Oh, yes, I'm sorry, but I hate false modesty. Everyone tells me I have a great figure. I was just assuming you *would* want to paint me.'

'I am a sculptor, not a painter, Angel.'

'Well, yes, of course – I meant *sculpt* me – but it's all the same from the model's point of view, surely?'

'Not in this case. I could never work by sight; I'm blind.'

She looked at his distant eyes. Of course! The window blinds he didn't know were closed, the careful layout of the house and studio... She could never feel embarrassed with him unable to see her naked body. She had been dreading disrobing in front of strange eyes; now she felt such great relief she laughed. 'Ha! How wonderful! Oh gosh, I'm sorry! It's not wonderful for you – but it's wonderful – *fantastic* – all that you have achieved!'

'That's okay, and thank you for the compliment! Would you like to see some of my work?'

She gazed at the life-sized women in his storeroom. All beauties, some in skimpy costumes, most naked. The range of poses was amazing – demure to blatantly sexual. Some of the nearer ones were similar. A lovely, petite girl with neat breasts. 'They are truly beautiful! These ones: were they from your last model?'

'You mean the closest four?'

'Sorry, I was pointing. Yes.'

'I still use her sometimes, but my market demands variety. I'm looking for…well, a bigger girl.'

'And you think I am bigger than her?' She enjoyed the advantage of him not seeing her.

He sounded irritated.

'She's quite small, so there's a good chance that you are, right? Anyway, judge for yourself – I've already roughed out a piece that could be transformed into you.' The clay was moist, recently daubed onto a wire frame, but the outline was there – a full-breasted young woman down on all fours.

She looked at 'her' clay breasts hanging down, the high bottom inviting penetration. Just like her when she was with Michael. It sent a *feeling* through her lower body.

'But how *can* you work from a model you can't see?'

He perceived the concern in her voice. The penny was beginning to drop. 'Apart from sound, I get most of my information about the world through my sense of touch.'

'You mean…'

'Yes.'

'What, you actually *feel* the model's body?'

82

'Of course.'

'What? So *that's* your game! You think that I'm going to let you touch and feel *me?* You got me here for *that?*'

He heard the clack of her sandals as she started to go. 'So that's it then, Angel?' He followed her into the hall.

'No way you'll get your slimy hands on *my* tits!'

'It *is* the only way I can work. I can't see them, hear them, smell them... I suppose I could taste them!' he laughed.

Silence.

'Are you still there?'

A pause. 'Yes.'

'Well, there's no point you staying if I can't touch you. I simply can't work any other way – my world is one of sound and touch. But before you go, just let me feel the contours of your face, then go home and think about it. Come again if you change your mind.' From the subtle reverberations of his voice he knew she had come up close to him. He reached out and found the side of her face.

He felt her facial muscles relax under his touch as he built up a mental image of her appearance. He took a long time and she became very calm. At the end, his hands briefly outlined the rest of her body. She was a beauty.

'I was just thinking what it must be like not being able to...well, *see* anything at all. And that shape you got before even touching me...'

'Perhaps the pose frightened you a bit?'

'It did, rather! But I'm not frightened now. I accept that you have to touch to see.'

They were back in the studio. He opened the window wide on to sunny countryside. She could hear bird song; see the secluded garden curving away down the hillside.

'Well, I'd better get stripped off.' She began to undress.

83

'Not so fast! Your interview... Come over here. Closer.'

He touched her face again, so lightly it almost tickled.

'You know that you are truly beautiful, don't you?'

'I'm okay. Some women are more...'

'Do *not* put yourself down!'

The anger surprised her. For the first time she felt the full strength of his personality.

'When you pose for me you will be the most beautiful creature on the planet, and I the best sculptor! I have been waiting to sculpt a woman like you all my life, Angel. Your perfect, sensual form will be immortalised in my sculpture.'

'Do you really believe all that?' she asked a little breathlessly. 'You haven't felt all of me yet.'

'I *must* believe it and so must you. Any doubts either of us have will diminish the work.'

While they were talking he'd been feeling her arms, her neck and shoulders, her collarbones – building a mental picture, she supposed. His touch was *so* delicate. She put her arms loosely around his waist; it felt the only natural thing to do. Concentrating, he hardly seemed to notice.

He turned her around, rather roughly, so she had to let go of him. She was beginning to realise that she was just a physical model for his main purpose – to form another work of art like the others she'd seen. He felt her back minutely through her dress, examining her shoulder blades, every vertebra.

'Go on talking.'

She did. About the studio, his work. He was quite capable of ignoring her questions, leaving them hanging in the air. She shrugged and chatted on.

'You're not wearing a bra.'

'Not today. Normally I do. It's a heavy-duty affair that keeps my boobs from wobbling about and attracting too much attention. I hate men ogling me. Today I felt like being free.'

'But you realise that although I can't see, I will be ogling you in a far more intimate way?'

'Well yes; but you are an artist – a sculptor... You won't be thinking of me in *that* way, will you?'

He sighed. 'I'm not a hypocrite. I don't want you running out on me again, but now is the time, if you must. I *am* an artist who sculpts, but I am a man first – a man who loves women's bodies. I will certainly be thinking of you in *that* way. I *will* be ogling you! Your body is a feast for a man. I knew it before we even met.'

The words excited her. She knew men wanted her, but put that way, thinking of her body as a *feast*...

'Remember what you said when you ran off?'

'Oh God, I'm sorry. *I'm* the hypocrite. I said 'No way you'll get your hands on *my* tits'.'

'*Slimy* hands.'

'Oh, gosh. I was a bitch!'

'Not at all. A very natural reaction to an unusual situation. And my hands *would* be slimy with clay! So are you *in* or *out?* It has to be wholehearted, we won't get anywhere with half-measures.'

A long pause.

'I'm *in*,' she said softly.

He touched her breasts. He felt them through her dress; felt their weight, mobility and softness. He opened her dress and pulled it down to her waist. He handled each upstanding breast separately, each nipple, feeling the change in profile, the rising cone of textured skin around each point; feeling the subtle differences between the pair. His sensitive touch was truly at a different level to a sighted person; his hands had taken over the function of sight. They felt delicious. She wanted him to squeeze her harder, wanted him to… He let go of her. No, don't let go now! she thought.

'I got them just right, didn't I?

'Yes, you did!'

'May I…?'

'Yes?'

'Suck them?

'Yes, you said you'd taste them…' That was what she wanted. He knelt before her and took each breast to his slightly bristly face. She leaned forward slightly, offering herself. After the scratchiness she felt the wetness as his tongue lightly trace the contours around each point; his teeth gently bit her nipples until she gave a little 'Ouch!' just before it would really hurt. Then he sucked on them. She felt gorged, swollen, as if full of milk. His fingers continued to knead. Gently he tried a little milk-stroking. She couldn't be sure, but she felt certain he'd tasted a little sweet fluid at one nipple. He tried to get some from the other… He came up for air.

'Well? Was that an 'Ogle' or what?'

She laughed, her breasts rising as her breath came quickly. 'You certainly know how to handle a woman… Do I pass?'

'You'll do.' He stood up abruptly, shook his head as if to clear it. It was as if he'd allowed himself to go too far and regretted it. 'Just sit down here.' He pulled up a cane chair. 'Sit down and watch me work for a moment.'

She sat down, feeling deflated. I guess that's how far his survey is going, he can't be bothered with the rest, she thought. He just wants to get on with the work. *You'll do*? Of course she would bloody do! She started to pull the dress up to her shoulders.

'No, don't do that!' he said, hearing the silky sound. 'You are my model; I need to refer to you.'

My God he can be a bossy insensitive bastard, she thought, but what a wonderful touch…

He wet his hands in a bucket and advanced on the waiting clay. After a few minutes the hanging breasts were smoothed to her exact shape – or so she thought. He came back to her, wiping his big hands on a towel. His hands were very cold with handling the clay. He felt her shape – very softly this time, touching the curves without pushing them out of line.

'No, this won't do. Your breasts are firm and stand out just like men would love all tits to, but I *do* need to feel the hanging shape. It's always quite different. Can you lean forward to get the top of your back level – almost horizontal?'

'Wouldn't it be better if I just got down in the same position as…as *her.*'

'It would, but I don't have anything handy for you to kneel on.'

'No problem, you don't have to mollycoddle *me*!' She would show him she was a trouper. She would be a professional. She knelt on the hard wood floor, almost in the exact pose of the clay, her dress hanging at her waist. He felt her position. 'Not quite right. Raise your head a little and look back over your left shoulder.

'Does that alter the shape of my breasts?'

'Oh, yes. Very much. Check it out in the model's mirror.'

'Yes, I see. It twists my boobs around quite a bit… Shall I take the dress right off now?'

'In a moment.' He got down under her torso. 'I still have this mental picture of you with it half on… Let me just get this right first.' She felt his hands touch her hanging body so softly it was almost like a caressing breeze – a gentle breeze that touched all over, all around. Then the touch was gone and he was working at the clay again. She heard his comments as he worked. 'Yes, that's it... No, sod it! Fuck! Do this curve again.... Ah... Right!

'Okay. Your knees must be killing you. Take five. Fancy a cup of tea?'

He sat sipping tea in his work coat. She stood close to him, her dress down to her waist and her big breasts pointing out at all angles. 'My boobs are chilly.'

His hand automatically touched her. It felt very natural being part of his tactile world.

'So they are, I'll warm them up a bit.' He rubbed his hands vigorously then warmed them gently with his friction-heated palms. That felt *so* delicious! He was fondling them now, taking their weight...

'And this interview, what next – my waist?' she said breathlessly.

'Well yes, but we must also look at you holistically – as a complete woman – once the details have been examined...' He stood up and held her waist.

Interview! This was such bullshit, she thought. 'No!' She was firm. She pushed a hand against his broad chest. 'You keep getting me going, feeling my tits like that and then letting me go off the boil... It's driving me nuts!' She paused, surprised at herself, but pleased with her boldness. She wanted to say something to him... Something outrageous. She had never had to *ask* a man in her life, but him being blind made it different. He couldn't see her face – she could never feel embarrassed with him. 'Let's *do* it... Right here!'

'Are you sure you want to make love to a blind man?'

''Make love! Christ! This is all about sex. Your sculptures, the women – they all *ooze* sex! I want you to get me from behind! That's how I want it... Now!' She could hardly believe she was saying this.

He pulled her dress down over her hips and bottom, all the way down. She felt gorgeously naked. 'No knickers either, Angel?'

She felt his hands slide around the bare expanse of her hips as her dress slid to the floor. 'Well, you have me bare-assed, are you going to talk to me or *fuck* me?' This was marvellous. She felt so liberated! When her face couldn't be seen, she could say and do anything she wanted!

'Okay, Angel, I'll fuck you.' He smacked her bare bottom, a single slap. She liked that! He pushed her into a corner onto a rug. She knelt down on all fours ready for him – just like the pose.

He felt her, separating her thighs a little wider, his fingers probing her wet labia, feeling up inside her. And while his fingers moved, he kissed her long back. She moaned a little. He found her clitoris and gently worked on her. She moved against him. Her breath came more quickly. His kissing had travelled down her spine, all over her bottom cheeks now, lower... She felt his tongue replace the finger. The tingling spread up into her loins...

She felt him pull back from her. 'No. Don't stop!'

'Only a moment, Angel. Don't move!' He was taking off his clothes.

Her dark hair blew around in the warm breeze from the corner heating vent, as she waited, legs parted. Then, through her flying hair she saw him approach. Naked. Rampant. It was wonderful. She got her head right down and prepared to receive him. Hurry, hurry... Through the narrow gap between her hanging breasts and between her opened thighs she saw and felt the broad cock-head touch her body. She was so wet she was dripping. She felt it separate her lips; push through; felt the deep, deep penetration. She cried out in sheer joy.

She had not had a man since Michael. She needed sex badly after all this time; raw sex for its own sake, just like this. That impulse had brought her here. But this man… This blind man. She had never had anyone like him. He was a far better lover than Michael had ever been – and it wasn't just because he couldn't see her – although that did give her this wonderful uninhibited feeling.

He gently touched her clitoris as he filled her deeper than ever. His big hands with their infinitely gentle fingers were always where she wanted them, touching, stroking, toying with her.

Often he would withdraw and she was free to suck and taste him (and her own taste on him), without being self-conscious about him seeing her doing such an intimate thing. But each time, the desire to feel him thrusting hard up inside her again forced her mouth to give him up. But now she sensed when he wanted her to touch him, gently holding his balls while she could feel the tip of his cock, high inside her belly.

Finally he held her to a howling climax with his mobile fingers, thrusting hard and coming freely, deep within her. She in turn powered his spurts with gentle squeezes of her hand.

Still he kissed her. Long after. Him spent, her leaking onto the rug. He kissed her shoulders, her back and bottom. Lightly, he bit the rounded cheeks.

'Ouch!' she cried in mock pain. 'That was *so* lovely…' She rolled over lazily on to her back, her breasts looking up at him – he unable to see them. She felt a brief sadness. Such a cruel handicap. Then admiration. 'How do you do it, how do you know *exactly* what a woman wants?' He just smiled. She looked deeper into his sightless, sensitive face. She reached up to touch it as he had first touched hers…

Then she heard something. Someone nearby! 'Hey!' she almost screamed.

'What?'

'Someone's here!'

'Where?'

'I heard something – behind us.' She frowned, unsure.

'Don't worry, that would be Bess, my guide-dog.'

She relaxed, but she still hated the idea of being watched while making love (she corrected herself – while fucking). 'You have a guide-dog?'

'Of course. She helps me out and about. I don't need to use her much inside the house where I know where everything is.'

'But I haven't seen her around.'

'No, you wouldn't. She's pretty shy of strangers. She keeps well out of the way. Maybe when you've been here a few times she'll come out and make friends with you. My models get on very well with her after the initial surprise.'

'What surprise?'

'Well, she's an unusual breed for a guide dog…' that enigmatic smile again. 'Would you like to see her?' He called out 'Bess! Come here Bess!' A sharp whine sounded from just outside the studio door.

'No, she's not ready to meet you yet – maybe next time; I won't force her. Look, can you come back same time tomorrow? I have to take Bess out for a walk.'

She was both peeved and intrigued. Her curiosity overwhelmed her. Driving just a short distance, she parked and watched for him to come out with his dog. Nothing. Maybe they'd walk in that huge garden of his.

It was easy to work around to the back, but not so easy to see in. She pushed her way into the high, scratchy hedge and finally managed to get a view of the steps leading down to the lawn from the studio.

Two minutes later she saw movement behind reflections on the glass studio door. It was opening. A beautiful, completely naked young woman led the blind man carefully down the steep steps. It had to be the other model he still used sometimes – the petite one! She felt a strong surge of jealousy at the sight of them together. Then she noticed the collar around her neck. They frolicked around the lawn a little. She mostly ran, but occasionally dropped to all fours when he was close, allowing him to pat her like a dog. She even squatted down to pee profusely on the lawn.

The sight sent a flood of conflicting emotions through her, but jealousy and anger rose above them all. Before she knew it she'd burst right though the hedge, tearing the front of her dress wide-open in the process. She didn't care. 'You perverted bastards!' she shouted like a tart. 'You should be fucking locked up!'

'Angel?'

She ignored him, focusing on the girl who covered her breasts in fright. 'And you, you little bitch – I suppose you saw everything when we were fucking in the corner? How dare you watch me!' The girl whined her fear but stayed down at his side. He held her collar.

'Leave her out of this!' He calmed his powerful voice. 'Bess and I have an unusual relationship, sure. I wasn't hiding her from you: I was going to show her to you, remember? And didn't you see my car in the drive? I thought you might have worked *that* out. A blind man can't drive any more than his dog can. She drives me around.'

'Yeah,' she shouted, 'and you *fuck* her around in return; all around the house, I bet!'

Turning on her heel she fought her way back through the hedge, leaving most of her dress behind.

He answered the door. 'Yes?'

'It's me.'

His made his voice hard. 'Well?'

'I'm *so* sorry. I was well out of order. I was just so angry when I thought of her watching me being so uninhibited with you, asking for it like that. I've never done anything remotely like that before. I could only do it because you... I thought no one could see me.'

'Are you coming in?'

'Yes. I want to apologise for what I said to her – and you.'

After he let her in, he touched her face to read her expression. She pressed against him and he was soon fondling her free breasts through the thin sweater. His body began to respond strongly. She smelt different. There was a pleasant leathery smell. 'You've missed something,' she said smugly. He felt over her again. She was wearing a studded collar around her neck.

'Does this mean...'

His need for her suddenly became urgent.

'It does. I'm going to be a *complete* bitch this time.'

Birthday Treat
by Alex de Kok

The curve of the female bottom is one of the loveliest curves in nature, and Harry was happy to see it. He glanced across again, taking advantage of the fact that she was looking away from him to adjust the press of his half-hard prick against his jeans. Even on a garden kneeler, bent over a flower bed, Janet Blythe was a very attractive woman. The fact that he was only nineteen and she thirty-two didn't alter that fact, it only made it just about impossible that anything would ever happen between them. Nothing, that is, except what seemed to be a genuine friendship.

In baggy shorts and a loose T-shirt, Janet was working in the flower bed, dead-heading her roses. He looked again, but there was no panty line to be seen. No panties, or was she wearing a thong? His prick twitched, and he grinned to himself. Think pure thoughts, Harry! Yeah, right. With a woman like Janet Blythe around, a chance somewhere between zero and infinitesimal. But he could dream…

'Harry?'

Reality intruded with a mental thud. 'Yes?'

'Would you bring that rubbish bag across, please?'

'Sure.' He picked up the bag and took it across to where she was kneeling. There was a pile of dead roses beside her.

'Hold the bag open, and I'll put these in. No, I'll do it,' she said as he reached for the flower heads. 'I've got gloves on and there may be some thorns.'

'Okay.' He held the bag open for her as she lifted a double handful of flower heads, glancing down to make sure he had the bag positioned right. His breath caught in his throat. Her loose T-shirt had fallen away as she leaned forward, and he could see down into it, see the sensuous cleft between her breasts, breasts that seemed unsupported by any bra, breasts that he could see almost down to the nipple. Lovely breasts: lovely enough to cause a stiffening in his pants.

'Harry?'

He dragged his attention back to the here-and-now. 'Sorry,' he said, feeling the heat of his face as she stared up at him, her flushed pinkness probably matching his own. 'I was miles away.'

'It's okay, I think I'm finished here. How about you?' Her smile seemed automatic, and mentally he kicked himself. Idiot! Staring down her shirt.

'Just need to put the mower back in the shed,' he said, relieved to hear the normality in his tone. 'The cuttings are in the compost bin.'

'Good man. Will you put these in the shed, too? I'll go and put the kettle on. Come into the kitchen when you've put them away. What would you prefer? Tea or coffee?'

'Tea, please.'

'Ready in five. See you in the kitchen.'

Putting the mower, the secateurs and the rake away only took him a moment or two. Mentally he kicked himself, but a rueful smile crept onto his face. Caught ogling her, yes, but by God, those tits were worth an ogle! When he went into the kitchen, Janet was just pouring the water into the pot.

'Wash your hands, Harry, and the tea will be ready. No milk, that right?'

'Please.' He busied himself washing and drying his hands, then turned to her and took a deep breath. 'I want to apologise.'

'For what? Peering down my shirt?' She smiled. 'It's me who should apologise to you, Harry. I should have known my top was too loose.'

'Even so, it was rude, and I'm sorry.'

She shook her head. 'Say no more, Harry. You're a teenage male and I'd be amazed, and probably wonder if you were normal, if you hadn't peeped. Um, I bumped into your mum when I was shopping this morning.'

'Yeah, she said she'd seen you.'

'She told me it was your birthday yesterday. Why didn't you say?'

He shrugged, embarrassed. 'I don't know.'

'I'd like to give you something. What would you like? Any suggestions?'

You, he thought, and for a horrified moment he thought he'd said it aloud from the startled look on her face, but she merely said, 'Well?'

'I don't know. Something small. A box of caramels or something.'

'Are you sure?'

'Yes. I don't want you to waste your money on me. I feel guilty letting you pay me for the gardening help I give you as it is.'

She laughed. 'Don't. My ex pays me substantial alimony. I think it's hush money.'

Harry grinned. 'Got something on him?'

Janet winked, touching her finger to her nose.

Harry laughed. 'I'll take that as a yes.'

'Tomorrow?'

96

'What about tomorrow?'

'You normally help me from two until four on a Friday, but would you like to come around here about one, say, and I'll cook you lunch as a post-birthday treat?'

He was surprised, but pleased, and didn't hesitate. 'Yes, please. I'd like that.'

'Don't put your working clothes on. It's a birthday treat, a paid holiday. We'll have lunch, perhaps a glass of wine, and a chat. Maybe a swim. You okay with that?'

'If you're sure, I'd love to,' he said, pleased at the thought of just the two of them at lunch together. Almost like a date. Then it hit him. 'Swim? Where?'

She laughed. 'You didn't know I had a pool, did you?'

He shook his head. 'Where? Surely I'd have seen it?'

'You've never been in the back wing, have you?'

'No.'

'Drink your tea, and then I'll show you.'

They chatted idly for a few minutes while they drank their tea, then Janet stood. 'Come on, I'll show you the pool.' She led him through the house, to the wing at the rear. He'd always thought it was bedrooms or something, but when she opened a door he realised it was an indoor pool. Small, maybe twenty-five feet by fifteen, but enough to swim a few strokes. A couple of screened-off alcoves for changing. 'What do you think?'

He grinned at her. 'Great! Small, but fun.' He bent, testing the water. 'And cold.'

She laughed. 'The pool technician is due later this afternoon. I haven't been using it as there's a problem with the heater. The maintenance people have been waiting for a spare part to be delivered. They phoned this morning to say it's in and they're coming to fix it. It should be working by tomorrow, ready for our swim.'

'I'll look forward to it.' And to seeing you in a swimsuit, he thought. I hope it's a bikini.

'Me, too.'

In bed that night, Harry thought back to the glimpse he'd had of Janet Blythe's breasts, and her invitation. Holding the image he'd glimpsed in his mind, embellishing it with his imagination, he began to masturbate. Had he known that, just over a mile away, naked on her bed, Janet Blythe was thinking of him as she slid a dildo into her wetness, he'd have been even harder.

Next day dawned fine and sunny. He had a lazy morning and just after twelve-thirty set out to walk the mile to Janet's house. It was only ten to one when he got there but Janet opened the door to his ring and quickly ushered him inside. No shorts and T-shirt today, but a pretty summer dress, sleeveless.

'Hi, Harry, come on through.' She led the way into the living room and gestured him to a chair. 'Here,' she said, passing him a gift-wrapped parcel. 'This is for you, from me.'

He smiled when he saw the box of caramels, surprised when he saw what else was in the parcel. He looked across at her and she nodded.

'I phoned your mum. She told me you'd got a digital camera, and the model, and I popped into the camera shop and asked what was the best idea in accessories. They said extra storage was never wrong, and nor was a good supply of rechargeable batteries. So.' She gestured. 'That's what I got. Did you bring the camera with you?'

He nodded. 'It's in my bag, along with my swimming trunks.'

'Good. You can take my photograph later. I checked the pool earlier, and the heater has the water back up to

98

temperature, in fact probably over-temperature, as I turned the thermostat up to make sure it was nice for us.'

'I'm looking forward to it.'

'In that case, it's decision time. I decided that, as it was such a nice day, a cold meal wasn't a bad idea, so I've done us a king prawn salad. We can have ice-cream for afters. We can eat any time, so would you like to swim before lunch, and maybe again afterwards, or do you want to eat now?'

'I think you should choose. It's your pool.'

'In that case, we swim now. But before we do, there's something I have to say.'

'Such as?'

'Harry, I've had that pool for four years, and in that time, there have only been naked bodies in it. If you're shy, and you want to put your trunks on, fine, I'll put my swimsuit on. If you can bear the embarrassment of me seeing you naked – and, Harry, I'm not planning on looking away – if you can bear that, well, I'll go naked, too.'

He stared at her for a long, long, moment, then managed to nod. He tried to speak, failed, and cleared his throat. 'Skinny-dip? Please?'

'Want to see what you didn't yesterday?' Mute, he nodded, and she grinned. 'Good! Come on, let's see if I've still got what it takes.'

'I'm sure you have,' he managed to say, and she flashed a smile over her shoulder as she led him to the pool. 'You use that side,' she said, gesturing to an alcove, 'and I'll use the other.'

He'd only managed to get his shirt off when she called him. 'Harry? Can you give me a hand?' Curious, he moved over to the other alcove. Still fully dressed, Janet turned her back to him. 'I think the zip's stuck. See if you can move it, please?'

'Sure.' He took hold of the slider, and the material next to it, and tried to move the slider down. It wouldn't budge. He peered closer, trying to see why, smelling her spring flower perfume, and something else, a musk. His prick twitched at the warmth of her that he could feel, being so close to her. He peered again, and could just see that the stuff of her dress was caught behind the slider.

'I think the dress material is jammed in the slider,' he said. 'I can't move it.'

'Damn.' Silence for a moment. 'It's an old dress, Harry.' She giggled, surprising him. 'Think you could rip it off me, he-man?'

'You want me to tear it off you?' He couldn't keep the startled surprise from his voice. Nor the excitement.

'It saves going for scissors. Like I said, it's an old dress. I'm fond of it, but if the material's got into the zip it's probably ruined, so yes, Harry, tear my dress off!'

'Brace yourself.' He took a firm hold of the material on either side of the zip, and pulled sideways. Resistance at first, and then the dress split down the seam next to the zip, and tore all of the way down to where Janet's bottom jutted out towards him. She gave a shake, the ruins of the dress fell away, and he was rewarded with a vision in peach silk. Half-cup bra, barely covering her nipples. Skimpy panties, little more than thong. Smooth, lightly tanned skin. A lot of skin.

Janet smiled as she turned to him. 'Thanks, Harry.' She put her hands to the front fastening of the bra, and it fell away. There they were, those breasts he had only 'nearly' seen before, in all of their naked glory. Rounded, full, erect nipples crowning puffy areolae, they were beautiful.

'Like them, Harry?' she murmured.

He managed to nod. 'Beautiful,' he said, embarrassed to hear the croak that his voice had become.

'Thank you. Go on, get the rest of your clothes off,' she said, letting the bra slide down off her arms, and reaching to push down her panties. She paused, thumbs in her waistband. 'Oh, you want to see me first, eh? Okay.' And she pushed the panties down, letting them fall, kicking them aside. She struck a pose, one arm in the air, the other on her thigh, weight on one leg, the other bent. 'Tada!'

He stared. She was lightly tanned all over, not a tan line to be seen. Her pubic hair, neatly trimmed to her panty line, was the same dark blonde as on her head, although slightly darker. Presumably from less sun, he thought, although considering the absence of tan lines, he wondered. She broke the pose, grinning at him.

'I think you like the view,' she said, her tone soft.

He swallowed. 'The most beautiful I've ever seen,' he managed to say.

'And I haven't seen you yet, Harry, so get your clothes off, please.'

He managed a smile and turned back to the alcove where he'd put his shirt, startled to find she'd followed him.

She grinned. 'You watched me; I watch you. Get 'em off!'

He swallowed the huge lump in his throat, and tried to ignore what he knew was almost a full erection pressing against the front of his jeans, unzipping them and pushing them down, then wrestling off the sneakers he'd forgotten about, kicking his jeans off. His boxers were tented in front and she looked down and then glanced up at him, a twinkle in her eyes. He managed a grin, and took a deep breath before he pushed the boxers down, breathing a sigh of relief as his prick sprang free, almost erect.

Her eyes widened, and she smiled, then her eyes came to his. 'Nice, Harry.'

He gestured, embarrassed. 'I'm sorry.'

101

'What for? Your body is paying me a compliment, and I'm flattered.'

He gave her a wry look. 'We both think you're lovely.'

Janet laughed. 'Thank you, both.' Her face sobered and she looked him in the eye. 'Harry, yesterday, remember, when I asked you what you'd like for your birthday?'

He had a sudden, horrible feeling that he knew what was coming and he could feel the heat in his face. 'I remember.'

'Do you remember what you said? Of course you do. When I asked you what you wanted, you said 'you'. I don't think you realised you'd said it aloud, or maybe you sub-vocalised it, but I have acute hearing, Harry, and I heard you.'

He gestured helplessly. 'It sort of slipped out. You're right, I didn't know I'd said it aloud.'

'Did you mean it?' There was a tone to her voice that suggested the answer was important to her.

Harry nodded. 'Absolutely.'

'And now you've seen the reality you could only imagine before? What now? Still feel the same?'

'More than ever.'

She smiled, stepping forward to kiss him lightly on the lips. 'Good,' she said. She paused, then, 'Harry, when you said 'you' when I asked you what you wanted, what was in your mind?' Harry flushed, and gestured helplessly. Janet smiled. 'Making love, perhaps?' He nodded, unable to speak, a huge lump in his throat. Her smile faded. 'Harry, love, after you left yesterday, I couldn't get what you said out of my head. I know I'm older, nearly twice your age, but I like to think I still look good.'

'Better than just good!'

'Thank you. Last night, Harry, after I went to bed, I lay there, just thinking about you, and what you'd said. And do you know what I did?' He shook his head, wondering. 'I masturbated, Harry. I got myself off. I got my dildo out for the first time in three years and I fucked myself to orgasm, pretending it was you.' He shook his head, helpless, and she reached out to touch his cheek. 'Do you want me, Harry? Do you want to make love to me?'

'Yes,' he managed to say, his voice hoarse.

'Well, I want it, too, especially now I've seen what you're offering me. And soon. I read somewhere that anticipation is the best aphrodisiac, so I want you to anticipate, Harry, I want you to anticipate sliding that lovely erection you showed me into my pussy and fucking me.' She smiled, and stretched across to give him a quick kiss. 'Have you fucked before, Harry?'

He shrugged, and nodded. 'Yes, but only twice.'

'Girls? Or women?'

'Girls.'

'Virgin?'

He shook his head. 'Not yet.' She frowned, and he laughed. 'Sally, my girlfriend at university, she promised me her cherry when the new semester starts. We're moving out of the halls and into a flat, with another couple.

Janet laughed, a fruity gurgle that made his prick twitch. 'Anticipation, Harry!'

He grinned. 'Yeah!'

'Kiss me, Harry.'

The kiss was tentative at first, as they learned each other's flavour, but deepened quickly, until their mouths were working on each other, lips parting, tongues probing, duelling, twining, breathing deepening, until she broke the kiss, panting. She took a deep breath, then gave a shaky laugh.

'Harry, we'll swim later. Now, we need a bed. Come on.' She took his hand and led him to her bedroom. Beside the bed she twined her arms around his neck and looked up at him. 'Touch me,' she whispered.

Hardly daring to breathe, he brought his hands up and cupped her breasts. She hissed in a breath as she felt his thumbs pass over her nipples, and he felt her pressing against him, trapping his hardness between them, her hips moving, grinding against him. Her mouth came up and captured his, opening to him, sharing his breathing. He moved his hands from her breasts and pulled her against him, feeling her breasts flatten against his chest.

She broke away and moved to the bed, laying herself on her back and spreading her legs. She held her hand out to him. 'Fuck me, Harry,' she whispered.

He moved onto the bed, kneeling between her legs, his cock held lightly in one hand and bent to enter her, feeling her cool fingers guide him to her opening, her wet, hot, opening. He pressed in, feeling her yield to his thrust, wishing he could see it.

'Push in a little, then pull back, lover, spread my juices, then push in again,' she murmured. Once, again, a third time, and he was deep inside her, his balls against her bottom. He pulled back, ready to push in again, but she stopped him, her hands on his hips.

'Just hold it there for a moment, lover. I'm enjoying this. Yours is one of the biggest cocks I've ever had in me, and I'm feeling good.

'Is it really?' he said, uncertain.

'It is,' she said, squeezing down on him with her internal muscles. She stretched up and kissed him. 'Fuck me, Harry,' she said, her voice a caress. He began to move. Gently, almost gingerly, at first. 'Feel good?' she said.

'Oh, yes,' he breathed. 'It's wonderful, better than I ever dreamed. Every time I –' he broke off, and she smiled.

'Every time what, Harry? Every time you jack off?' He nodded, a little embarrassed. 'Every time, then, Harry? What?'

'Every time I jack off, I imagine doing this, with you.'

'I'm flattered,' she said, smiling up at him. 'Come on, let's make that dream true.'

He laughed, and began moving a little faster. She squeezed him again, and pulled her knees up, opening herself to him. He was moving easily now, audibly, in her juices and she hugged him, urging him on with wordless little cries, but the moment got to him and he stiffened, and cried out, shaking as he came, too soon. Far, far too soon.

'I'm sorry, M—' he began, and she giggled, putting her finger across his lips.

'I think it's probably time you called me Janet,' she said, smiling up at him. 'You came?' He nodded, and she stretched up to kiss him again. 'Don't worry, lover. I'll get you hard again and the second time will be better.'

'You make me too excited,' he said, with a wry grimace.

'Pull out and lie back,' she said. 'Let's get you cleaned up.' He eased himself from her, feeling the cooler air on his half-hard prick, and she came up onto her knees beside, his gasp echoing her soft moan as she took him into her mouth, her lips and tongue moving on him, cleaning him, stimulating him, so that it seemed but moments before he was hard and pulsing again. She sat back on her heels, holding his erection lightly between her fingers. He reached for her other hand, squeezing the fingers, and made to get up. She stopped him with a flat hand on his chest.

'Lie back and enjoy, lover. It's time for Janet Blythe to ride!' Slightly startled, he lay back, feeling the grin spreading across his face as she shuffled astride his thighs, moving so that her pussy was poised above his hardness, lowering herself until he just entered her. She took her hand

105

away, reaching for Harry's hands and placing them on her breasts. He cupped the soft mounds, enjoying touching her, the weight of her in his hands, and she held his eyes as she lowered yourself onto him. She was wet, still full of him from before and it took no more than a wriggle before her bottom was resting on his thighs.

'Feel good?' she said, brow arched, and he nodded, grinning up at her.

'Feels fucking fantastic, pardon my French,' he said. She bent forward to suck his nipple, and he shuddered. She laughed.

'Never had your nipple sucked before, Harry?'

He shook his head. 'It felt incredible.'

'Not today, but sometime soon, Harry, I want you to suck my nipples, and I want you to eat me, because I don't need a prick inside me to make me come, just a caring man treating me right.'

'Are you saying you want to do this again?' he said, scarcely daring to hope.

'Fuck yes, Harry, I most certainly am. For now, though, let's you and me concentrate on both of us getting to come.'

'Just tell me what to do.'

'Lie back and enjoy, lover,' she murmured, and began to move, easily, because she was so wet, and Harry played gently with her breasts as she moved, audible now, a liquid slither of sound. She giggled as trapped air escaped with a blurt of sound. Harry could feel the sweat on his face, feel it between them, and she changed her angle slightly, her breathing quickening, bringing them both up the slope of sensation. Harry could feel himself getting closer and gritted his teeth, willing himself not to come until she was ready, but pushing back up at her as she rode him.

'Close, lover?' she gasped.

He nodded. 'Very, Janet, very close.'

'Good,' she said, and he saw her fingers move across her clit. She gave a tight scream, her pussy clutching at him, milking him, and he pushed up hard at her, letting her take him over the precipice of climax and into the miniature death that is orgasm.

Slowly, slowly, awareness returned. He was gasping for breath, as if he'd just finished a marathon, and Janet too was dragging oxygen from the air. Gradually, normality returned and she bent forward to kiss him, a long kiss, filled with warmth, with pleasure. She broke the kiss and sat back, Harry still inside her.

He smiled up at her. 'I think without any doubt at all, that will be my best late birthday present, ever,' he said.

Janet grinned. 'Don't bet on it.'

Backstory
by Frances Jones

Moments after the mayor's gavel-stroke marked the adjournment of a blessedly brief City Council meeting, my competitor and I were locked in a City Hall janitor's closet, fumbling with each other's clothes.

His teeth studied my neck as I unbuttoned his corduroy trousers, the heat rising from his groin. I dove in with my hands, then backed up against a sturdy shelf and propped myself against it before pulling him inside me. There was no floor space to speak of, and his reporter's arms were too damaged by years of high-speed typing to lift my sturdy frame. Besides, we were both on deadline and there wasn't much time.

We weren't always like this. I faintly hated him the first time I saw him. He was there, in the back row of a gossip-filled neighbourhood meeting I thought only I knew about, whispering with residents and taking pages of notes. He never looked at me, never saw the barbs in my eyes.

My scorn only grew as he managed to dig up just as many exclusive stories for his newspaper as I did for mine. His name and by-line were the reason I swore under my breath each morning and worked late each night, trying to beat him in the next day's edition.

We were thrust together – literally – during a standing-room-only press conference at the international airport. Dozens of reporters crowded around the talking heads as they brought hurricane victims' pets in by plane and took them to local animal shelters. He was standing just behind me – towering over me, more precisely, since he is nearly a foot taller than I am.

I'd never been so close to him; one tends to keep a safe distance from one's imagined nemesis. We were both scribbling frantically in our notebooks when the network-news cameraman in front of me stepped back, bumping me directly into the man I'd worked so hard to avoid. I started to mumble an apology, but when I felt his erection pressing against me I lost all powers of language.

I looked up at him, studying his liquid mahogany eyes, three-day stubble and tangle of dark, curly hair. With a quick tilt of his head and a tug of my hand, he beckoned me to follow him. He led me silently down a hall and into a small office whose floor space was nearly filled by a desk and two armchairs. There, with the late-afternoon gloom shining in through the venetian blinds and the planes roaring on the tarmac outside, he sat down in one of the chairs and unbuttoned his khakis, letting his cock spring free. He quickly sheathed it with a condom, and then raised my skirt, slid my underpants down, and lowered me onto his lap.

I squeezed his legs together between my thighs and rode him as he clutched my breasts from behind. His gasping breath jetted hot streams of air across my shoulders. With one hand on my clitoris, my orgasm came quickly, subsiding just in time for me to feel him spasming inside of me.

We both settled backwards into the chair for a few breaths. I twisted around to kiss him, keeping his organ buried deep. As I pulled away he started to speak, so I put my musk-scented fingers against his mouth. Any conversation might lead us to spill our sources, reveal our leads, ruin our competitive edge, or even make friends. It was better to say nothing.

I kissed him once more, tugged my panties back on, and found my way back to my car. Then I raced back to the newsroom and composed the best orphaned-pets story I'd ever written. The whole time, I imagined the stream of profanity that would emerge from my lover's lips the next morning when he saw it on the front page of my newspaper.

A handful of reporters from local papers regularly reported news in the city I covered, but my competitor and I were the only ones consistently assigned to the same City Council meetings, ribbon-cuttings, and press conferences. On evenings when he didn't show up, I made sure I wrote a story that would make him sorry he missed it.

When he did show up, he always found a way to tryst with me in some abandoned room, closet or secluded garden. We were never together more than 10 minutes – we were on deadline, after all. How he knew every hidden spot in every location in the city, I could only imagine. Perhaps he had his way with every female reporter, sooner or later. Perhaps at home he kept a master map, marking down new spots as he discovered them. That would explain why he always had a condom or two in his back pocket.

After a gruelling meeting in which a 35-member committee bickered for two hours about the benefits and drawbacks of artificial turf, he showed me into a darkened office with a planner's name on the door. There, he bent me over the desk and entered me from behind, his soft hands knotted into my hair, while I eyed a photograph of the office's owner posed with a wife and two young children. They beamed blandly back at me. After my lover left, I

110

swiped one of the planner's business cards – I needed to interview him for an investigative piece I was pursuing.

We met as often as chance brought us together. At a garden-party for a new wing of the local college, he pulled me behind a tall hedge and laid on his back in the grass. As I straddled him, my long skirt shrouding our nakedness, we covered each other's mouths with our hands to muffle our moans. Watching him at the banquet table that morning, I learned he subsisted (as many poorly paid reporters do) on nothing but coffee and catered food. Meanwhile, he learned that I had the Dean in my back pocket.

To pass the dull prologue of a school-board meeting, we found an unlocked classroom and fed each other bites of a teacher's apple as he hoisted my legs over his shoulders and plunged into me. Since then, I haven't been able to eat an apple – or interview that teacher – without remembering the ferocity in his eyes that night, as though he were exacting some revenge on every dull classroom he'd endured.

Remaining wordless turned out to be wise. Our news reporting became smarter than ever, fuelled by the silent chemistry between us. Each of us found juicier angles, sweeter sources, and sharper tongues the more we trysted. As we grew more incisive our editors sent us out into the field more and more.

Eventually, he invaded my dreams. One month after that afternoon at the airport, I dreamed that another reporter had stumbled upon us in a City Hall broom closet, then jotted notes briskly in her notebook while we continued fucking. The next morning, her headline proclaimed that our papers were secretly in bed together. Page designers can never resist a bad pun.

A few weeks later, I dreamed that my lover had written an article in which the capital letters of each sentence spelled out a secret message to me, although when I woke I could not remember what the message was.

I never once felt guilty for my moments with him. Now and then I craved the feel of his hands, his mouth, his breath on me as I went through my workday. Sometimes it was all I could think about.

If my bureau chief thought my competitor would be somewhere, she'd send me to make sure we had the story, too. Meanwhile, he and I got to know each other in the way our field has the most trouble conveying. Journalism is good with facts and ideas – less so with intangibles. Like the spark you get when you climax with your nemesis and then return to the newsroom sated, clear-headed, and ready to wipe the floor clean with him.

One afternoon, a stormy wind blew down a concrete wall at a demolition site. According to the dispatcher whose voice crackled on the police radio, the 10-foot-tall structure had collapsed onto the car of a woman who pulled over to look at a map, and had taken down an electricity pole in the act. I jumped in my car and sped to the address.

The scene was a confusion of fire engines, urban-search-and-rescue trucks, firemen in yellow jackets and hardhats, and curious neighbours gathering beyond the line of yellow police tape. My lover was already there, taking a statement from the police department's spokeswoman. She was dressed against the frigid gusts in a long black trench coat. When I stepped up to ask her what she knew, I caught the haunted look in my competitor's eyes.

'No, we don't know who she was,' the spokeswoman said, her voice already hollow with repetition. 'No, we're not sure how many neighbours are without power. Yes, we think one of the other walls might be in danger of collapsing. We've evacuated the house next door, just in case.'

I jotted notes, but my mind was on my lover. Out of the corner of my eye I watched as he walked toward the demolition site, his figure receding into the shadows of a nearby alley.

As soon as I could, I followed him. My cell phone rang; it was my editor. I silenced the call, then approached the gruesome place where a half-block of concrete lay in a peculiar hump over the shape of a crushed automobile. Rescue crews were using a jaw-toothed crane to pull pieces of rubble aside. The coroner's white van waited patiently nearby, its back doors ready to receive the dead woman's body. Grief stuck in my throat. I shook it from my head and walked on.

The alley was dark and smelled like dust and ozone. Before my eyes adjusted I felt his hands clutch the heavy fabric of my coat and pull me into the shadows. I kissed him and tasted the tears that wetted his face and throat. It was all I could do not to cry, too – for that lost woman, for all the pleasures she would no longer know. Suddenly it felt important to make it up to her. I could tell my lover felt the same.

His crushing embrace made it difficult to breathe, and he kissed me so sharply that his teeth bruised my lips. His icy hands sought their way under my long woollen skirt, roughly pushed aside my panties. I gasped as he penetrated me with three fingers of one hand and unzipped the fly of his corduroys with the other, pulling his red, stiffened cock free.

We switched places. I leaned against the masonry; he bent his knees and slammed into me, wrapped one of my legs around his waist. Hard kisses muted our sorrow-laced moans. Our orgasms rushed over us like the frozen wind, hurrying with need. A moment later, he re-bundled himself against the cold and rushed off to get more quotes. I went to my knees and brushed the gritty sidewalk with my hands, unready to return to the world just yet. Few understand what these scenes are like, and I was thankful beyond words for his knowing company.

Our articles were nearly identical in the next day's editions. That was okay; I would keep closer tabs on the police department's follow-up investigation than I knew he had time to do.

Tonight, among the mops and buckets, as he climaxed inside me, he laid his rough-shaven face against my breast and I held him like a child. I wondered what thoughts rattled around in his mind when he recalled or longed for these trysts. I wondered what exclusive story he had in store for tomorrow's edition.

He zipped his corduroys, kissed my vulva and then my mouth, and stole away quickly. The door had clicked shut behind him before I opened my eyes.

Sometimes, when I return to the newsroom after seeing him, my editor notes my enthusiasm for late-night meetings and compliments the speed and incisiveness with which I write about them. When she asks what keeps me interested while our other reporters are passing out at their desks, I tell her only this: our work is made up of the words that people say, but it's what happens between the words that makes the story come alive.

Brown Nosing
by Richard Terry

I just couldn't think straight. It was her heels. Not the heels per se, but the noise they made. You'd think my new boss would just respond to the emails in kind in those first few days. Instead, she'd actually appear in my doorway. No one wanted that much personal contact with her, least of all me. Her heels terrorized me.

Marisa scared us, more to the point, she scared me. I couldn't understand it. Maybe it was because we were the only folks of colour in the corporation this high up – she being Latina and me Black – we kept a look out for each other but I could swear she was watching me as much as I was watching her. More and more she became the North Pole the compass in my pants pointed to. I could see where this was headed so I made attempts at being unavailable. Well, I tried, kind of. In actual fact I made up some reason to be at her end of the floor every chance I got.

The thing is I didn't expect it. Her. She's a big girl, all round and brown. But tight and toned, like, you could tell she worked out but only so she could maintain just the right jiggle. She's not like Sheila, actually, who's lately been subsisting on cigarettes and water, in fact quite the opposite. Or is it vodka? I can't tell. All I can see when I walk in the door is the TV on, a tumbler at her side, an ashtray overflowing with cigarette butts and her cradling the cats. Damn those things. They're nestled in places I could hardly remember feeling.

Marisa, on the other hand is ample, something over 180 and hitting almost 6' 2" what with those slides she wears. She paints her toes mauve. You wouldn't think something so small would make me flub my words. She stands close to me when she talks, and I get hard of hearing around her what with that full mouth of hers. Her hair cascades in honey blonde locks like some Medusa Colossus. She had to be older than me but you couldn't tell by the way she dressed. Take this morning for instance: she came in wearing a crisp cotton shirt – not a blouse – a shirt. White. Starched. Open to the third hole. My height gave me an advantage: fucking teal lace bra barely held it all in. I could feel those scalloped edges between my legs. Damn if she didn't have a tiny mole just up to the right of her heart. She tucked all of this in black linen slacks which did a good job making everybody know she had enough back you could strap luggage onto. I coulda shaved with the crease in her pants. Okay, you could say I was scoping her out.

As if on a whim, she threw us a party. On the pretext of calling an emergency meeting she informed us to join her in the conference room. We all squeezed through the door to find the room transformed with holiday decorations and Christmas lights. The room length table was overwhelmed with all sorts of fowl, meat and sweets, and the caterers were at attention ready to dole all of it out.

The DJ kick started the spot playing Christmas tunes. I mean, c'mon, in July? It was around my second eggnog when she threw in Modern Jazz Quartet and some other shit she must've gotten off some smooth jazz radio line-up. Then, dumped right in the middle of that mix – a little

Teddy. When *Turn Off The Lights* filled the room Marisa strutted towards me wearing a leopard print scoop neck and black pleated mini. For this occasion she had her locks erupting out of an ivory barrette. I could sense her legs before I saw them. Toned, creamy – no hose mind you – she rubbed them down with something that filled my nose and imagination. All of that teetering on the most precarious slides. Toes wriggling fucking red nails. They were tickling the edges of my retinas. I had to force myself to breathe.

Marisa grabbed me by the hand and led me to the floor. Things were just about to get really going when she broke from me, signalled the DJ to stop and made some speech about how what we were doing was good for the company and her rep. Of course we'd heard all this before, but these pronouncements came with bonuses and shit. After that, after the whoop, whoop and applause, the DJ put *Hey Pocky Way* on and cranked it up to 11; it looked like everyone just up and started rubbing against each other, we were so happy. An octopus couldn't have served the drinks fast enough. Still it was hard to get into the scene what with taking in all the drama Marisa was flexing. I can still smell her from our embrace. I can still smell a lot of things.

She came back to me and we resumed dancing. I did what I could to show her I knew what I was doing. She didn't take it lying down and gave it right back. And whenever we looked at each other it was almost impossible to look away. I'd try and, instead, became mesmerized by the way her chest shimmered under the Xmas lights. Before I could regroup the song ended. I thanked her and went back to my office on the pretence of grabbing my shit and heading on home. But I didn't. I went to hers.

Now it may sound like I know what I'm doing, but I wasn't thinking with the right head, if you know what I mean. Even though I went to her office I still wondered if I got the signals right. I was so nervous I didn't know whether to stand or sit. Like, I couldn't decide whether to leave the lights off or turn them on. If I turned them on, what if someone barged in? What reason could I give for being there? On the other hand, if I left them off and she came in, she'd probably wonder why I was standing there in the dark. How could I stay there? How could I leave? What was I doing? My mind wandered. I began to notice all the LCD's that dotted her desk. It was like I was looking down on a little dark town. But all those thoughts flew away when the click-clack of high heels ricocheted down the hallway. Even though I knew it was her I was still relieved when she appeared at the end of that cadence. She closed the door, locking it even. I didn't think my heart could pound any harder than when she came over to me. We grabbed each other with our mouths. I couldn't feel my tongue but could tell what hers tasted like. She was hungry. So was I. I felt her up as we moved across the room, kissing all the way. Couldn't get enough of those lips. Reached into her top but couldn't decide which breast to suck on, so I did them both. Those nipples! Man, I sucked them till they could stand up all by themselves.

I wanted her up on the desk, legs up on my shoulders but she didn't submit that easily. Instead, she turned around. Teased me by ceremoniously lifting what little skirt she had on to her back. All I imagined was staring right at me. The sound of my zipper made her look over her shoulder and told me to hold up. Said she could get that at home. Bigger even. She needed something else.

Didn't give me a second look as she put her elbows back on the desk, turning the lamp on and wiggling her ass in the process. Her telling me what to do sparked something inside of me and made me shiver. And since her ass was everything I imagined and more, what I couldn't do with my dick I'd do with my mouth. I grabbed her cheeks – not an easy thing to do given their size. They were firm – but, I dug into them just the same. I'm sure I left marks. I held on to them when I dropped to my knees. Wasn't too comfortable neither, those floors were concrete. But the way her thong fit in the snug of her crack made me forget how hard it was. I hooked the strip with my finger and pulled just enough of it away. My nose flared, the fragrance her legs gave off was even more potent between her cheeks and made for a heady mix. I pressed my face in there so far I couldn't tell where I ended and her ass began. I tore it up, first her pussy, then, her ass, especially her ass. I sucked it, laved it, drew sustenance from it. The more I licked the deeper I dug it; her ass had a special tang. I plain wallowed in her.

It's unbelievable I know. Like how can I be on my knees with a face full of my boss's ass? Well, finally, at last, unlike most situations, this time I made sure my ass was covered. I gotta hold of my phone, called myself and recorded the whole thing:

Oh God I can't believe I'm doing this. Show me you love it. I want to hear it. That's right. Smell me. That's right blow on me. Shit that feels good, yeah, oh God, use that tongue. Lemme back up onit. I'ma whore for that tongue. Yeah lick it lick it all around. Unnh, bite it, bite it bitch. Lemmee spread myself s'more I wanna feel it all at once. That's right, run it around in circles. Don't forget the other hole. You so good, bab. Yeah one finger, move it around. Lick that finger as it goes in, keep that up. That's righ. Oh, oh, now, yeah, put two in, that's it. Goddamn, those fingers. Get it in me. Your tongue, move it in and out, yeah! God you getting me so wet. Yeah, go deeper. I'm loose enough now; slow up, okay? Yeah, that's it. Put two more in, yeah, open me up, spread me wide open, goddamn you nasty. Don't stop! Don't stop, yeah, move that tongue, sweet, yeah, this is so sweet, yeah tongue fuck me baby, get me juicy, oah I don't want this to stop. Shit, this is good, stretch me muthafucka, yeah that's it, give me more fingers; how many you got in me? Here, use soma this I want more in my hole. I love saying that. Goddamn, gimmee some more. I want to feel you in my guts. No no, let me take care of that part, you just keep doing what you doing. Shit, I gotta use my fingers now; can you feel it? Yeah I'm close. Don't pull out harder I don't know if I can take it. Yeah, a little more; here, let me help you. That's it. Uummm, good, get in there, yes. A little more, God, now don't move, gotta get used to it....okay, now move it in a little more, pull it out...yeah, that's it, slooowly. Some more, yeah, keep that up. Oh God, yeah, fuck me, that's it. I can feel you now. A little more! Faster, deeper, shit this some sweet shit, fuck me, deeper, faster. Yeah, fuck my ass. Fuck me nigguh give me all you got! Keep doing that, yeah, fuckmefuckmefuckme. Yes! Fuckme harder, fuckmehardermutherfuckahfuckme f. c . .!

The rest of it don't make sense. By the time I got up off that floor my pants were sticking to me. But you know what? I must've done a good job because she invited me to her place. I savoured her taste in my mouth as I got in my car and followed hers. It was late. Had to think of an alibi. But that would be later. I was gonna get mine.

Farmer's Daughter
by Landon Dixon

When Mr Loewen handed me the Fraser assignment, I was about as happy as a pig in water. It was the dog days of summer – howlingly hot, with a hell-like forecast extending well into the foreseeable future – and the last thing I wanted to do was leave a nice, quiet, icebox of an office in Sioux Falls to go driving off in an unair-conditioned beater down a melting asphalt highway to some sun-scorched farm a hundred miles south of the middle of nowhere. But when you're a first-year staff assistant (i.e. grunt) at Loewen and Loewen, CPAs, these are the kind of jobs you get.

So, I yanked the Fraser box out of the file vault, pulled a ream of Federal agricultural subsidy forms from the supply room, and phoned Elmer Fraser down on the farm to confirm the firm's bi-annual visit. Only, Elmer wasn't ploughing gumbo anymore; he'd been ploughed under himself.

'Dad died two months ago, Allan,' his daughter told me, a hint of a southern accent other than South Dakota in her husky voice. 'I'm running the farm now, and frankly, I could use all the help I can get.'

I rolled my eyes, picturing a festering pile of unfiled documents and unpaid bills, a painful lesson in accounting

101 to come. 'Okay,' I gritted. 'I'll be out there at nine tomorrow morning.' She agreed and hung up, and I slammed the phone down. Then I was jolted by a shoulder slap of commiseration and derision from my buddy in the adjoining cubicle; he was flying off to a fishing lodge in Canada on Friday.

Early the next morning, with the temperature climbing into the mid-nineties, and the sky the limit, I let my backbone slide into my furnace-hot '85 Monte Carlo, started it up, and hit the open road. One fractured fan belt and two steam breaks later, I pulled off the highway and drove down a long, dirt road that led to the Fraser place.

I'd never been there before, but it was typical farm fare – white, three-storey clapboard house, long metal Quonset in back, sprawling fields of sun-ripening grain in all directions. I shut off the spluttering car and peeled myself off the torn leather upholstery, hoisted my audit bag out of the spring-sprung backseat and trudged across a yellow lawn to the front door of the farmhouse. I knocked on the screen door, the blazing sun firing up my charcoal, polyester suit like I was a mobile solar panel. A woman eventually answered my knock, opened the door of the house and walked out on to the porch. And that's when things really got hot.

'Allan?' she asked.

'Nadine Fraser?' I replied, heavy audit bag slipping out of my sweaty hand and thumping down onto the stoop, along with my jaw. Even through the dense, wire mesh of the screen, I could clearly see that this was one good-looking babe, with a figure that really added up. And when she pushed the screen door open, giving me an unobstructed view, my body temperature bubbled up to a new daytime record.

The forty-something lady was tall and tanned and full-figured, with sky-blue eyes and straw-blonde hair pulled back in a blue-ribboned ponytail. Her over-ripe physique strained every stitch of the plain, white tee and faded pair of blue jeans she was wearing, the voluptuous farmer's daughter all mouth-watering hills and valleys – the exact opposite of the surrounding flatlands.

I stumbled inside the house, followed Nadine's round, twitching butt into the kitchen, where she invited me to set up shop while she busied herself whipping up some lemonade. I fumbled files onto a table already groaning under the weight of numerous accounting records and ledgers, my eyes glued to the blonde sexpot's body-in-motion. Sure, she was close to twice my age, but I've never held that against a lady – especially one I'd love to hold against me.

She carried a pair of tall, sweating glasses of lemonade over to the table and then sat down next to me, her boobs brushing the edge of the Formica top. Sweet perfume filled my head and clogged the pores in my brain, and I shrugged off my sweated suit jacket to better feel the heat of the five-alarm hottie.

'It's been rough since Dad died,' she stated, looking me in the eye, breathing into my face. 'But I'm determined to carry on where he left off.'

There were crow's feet etched into the corners of Nadine's eyes and mouth, but they only added to her well-seasoned attractiveness. 'Uh, you don't have a husband... to help you out?' I asked, glancing at the ringless third finger on her left hand.

'No, I'm divorced,' she said. 'My daughter helps out when she can, and I hire men when I need them.'

I choked on a mouthful of lemonade.

'Shall we get to work?'

I vaguely nodded, picking up my mechanical pencil and fumbling my calculator to zero, my eyes resting uncomfortably on Nadine's rising and falling chest.

By noon, we had most of the subsidy forms filled out and her father's antiquated books almost up-to-date. My libido had been throbbing like a John Deere tractor all morning as a result of working so closely with the gorgeous MILF, and when she came up behind me and rested her warm brown hands on my shoulders, I just about spontaneously combusted. 'You better clear off your stuff, so I can set the table for lunch,' she said.

'S-sure,' I mumbled. I scrambled up out of my chair and took a step to the left, directly into her path. Her bodacious bumpers bounced against my chest, my tent-city cock striking her jeans.

She laughed. 'Shall we dance?'

The sexual tension inside me snapped, and I grabbed her and planted my lips on top of her startled, scarlet pucker. I clenched her hot, soft body against my hard, sweat-soaked body and chewed on the mature mama's lips, my steel ruler of a cock pressing into her stomach.

'Wow!' she exhaled, when I finally pulled my head back to catch my breath. 'Someone has worked up quite an appetite!'

'Sorry, I-I didn't mean to –' I started to stupidly stutter, till Nadine quickly shushed me by cradling my red face in her hands and mashing her mouth against mine.

Mercury rising! We clung to one another and kissed hungrily, ferociously, my damp hands travelling all over Nadine's all-woman body, sliding down onto her jean-clad bottom. I squeezed her plump ass cheeks, and she moaned into my open mouth, her fingers roaming through my hair. Then she slid her tongue into my kisser and we frenched like a couple of high-schoolers, slapping our slippery tongues together over and over, our strangled breath steaming out of our flared nostrils, our frantic hands gripping and groping.

She pulled her tongue out of my mouth and stared at me, her blue eyes blazing and her thunder chest heaving. Then she kissed me once more, wetly and deeply, before breaking away and clearing the kitchen table with a sweep of her arms, files, forms, and accounting records flying all over the place. She yanked her T-shirt out of her jeans and pulled it up over her head, and I stared, open-mouthed and bug-eyed, at the luscious lady's freckled, sun-burnished chest, her big, bra-cupped titties.

She wrestled her tit-holder open in the back and flung it aside, and her bare, brown jugs dangled directly in front of me, thick, caramel-coloured nipples jutting straight at me. Those tawny mounds sagged more than a little, sure, but whatever their slippage, they more than made up for in volume. I grabbed on to them, began feeling them up with my nervous hands, revelling in the smooth, firm texture of that heated tit-flesh.

'Yes!' Nadine cried, tilting her head back. 'Suck my breasts!'

I'd learned long ago not to argue with my elders – especially when they're built like brick Pamela Andersons – so I quickly hefted Nadine's left hooter and bent my head down and licked at her fat nipple.

'Fuck, yes! Suck my fucking tits!' she dirty-mouthed me.

I swallowed her rubbery tit-cap and urgently sucked on it, swabbing the underside of her boob with my tongue as I did so. Then I popped the one gleaming nip out of my mouth and wet-vacced up the other honey-dipped nipple. I bounced my head back and forth between the groaning lady's awesome hangers, sucking and licking and biting

125

meaty nipple, squeezing and kneading mountainous mam, righteously milking her jugs with my hands and my mouth.

'Fuck me!' she screamed, when she could take my wicked tit-play no longer.

I reluctantly unhanded and unmouthed her glistening floppers, watched them bob and bounce around as she peeled off her skin-tight jeans, pulled down a pair of pink panties and tossed them aside with a flick of her foot. She showed off her searing bod for a moment in that superheated kitchen, then jumped ass-backwards up onto the table and spread her legs.

Her pussy was old-school – plenty of springy, blonde fur for a guy to cushion his balls on – and soaking wet. She plunged two of her fingers into her gash and started pumping, as I somehow managed to untangle my belt buckle and zipper, my feet from my dropped dress pants and drawers, my eyes never straying from the sexpot's pistoning hand. And when I was as rudely nude as she was, she unplugged her dripping fingers, briefly showed them to me, and then stuck them in her mouth and sucked on them.

My rock-hard cock vibrated with anticipation, a seven-inch spear of pulsing, pink flesh with an eye intent on stabbing Nadine's moist pussy. She pulled her fingers out of her mouth and grabbed on to my throbbing dong, tugged on it with her hot little hand, my body jerking at her warm, wet touch.

'Fuck me!' she hissed.

I pushed her back onto the table, shouldered her legs, and split her pussy lips wide open with my dickhead. She cried out with joy, and I grunted with satisfaction, sinking shaft deep into her twat. I started churning my hips, sliding my pole back and forth in the woman's amazingly juicy, gripping sexhole. She held on to her jouncing boobs and rolled her flared nipples, as I licked and bit her calves, pounded cock into her cunt like a man possessed.

And just when I was about to blow my load, salute the MILF's ultra-hot body and lovin' with a shower of sizzling sperm, she decided to switch positions. She jerked my prick out of her pussy and jumped down off the table, spun around and bent over and stuck her big, bronze ass out at me. 'Fuck me now!' she demanded, gripping the edge of the kitchen table.

I grabbed ahold of my slickened member and smacked Nadine's brazen ass cheeks with its bloated head, watching the twin, golden orbs ripple with delight. Then I felt for her greasy slit with the tip of my dick and found it, slammed my dong home again. I grasped her waist and brutally pumped her, the table skidding on the linoleum tiles, our bodies smacking loudly and wetly together, in time to my frantic cock-thrusts.

'Yes!' Nadine shrieked, her body trembling with orgasm.

'Mother-fucker!' I bellowed, the stifling room spinning, my balls boiling over. I grabbed on to Nadine's ponytail and jerked her head back, her mouth breaking open in a silent scream, sperm cannonading out of my cock and pulsing deep into her sopping sex. I desperately thumped her bottom, riding the gasping, lathered lady like a horse, riding out the electric storm of our ecstasy.

Later that sultry afternoon, after we'd cleared up the remaining paperwork, Nadine suggested that we have a picnic dinner down by the stream that ran through her property. I agreed, then waited impatiently while she packed a wicker basket full of eats and then changed her clothes.

It was worth the wait, though, because when she finally emerged from her bedroom, she looked absolutely spectacular in a white, summer, almost-see-through dress and a big, floppy, white summer hat with a blue ribbon around its crown. Her bare, brown arms and shoulders and legs and chest were mouth-wateringly highlighted against the filmy white background of her dress, her long blonde hair loose around her shoulders. And I could've died a happy death from sexual suffocation in the depths of her plunging bronze cleavage.

I tucked the wicker basket under one arm and the wicked MILF under the other, and we strolled out the back door. We walked across a field, through a scraggly cluster of elms, and then down a hill that led to a shallow stream. And when I dropped the basket down on the grassy bank of the creek, Nadine curled around in my arms and embraced me with her lips.

'Come to daddy!' I murmured, tasting her glossy lips, gripping her full, only-slightly-drooping bottom through the skimpy material of her dress.

We kissed passionately under the blistering sun, rekindling our nooner fire, the only sounds the babbling brook, the twittering birds, and the wet smacking of our lips and tongues. Eventually, Nadine slipped out of my grasp and pulled her dress up over her head, revealing Nadine and nothing else underneath. Her curvy, sun-kissed body shone ripe and delicious for the picking, and I quickly dismantled my own duds, my cock springing up and sniffing the air.

'Looks like you could use some cooling off, young man,' Nadine laughed, her eyes twinkling. She flipped off her shoes and stepped into the creek, scooped up some water and splashed me with it.

I took it on the chest, like a man, my nipples hardening on impact. Then I strode into the gurgling brook after my motherly lover, till we were both up to our knees in the cool, crystal-clear water, our hot, naked bodies glued together.

We kissed and frenched some more, Nadine's tits surging against my smooth chest, my dick pressing hard into her flat stomach. Then she abruptly broke away and bounded further up the stream, plopped down on a large, sun-heated rock that stood squarely in the middle of the water. She spread her legs, opening the furry gates of heaven, and beckoned me to come forward. 'Eat me!' she hissed.

I waded over to her like an obedient, anxious little boy, then stopped and stared at her pussy, at the moisture glistening on the swollen pink lips that peeked out from under her downy, blonde thatch of fur. Then I dropped to my knees in the water and grabbed on to Nadine's baby-bottom smooth thighs and dove tongue-first into her twat.

'God, yes!' she wailed, her body jumping when my tongue touched her slit. She leaned back on the rock, fingers gripping the jagged edge behind her, splayed jugs thrust out to the glaring sun.

I earnestly licked her pussy, savouring her tangy juices, amazed, again, at how wet the old-enough-to-be-my-mother babe could get. Then I clawed her slick, engorged lips apart and speared her juicy pink, fucking her with my tongue, rubbing her puffed-up clit with my thumb. I sank deeper into the water, into the sandy creek bottom, as I lapped and lapped at the lady's soaking wet snatch, Nadine moaning low and long, her body rippling with sexual electricity.

I pulled my tongue out of her slit and latched my sticky lips onto her clit, sucking hard on it. She howled with joy and her sweat-dappled body arched off the rock, her locked muscles standing out in stark relief, her powerful thighs crushing my head. She was jolted by orgasm again and again and again, girl-juice gushing out of her gash and into my mouth.

It took a while, but once Nadine and I had gotten our breath back, she instructed me to stand up on the hot rock. I climbed onto the now-slippery stone while Nadine stood in the creek, facing me and my steel-hard prick. She looked at my twitching rod for a couple of sex-charged seconds, moist lips only inches away from my mushroomed hood, and then she smiled up at me and vacuumed my cap into her warm, wet mouth, started tugging on it. She sucked expertly on my dickhead, her tongue scouring the sensitive underside of my prick.

'Yeah, momma!' I groaned.

Nadine juggled my balls with her right hand while she slid her left up my sun-blasted chest and played with my nipples, her puffy lips inching slowly and inexorably down my pulsating pole. She consumed more and more of my turgid meat, till she had a throbbing two-thirds of it secured in her experienced mouth. That's when I thrust my hips forward, throat-burying myself to the bone.

She didn't even gag, so I grabbed on to her blonde tresses and mouth-fucked that mother, plunging my cock down her throat repeatedly. She dug her claws into my ass and hung on for the ride. And within a short, sunstroked minute or so, my throat-diving dick exploded.

'I'm coming!' I hollered, frantically pumping my hips, wildly throating my old lady. I clutched her hayseed locks and sprayed her mouth full of sperm, my sweat-slick body shaking like a wheat stalk in a tornado.

Nadine doggedly gulped down just as much of my spurting jizz as she could, the rest spilling out of the whitened corners of her mouth and running down her chin. And when I finally yanked my slimy, spent cock out of the sexpot's hell-blazing mouth, I glanced up and saw a girl standing on the ridge above us, a shotgun cradled in her arms.

'W-who's that!?' I yelped, pointing at the armed girl staring down at the obscenely naked pair of us.

Nadine nonchalantly gathered up some cum from around her mouth, licked her fingers clean, and then gripped my sodden cock and looked at where I was pointing. 'Oh, that's my daughter, Janine,' the sensuous farmer's daughter remarked, licking her lips and swallowing, swirling her hand up and down my dong. 'She doesn't like it much when I take up with strange men.'

First Time For Everything
by Mary Borsellino

I lost my virginity on New Year's Eve, 1999. It's very likely that I'm far from the only person who can claim this. Everyone was a little crazy that night. I think some people thought it was the end of the world, or maybe they just wished it was.

I was eighteen years old, fresh out of high school, and I'd never been kissed. All through my junior and senior year, I'd harboured a desperate, profound crush on my best male friend, Andrew. He'd come over to my house in the mornings before school and play video games with my little brother.

I'd watch his hands, wrapped around the joystick on the game controller. It sounds absurd in hindsight, but eighteen is still a teenager, and my hormones were going wild. Watching his long, clever fingers cradle the slick black plastic of the controller's shaft was enough to leave me flushed and distracted all through my morning classes, the dark navy panties of my school uniform soaked damp.

Sometimes, if I could convince a teacher to let me out before the bell, I'd escape to the girls' bathroom and masturbate in one of the stalls. I'd bite my lip and rub furiously at that wet, uncomfortable cotton, my breath panting as I silently imagined Andrew's slim, clever face and beautiful hands. It never felt like a relief, though. Nothing did.

I was an undersexed mess, and Andrew was none the wiser. He had girlfriends from time to time, but never seemed as interested in them as he was in me. The trouble was, it seemed like all he wanted from me was friendship. Honestly, I have no idea why he even wanted that; I was a babbling, silly idiot when he was nearby.

So there we were, on New Year's Eve, walking up the high hill near our friend Justine's house toward the local liquor store. It was after ten already, and our party had been going full swing for hours. All the drinks were used up, so we'd been sent out for more.

'What's your most embarrassing confession?' he asked, for no particular reason.

I'd already had two vodkas, and the words slipped out before I could stop them. 'I'm a virgin. I've never even been kissed.'

He stopped, and turned around. His eyes glittered in the low light of the streetlamps. His breath, beer-bitter, was hot and damp on the air between us in the second before his lips touched mine.

'You?' he murmured, a little slurred from his own drinks. 'Never been…'

My first kiss. A warm, heavy press of his mouth on mine, closed and almost chaste.

Then he grinned, stepped back, and started striding up the hill again.

'Now you have!' he called back to me. 'Hurry up!'

I brought my fingertips to my tingling lips, and ran after him.

My second kiss was five minutes later, on the walk back down the hill, two wine bottles clinking in a plastic bag against my thigh as I pulled Andrew's face to mine with a hand twined in his hair. Our mouths opened against each other. It felt like a part of me was melting.

Back at Justine's house, we gave our hostess the drinks we'd bought and then, our fingers laced together and laughter zipping in the air between us, we crept down the hallway to the unused guest bedroom.

'You'll miss the best parts!' someone called after us, but as far as I could tell that's exactly what I was finally going to find.

The sheets were a plain rose cotton, a dull delicate colour. I shoved Andrew down onto the mattress, preferring the wild flush of his cheeks to the fabric's shade.

I could feel his pulse on my tongue when I sucked at his neck, my thighs straddling his lap, and it made me wonder if I'd be able to follow his heartbeat while I sucked his cock later, when we had our energy back.

His hands were behind me, unhooking the catches of my bra. Those clever fingers had done this before, with the bras of other girls, but I didn't feel inexperienced or stupid compared to him. It was like my body knew exactly what it wanted, and how to get it.

I stood up, glad that I'd worn a skirt to the party. My breasts, heavy in their unhooked bra, swung forward as I bent down a little to slip my underwear off my hips. Andrew seemed transfixed by the sight of my shifting cleavage, so I leaned forward and bent lower. He could see my nipples now, peeking out of the slipping tops of the bra cups; hard as bone and aching to be touched.

'Please,' I begged, not knowing how else to ask. Half an hour before I hadn't even known what kissing was like, and now I needed his mouth more than anything. He cradled one of my breasts like a full, weighty piece of ripe fruit in his palm, the callus of his thumb tracing lightly over the

134

pebbled pink of the areola. I pressed in closer, urging his face towards my breast. The flat, thin edge of his teeth grazed the nipple, barely a touch, and I felt so wet and open and ready for him that I think I moaned aloud.

I had to step away. It felt too good. I was going to fly apart, like a puzzle dropped off the edge of a table, pieces in all directions. I couldn't cope with something that good, not unless I had something solid to grasp and ride through it.

I pulled my shirt and useless bra over my head, and kicked my panties away. Still dressed in my awkward first pair of high heels and knee-length charcoal pantyhose, my black skirt sticking to my sweaty thighs, I reached into Andrew's pocket and felt around until I found the crinkling packet of a condom. I knew he'd have one. I knew everything about him. He was my best friend.

He unzipped his jeans and shoved them down off his hips. Skinny, pale hips – Andrew was the kind of boy who loved computers, not football. His knuckles were white against the mattress as I rolled the condom down onto his thick, blood-full cock, and he made a choked, whimpering sound in the back of his throat.

'Shh,' I soothed, touching his face, even though I was the virgin of the pair. I moved my hand up and down over the delicate-looking latex of the sheath, marvelling that something so thin and weightless could offer such protection, such security. It was flavourless, and tasted faintly like party balloons when I lathed my tongue up the length experimentally. Andrew's heart was racing. His pulse felt like the wings of a tiny, frantic bird. I wanted to keep tasting and exploring, but knew he couldn't last through it to my own pleasure if I tried. Experienced he might have been, but he was still a teenage boy.

It hurt as I sank down onto him, a dull stretching ache that wasn't as bad as I'd expected. I needed him too much. I wanted him too much. Nothing could hurt me.

'Oh,' was all he said. We were both too overwhelmed for dirty talk or even for each other's names. I rocked up, experimentally, letting him almost slip free as I clenched my muscles and held him in. The push back down made the length of his cock stroke the upper wall of my cunt, and I felt a wave of amazing sensation shudder through me.

The G spot, I remember thinking to myself. That's called the G spot. It made me wonder what other magnificent buttons my body might have that I didn't know about.

'Squeeze my tits,' I managed, raking my nails against his arm. He cupped them, shoved them, pinched the nipples hard. I'd never thought to treat myself so roughly. It felt like nothing on earth. I began to understand why people claimed to see God when they were having sex. Every nerve ending in me seemed tuned to some divine channel. Andrew rolled my nipples between his thumbs and forefingers, quick and sharp, and I screamed with pleasure.

'I'm not gonna last,' he warned me, but I wasn't either so I didn't care. We stared at each other, too trapped in the feelings passing between us even to do something as simple as kissing. Then we fell off the edge of the world and into climax, him first and me following after. I wondered if someone could really have an orgasm that strong on their first time, but at the same time I knew it couldn't have been anything else. It was like champagne. It was like... fireworks.

'Hey,' I said, still sitting on his lap, still feeling aftershocks through my body like lightning. He was still inside me, and I didn't want to ever be without that fullness again. 'Hey,' I repeated, glancing out the window at the empty night sky outside. No fireworks split the black out there. They were all inside me, and my new lover. 'Look. It's not even midnight yet.'

High Heels And Monster Bikes
by Kitti Bernetti

They were deliciously understated. You can tell real class by whether a woman goes over the top. And these weren't. They were just right. I was picking a receipt off the floor when I first glimpsed them. It was the heel connecting with the floor which caught my eye. Rubber against granite tiles. Practical but beautiful too in the mixture of textures. I had to stall, pretend I was gouging a bit of chewing gum off the floor with my fingernail, while I studied the heels. They were high. Of course. I can't be doing with flat shoes. They ruin the line of a woman's leg. These must have been at least three inches long and black patent. Amazingly, there wasn't a scuff or a mark on them. They were virgin, pristine, shiny, and black. Like the surface of new gloss paint when you take the lid off. I could have got down on all fours then and there and licked them. What would they taste of? A little bit of leather polish. Oh yes, these were real patent leather, not plastic. I can tell. For goodness sake, I'm a connoisseur aren't I? Some men go for fine wines, some for Cuban cigars. My passion is shoes.

*   *   *

I lingered a little too long. My manager saw me and asked what I was doing. Arse. He's got less finesse than a bucket of pig pooh. I gave him a look and walked away. I just hope she didn't hear. I don't think she did, she'd paid for her stuff and was clicking her way out by then. The whole of the rest of the day, I relived that moment. I thought about how it would feel to have my hands running over that black leather, to feel its shininess under my fingers. They were cute-sexy, round-toed, with a strap over the ankle and fastened with a black pearl button. And yes, you've guessed it. Fish-net tights or stockings. I don't know which. I don't care much either. It's the foot that's the thing and the shoes. Once I've passed the ankle I don't give a stuff. Feet must be the most erotic parts of a woman's body. It amazes me how many people pass them by. They never even look down. Can you imagine that? Nope, neither can I. They must be sensorily redundant if there is such a word. Search me. What does it matter, you get my drift. As I stacked the tins and swept the floor – that day, unlike all the others – seemed to fly by. She kept me going. My high heel girl. My high heel lady.

The next day, of course I waited. Hovered near the tills. I'd managed to get myself on vegetable stacking duty. You should have seen my manager's face when I volunteered. It was a picture. He couldn't believe I'd put myself forward to do anything. 'That's not like you, Matt,' he goaded. 'I usually can't prise you off your coffee break. Are you sickening for something?' He'd put his greasy mitt on my forehead to get a better laugh from the girls. Oily jerk. I could have whacked him in the teeth.

I'd learnt to keep my cool though. A spell inside teaches you that. I wasn't in long, mind. I played Mr Nice Guy and learned my lesson. It's tough when you're a street-wise kid. You have to prove yourself to your mates. It was stupid idiot stuff which got me my stay at Her Majesty's pleasure. We actually took the trouble to go to Richmond to break into a cricket pavilion and smoke fags. Only trouble was, some dick chucked his dog-end onto a pile of papers and the whole pavilion went up like the great fire of London. We were sitting ducks when the police caught us. I was sent down and I did my few months in the university of human nature. The main thing I learnt was don't get angry. So now I don't. I have other interests. I'm squeaky clean now. I even gave up smoking. One of these days I'm going to open my own motorbike shop. Just a local one. I'll sell a few and fix a few. I know what I'm up to. Funnily enough they taught me that inside too. School'd taught me bugger all. It's ironic that I had to commit a crime to get my three month crash course as a mechanic. Still, that's cool if it gets me where I want to go someday.

So there I was, hovering, taking my time over stacking the satsumas, when I heard her walking behind me before I ever saw her. Clack, clack, click, click. I turned around as if I needed to open a new box and nearly collapsed with desire. How do women wear heels that high and still walk? They were absolutely gorgeous. Red. Now there's a colour. The colour of passion, tango, wine. Red roses for love. Red light for danger. Imitation crocodile skin, and pointy toes. Delicious. I had to swallow hard and keep fixed on my work. It's quiet in the supermarket that early in the morning. I'd been there half the night but she was fresh as a daisy. Those red shoes kept me going all day long. And half the night too if I'm truthful. Don't get me wrong. I'm not in favour of your all-night-long five finger exercise. A little do it yourself is inevitable when you see something like that. It's like look but don't touch. A single bed with one occupant's a lonely place, or at least mine is since I split up with Sarah. Five long years together and now alone. So I dream a bit and I cuddle up a bit with thoughts of those red shoes.

I'll tell you something to make you laugh – I couldn't wait to get into work the next morning. I revved up the bike and there I was champing at the bit before they opened the main staff door. We have to go in round the back in case the punters see us. Like we're lepers or something. That's how these big supermarkets treat you. They want your labour and they want it cheap. But they'd rather you didn't come in through the front and scare off the precious customers. Lucy was there too. Little Lucy whose Mum talks for Britain and who can't wait to leave home, if only she could get someone to take her on. She's sweet, I like her but I don't fancy her. I've got a feeling she might have the hots for me though. When we were standing outside, she lit up a fag and said, all coy like, 'your manager's got it in for you hasn't he?'

'I guess so.' I replied. 'We're not exactly bosom buddies.' She giggled at that. She's not much more than a child.

'You know what I think his problem is. I think he's jealous of you.'

'Why should someone who's earning twice as much as me be jealous of me?' I asked. Not unreasonably I thought.

'Cos you're good-looking I guess.' She let that sink in for a second. For effect like, and blew a cloud of smoke to the side of her. 'It stands to reason. It doesn't matter how much he earns. He'll still be a balding fat git and you'll still be young and blond with huge broad shoulders.'

I guess that was a compliment. Luckily they opened the door then. She's jail bait, little Lucy. Too young for me. And besides I'm afraid I couldn't get turned on by those big flat chunky Goth boots she wears. As soon as I'd got out of my leathers and into my uniform, I went off to search for my high heel lady.

I didn't have to wait long. If I didn't know better, I'd swear she was looking for me. We sort of 'meet' at more or less the same place each day. That's rubbish of course. Classy chicks like her don't look twice at shelf-stackers like me. Maybe if I'd already got my bike shop and everything, I'd have a bit more confidence to go up to her and start chatting. But, as it is, she and I are worlds apart. The tension sort of turns me on a bit. The thought that I'll never possess her, never go to her house, never look in her wardrobe and see all those shoes tantalises me. But I've still got my fantasies.

For the first time, it was her face I noticed first, before the shoes. It was a glowing face. Slightly tanned, cutely freckled and framed with long straight brown hair that curled at the ends. She wears glasses, I've seen her peering at the labels on stuff. Executive type glasses with cool green frames. Today, she looked like a pussycat. She had this just below the knee mock leopard print coat. On anyone else it would have been too Bling Queen meets Zena, Warrior Maiden. But on her it looked just right. And, to go with it for your delectation today, sir? Long, long, lace up brown boots with a kitten heel.

I felt a surge of adrenalin zap straight to my cock. I imagined taking the top of the laces between my teeth and pulling them undone. Then I pictured myself mouthing each lace laboriously out bit by bit. It would take ages of course. But in my fantasy, I and my glorious high heel lady would have all the time in the world. As I did it, she'd sit on the side of the bed, in that coat and only her underwear, and watch me. As I unlaced, the smell of leather and a slight whiff of female sweat would tease my senses. I would breathe in, ease the boots slowly off her feet and start sucking on her toes. Heaven. Pure heaven. Glassy-eyed, I let my mind drift and imagined her guiding me over to her bed, her pert arse lifting up and down like a boat on a gentle swell. She'd point me to one of those expensive duvet covers, all plum coloured satin, inlaid velvet and sequins. With eyes that said 'I'll do anything for you,' she'd push me back on the cover and start to run her hands over my chest. She'd kiss my eyes closed and whisper, 'I've got a surprise for you. Relax.' Then, I'd sense her lying down, so her feet met mine and then with those gorgeous, sensuous feet, she would start to rub her heel up the inside of my calf. My imagination would go wild, hoping upon hope that she would do that one thing that I've always wanted. I'd feel her toes, the soles of her feet, not rough but soft, move up between my thighs. Then, unbelievably, she'd do it. Take my cock between her feet and expertly grip it just right. At that point, I would give myself a treat. I'd open my eyes and see her superb pink pussy exposed before my eyes, glistening and moist as she held her legs open. Then I'd watch those magic feet doing their business. Back and forth, back and forth they'd go and she'd watch me, cool as a cucumber, a smile playing on her lips as she controlled me like no woman had ever controlled me before. Trying to hold back, I'd look away. But it wouldn't be any good. Feeling the power surge down my prick, I'd look back again to watch my warm salty come erupt and shoot all over those cute little toes.

Breathing a bit too heavily for comfort, I was shot back into the real world. My high heel lady had paid for her goods and was gliding off, just a memory to brighten my same old, same old day.

I'd volunteered to do overtime. It was late, maybe 11pm by the time I'd finished and was easing into my leathers. I pulled my hair out of the collar. I know it's old fashioned and all that to wear it long but I keep it squeaky clean and it's nice man-hair. Not straggly or greasy or tied up in a pony tail. It's just long enough to sit on my shoulders with a gentle curl. An old girlfriend once told me I looked like the captain of a pirate ship. A pirate in bike leathers and a black helmet. She had a wonderful fertile imagination, that girl.

I'd kicked the bike into life and was purring through the car park when I had to blink twice. I lifted my visor and frowned. There she was. My high heel lady. Standing all alone in the car park in the dark. It was dangerous, she shouldn't wait there all on her own. I slowed the bike down to a crawl as I got near. I couldn't speak to her, I didn't know her. A six foot geezer on a monster-bike approaching a lone female just wasn't on. And yet, and yet. Something about the way she looked at me, and smiled, made me pull on the brakes and stop in my tracks. I glanced behind me expecting to see some massive geezer in a Lexus revving me off the scene. But no. It was deserted apart from a blue carrier bag whirling frenziedly on the breeze. I felt just like that lost bag. Nowhere to go but round in circles. Maybe today I'd get cracking on starting up that bike shop, maybe not. Maybe today I'd win the lottery, maybe not. Maybe today some gorgeous woman would choose me. Maybe not. Round and round in circles my head seemed to whirl. Until I heard a voice in front of me.

'Hi,' it was female. Sweet as pink candy floss at the fair.

'Hi,' I answered. Not a great line I admit, but even Mel Gibson has to start somewhere. She shifted from foot to foot. Could she be as nervous as me or was it just the cold? From foot to foot. I was reminded of those feet and looked down. There they were. Brown boots with laces begging to be undone. I exhaled. They could have been no more than size fives, my favourite size. I lifted my eyes up to hers. My blue ones locked into her hazel ones. Please say something I thought. Please, because it's your turn, and you started it and besides, I'm not too good at this.

'You work in the supermarket, don't you?'

'Yes.' I tried a smile. In the absence of the ability to speak I have found, like strangers in a strange land, that a smile can be useful. Brainwave. I loosened the strap and gently took off my helmet. Now I could hear her better; now there wasn't that barrier between us. Now I was less of a scary guy and more just a bloke on his way home. Except it seemed maybe I wasn't on my way home just yet.

'Well, this may seem kind of strange. And I don't usually do this, and my friends would kill me if they knew I'd done anything so stupid as wait for a complete stranger in a car park in the dark.'

She was babbling nervously. She couldn't possibly be as nervous as me, could she? If I was going to be Mr Scary Psycho I'd have pounced by now. I'm not, believe me, gorgeous girl. I'm just an ordinary guy.

'But, I wondered if you fancied going for a drink now you're finished.' This last jetted out like water cascading down the side of a cliff, like she'd been thinking it but couldn't believe she'd said it. I could have opened my arms, folded her size ten frame inside them and kissed her. But that, I hoped, would come later. Much later when she knew me and I knew her and the time was right. Until then, for the first time in my life I kept cool, but not chilly. I plastered a smile over my stupid face and said, 'Have you ever ridden pillion?'

'No.' She shook her head and those ribbon falls of hair waved and bounced.

'Would you like to?'

'Yup,' she nodded. 'I've always had a bit of a thing. Well, a big bit of a thing about bikes.' And shoes, I thought, dear, dear lady. And shoes.

'Then this is your chance. We could go to McClusky's if you fancy it,' I said. A frown spread over her face and I thought nooooooo. You've blown it. You idiot. You said something wrong. It's not going to happen. She's going to walk away in those gorgeous suede boots and out of your life for ever. 'If you don't fancy McClusky's, suggest anywhere else,' I blurted.

'It's not that,' she said. 'It's just I'm not sure if I can get on your bike with these boots. They are a bit high.'

I could have punched the sky, I was so high on the evening, on the breeze, on this wonderful female talking to me. 'Don't worry,' I hope I sounded cool as a cucumber although my heart was thudding louder than the bike's engine. I reached backwards to the box, lifted out the spare helmet and started at the softness of her hair as I helped her into it. 'Just hold on to my shoulder and jump on.' She did. We moved off and I left my stomach behind as she gripped my waist, her head leaning on my back. As we rounded the front of the supermarket I shouted, 'What do you do for a living?'

'I'm a financial adviser. I advise people setting up in small business. Get them loans, advise them on premises, all that boring stuff.' Boring, I thought. No: as I pictured my little motorbike shop. This might just be a relationship made in heaven. Then, I saw in the dark shop window as we stopped at the lights, our reflection in the glass. Her eyes were dreamy as she leant into my shoulder and I could see her admiring the reflection of her shoes next to the chrome of my bike. I grinned like a kid on Christmas Eve and rode off with my prize holding me tight, so tight.

Neighbourhood Watch
by Stephen Albrow

As soon as her husband had left for work, Rachel carried the chair to the window. She drew the curtains, leaving a tiny gap through which to peek, then waited for the entertainment to start across the road. It was now almost a fortnight since the mystery woman had moved in opposite, ever since when a succession of men had been turning up on her doorstep at every hour of the night and day. The neighbourhood had never seen anything like it before – a call girl working right in their midst!

It was almost nine o'clock in the morning, which meant the day's first client would be arriving soon. Most of them were businessmen. It was a high-class operation, nowhere near as squalid as Rachel had always expected these things to be. She sipped on her coffee, growing excited at the prospect of what was in store and glad for any excuse not to tackle last night's dirty dishes. *I bet she doesn't have to wash the dishes*, thought Rachel, as she pictured the woman over the road – a tall brunette, with hourglass curves, who was permanently clad in thigh-high boots and shiny black leather.

A car came crawling down the street, then parked in the woman's driveway. Rachel stood up to get a better look, peeking through the tiny crack in the curtains and watching as a middle-aged man walked up to the front door and rang the bell. He gazed back at his car as he waited on the doorstep, desperately trying to appear nonchalant, but Rachel could see the tension in his eyes. All the men who went in the house seemed nervous, but they always emerged contented and calm. The mistress of the house had a way about her – there wasn't any doubt about that!

After a moment's wait, the door opened and Rachel glimpsed a swathe of jet-black leather. The tall, elegant woman beckoned her client inside, then she took a quick glance up and down the street, before closing the door behind her. She always glanced up and down the street – she'd even caught Rachel's eye once or twice – but Rachel could never work out the reason why. At first, she'd thought it was an anxious look, a check to see if anyone had worked out what was going on, but it had grown into a look of defiance, as if the woman was saying, *yes, what you are seeing is true, but there ain't nothing you can do about it*!

And yet, as secretary of the local Neighbourhood Watch, there was plenty that Rachel could do about it. Thanks to her prime location, she'd been asked to take note of all the comings and goings, but it wasn't that which made her sit by the window all day – it was a deep, growing fascination with the beautiful, powerful woman across the street. Rachel had never liked the Neighbourhood Watch, but Mike had forced her to join the group. She'd always seen them as a bunch of snoopers, hypocrites and killjoys, keen to stop anyone from being different or having too much fun. To them, the woman across the road was a nuisance, a danger and a threat to house prices, but Rachel had seen the changing look on the faces of the many men who entered her lair. She'd seen their edginess replaced by intense satisfaction, and she longed to experience the change herself.

148

It was an hour before the first customer left, emerging with a newfound spring in his step. His visit seemed to have set him up for the day, allowing him to face another boring shift at the bank or office. Rachel thought of all the housework she was meant to be doing, and then of how quickly her husband had hurried off to work that day. He could have set the alarm a little earlier, then they could have made love before he left. The chores might have seemed more approachable then, with the afterglow of orgasm still in her system.

Sex is a positive force, thought Rachel, as a second car pulled up outside. She stood up again, leaving a bigger chink in the curtains this time, almost as if she wanted her mysterious new neighbour to know that she was keeping watch. The client walked up and rang the doorbell. His body was trembling with nervous tension, but the mistress of the house would know how to relieve it. She opened the door and beckoned the man inside, then her piercing eyes flickered up and down the street. Her gaze skipped straight past Rachel's house, but then something clicked and she looked straight back. Eye contact was made, their gazes met, but it was all too much for Rachel to take. Ashamed of being caught, she stepped back from the window. Her heart was beating almost twice as fast, but something even stranger was going on.

Rachel had no real awareness of what had made it happen, but her hand had crept inside her knickers. Her middle finger was rubbing against her clitoris, the soft, circular motion causing sticky juices to ooze from her gash. She regained her senses for a second, telling herself what she was doing was wrong, but then something made her reach for her cleavage. Her hands cupped each of her breasts in turn, feeling how swollen her nipples had become.

'What's happening to me?' Rachel mumbled to herself, turning to gaze in the mirror above the fireplace. Her face was flushed, but it was the look in her eye that really gave the game away. It was the same look of awkward edginess that all the men who visited her neighbour had. She did some mental reckoning – she and Mike had not made love for over two months, so the tension inside her clearly needed some release. She thought of taking a bath and masturbating, but that meant going upstairs, and for some strange reason she couldn't bear the thought of tearing herself away from the window.

'Pull yourself together,' Rachel told herself, then she decided it was best to get out of the house. Being cooped up at home for days on end wasn't good for a person's well-being, so she fetched her coat and then wandered towards the newsagents on the corner of the street. She browsed through the racks of magazines, occasionally glancing at the clock above the counter, waiting for the right time to head back home. She knew her neighbour's routine like clockwork by now – when each client arrived and how long they stayed. She could make it look like an accident, just wander by and see what happened.

At five to eleven, she picked up a newspaper, paid the girl behind the counter and stepped into the street. Normally she crossed the road straight away, but for once she stayed on the opposite side – the mystery woman's side of the street. As she neared the woman's driveway, she heard goodbyes being said, then a car engine started and the second client drove away. Rachel peered at him through his windscreen, spotting the satisfied smile upon his face. The mystery woman was still on her doorstep. On seeing her, Rachel crossed the street for home.

'Wait,' shouted the beautiful dominatrix, her words making Rachel stop dead in her tracks. There was something in the woman's tone of voice that made it clear she was giving out a definite order. Disobeying her wasn't an option, so Rachel slowly turned around. The domme crooked her finger, beckoning Rachel towards her, with a magnetic force she couldn't resist. 'I don't like snoopers,' the leather queen snapped, as the housewife neared her doorstep. Reaching out, she grabbed Rachel's hand and tugged her, forcefully, over the threshold.

Rachel was struck dumb for a second, surprised by the woman's obvious strength. She gazed up and down her leather-clad body, instantly understanding why so many men were happy to worship at the feet of such a striking, statuesque woman. Her powerful thighs and voluptuous breasts were truly Amazonian, but it was the thigh-high boots that really did it! The six-inch heels left her towering over Rachel's body. It was impossible not to look up to her!

'I...I didn't m-mean to spy on you,' Rachel stammered, keen to get in the domme's good books.

'I didn't mean to spy on you, *Mistress*,' the domme corrected her, pointing towards a door at the end of the hallway. Rachel knew the doorway led to the cellar, because the house was the same design as hers. Mike used theirs for storing wine, but the Mistress of this house was sure to be different.

'Down there, bad girl,' shouted the domme, then she waited to see what Rachel would do. The front door was still open, so she was easily able to leave. Her own house was visible just across the street, but instead she headed for the cellar door. As she opened it and climbed down the stairs, the domme shut the front door, a smile breaking out upon her lips. She was thrilled at the prospect of having a brand new toy to play with, especially one with so much pent-up sexual tension inside her body.

Being attuned to such matters, the beautiful domme had been able to sense Rachel's tension even from across the street. Whenever she moved to a new area, there was always someone who took an unhealthy interest in her affairs. Often it was under the guise of the Neighbourhood Watch, or some other prurient body, but the prurience always seemed to conceal an inner submissiveness. Following Rachel down into the cellar, she knew her new slave would be like putty in her hands. Rachel had waited her whole life to meet someone like Mistress Becki, someone who could unlock the darkest desires within.

'Welcome to my dungeon,' said the tall dominatrix, flicking a switch to turn on the light. All the hours Rachel had spent spying on and thinking about the dominatrix had not prepared her for such a sight. Her imagination was not wild enough to envisage all the whips, the chains, let alone the furniture – a medieval rack and an iron maiden. A nervous tingle ran through her flesh, turning it to goose bumps, as she eyed up the tools of Mistress Becki's trade. She was out of her depth, but she rather liked the feeling. It was exciting to place herself completely at the mercy of this fascinating creature.

'Get naked, slave,' commanded Mistress Becki, fetching a long-handled whip from a corner of the room. She lashed it through the air, producing an ear-splitting crack, which prompted Rachel into action. She was terrified of disobeying the whip-wielding dominatrix, but just as scared of the damage the whip could do to her naked flesh. Trembling inwardly, she removed her skirt and blouse, but the dominatrix wanted more. 'And your underwear,' insisted Mistress Becki, hovering over her submissive slave.

'Do I have to, Mistress?' Rachel asked, immediately regretting the question.

'Do exactly as I say, you stupid slut,' shouted the furious domme, then she lashed the whip through the air again, close enough for Rachel to feel the breeze.

Shocked into life, Rachel slipped out of her bra and knickers, a mix of motions tumbling through her mind. A part of her was wracked with terror, but a bigger part of her was enjoying her intense vulnerability. Her naked body, which hadn't been pleasured in over two months, was now fully in the hands of this strong and gorgeous bitch-goddess from hell.

'That's better,' said Mistress Becki, slowly circling Rachel's naked form. She stopped behind her, then stroked her buttocks, gently scratching the housewife's flesh with her long, manicured fingernails. 'I've seen you watching me,' she said, applying subtle pressure to Rachel's back and forcing her to lean across the medieval rack. 'Do you wonder what I do to make those men all feel so happy?' she asked. 'Well, the time for you to wonder has stopped. You're not spying any more, you bad, bad girl. The time has come for you to experience everything for real.'

Rachel took a deep breath and closed her eyes, afraid but excited about what would happen next. Her buttocks were poking up in the air, defenceless against Mistress Becki's whip, which lashed through the air and smacked into her flesh. She screamed at the point of impact, the sting of the lash unbearable, although something made her hungry for more. She raised her buttocks even higher, as if enticing the domme to flay her again. She heard it first, the menacing crack of the whip, then once again she felt the sting.

'You're a bad, bad girl,' yelled Mistress Becki, raising her hand to shoulder-height. The tail of the whip coiled around her arm, just like a snake being charmed by its master, then the length of cord straightened out again, as she thrashed it towards Rachel's bare behind. It struck her on

153

the top of her thighs, bringing with it a ferocious burst of pain that caused an agonised scream to spill from her lips. Unable to cope with the thought of another painful blow, Rachel begged for mercy. But she got no mercy, just another firm lash – the decisive one, which carried her over the threshold into a whole new world of intense fulfilment.

'Can you feel it now?' asked Mistress Becki, training the whip upon Rachel's back.

'Yes, Mistress,' she groaned, as the lash sent a wave of endorphins coursing through her veins. Her body's self-defence mechanism had been triggered into action, causing a wave of euphoria to overwhelm her senses and turning the painful torment into blissful pleasure. The domme raised her whip on high again, then thrashed the hell out of Rachel's buttocks, but the endorphins were now everywhere inside her, overpowering the painful sting. Suddenly, her body felt strong enough to take whatever was thrown at her. She felt alive in a way she'd never felt before, the outward sting of the lash and the inner tingle of her body fighting back, causing a pain/pleasure mix that blew her mind.

'I can feel it,' she yelled, as the tingling reached her pussy, shivers of pleasure making her insides tense up tight. She ran her fingers over her cunt lips and was amazed by just how wet they were, a sticky sheen of juices covering the whole of her erogenous zone. Mistress Becki saw her touching herself, then tossed aside the whip and demanded Rachel turn around. Placing her hands on Rachel's shoulders, she shoved the housewife to the floor, before hitching her shiny leather skirt above her bare cunt.

'Mistress always gets pleasured first,' explained the dominatrix, pressing her cunt into Rachel's face. Wielding the whip had made her pussy drip with juices, so Rachel obediently stuck out her tongue and started licking the cream from Mistress Becki's gash. Driving her tongue back and forward, she repeatedly entered the domme's hot, wet cunt, desperate to make her climax so that she would then be allowed to climax herself. The domme's hands were on the back of her head, keeping Rachel's mouth pressed tight to her sex. Her tongue reached deeper, feeling the spasms of pleasure in her Mistress's cunt, which grew stronger as the domme got closer to a climax.

'Now lick my clit,' commanded Mistress Becki, moving her hips so Rachel's mouth was in the right place. She stroked the housewife's hair, as Rachel's tongue lashed out at her clitoris almost as forcefully as she had lashed the woman's bottom with her whip. Intense pulsations started shooting through her clitoral zone, echoing the pre-orgasmic spasms in her cunt. Knowing she was just seconds away from a heart-stopping climax, she gave Rachel permission to touch herself.

'Thank you, Mistress,' Rachel whispered, pressing a hand between her legs. As she stroked her own cunt lips, she gave the domme's sensitive clit another firm lick, instantly hearing a tell-tale roar burst out of the leather-clad beauty's lips. Mistress Becki's body spasmed, making her almost double over, as a violent shudder ran through her cunt. She came all over Rachel's face, the sudden outpouring of lush, sticky liquid eliciting an instant, copycat response from her submissive slave.

Rachel dug two fingers inside her own cunt, as the first wave of orgasm overtook her body. Her mouth was still locked tight to Mistress Becki's pussy, muffling her ecstatic yell, but nothing could muffle the throbbing in her pussy, nor the endorphin-happy tingle surging through every inch of her exposed flesh. She gazed up at her Mistress, overwhelmingly happy to have served at her feet and to have brought her to such a magnificent climax. For all its blistering intensity, her own climax seemed to matter less, as though it were no more than a slavish echo of Mistress Becki's joyous release. Yes, it was Mistress who mattered most of all, but Rachel was happy to bask in the reflection of her glory.

'Good slave,' said the domme, patting Rachel's head, and the acknowledgment of a task well done was enough to revivify her climactic rush. Her pussy contorted around her fingers, spilling juice into the palm of her hand, but it was the sudden change in her facial features that proved to her how much it all meant. She didn't need a mirror to know that her initial look of edginess had vanished, to be replaced by the patina of intense gratification and relaxation that characterised the faces of the many men whom she'd seen exiting Mistress Becki's house. Pent-up tension had given way to a sense of calm fulfilment, such as follows an all-over body massage or the 'making up' sex that comes straight after a bitter marital argument.

'Happy?' Mistress Becki asked, pulling her sex away from Rachel's lips.

'Very happy,' Rachel replied, staring up at her Mistress, a look of adoration in her eyes.

'So, there'll be no more spying,' the domme demanded, issuing a firm but gentle warning. 'No more peeking from behind the curtains. If you want to see what goes on here, then you just make an appointment like all the rest.'

'Yes, Mistress, I understand' said Rachel, already aware that she would be coming back. She would lie to the Neighbourhood Watch committee, insist that nothing untoward was going on at Becki's house, since the last thing she wanted was for the beautiful domme to be hounded out of the area. A whole new world of sexual possibilities had appeared right on her doorstep and she wasn't going to waste the opportunities it offered. Rachel had a chance to find herself, just like all those men who turned up nervous, but who left in a state of satisfied bliss. Her rightful place was at Mistress Becki's feet, where she could do her slavish duties, bringing pleasure to her Mistress and so also to herself.

Cherry Bottom
by Shanna Germain

'You okay, babe?' Andrew's voice above me was half sexual rasp, half concerned. His warm, oiled hands had moved from the outside curves of my ass to the inside of my thighs, and they were resting there, not pulling or teasing, just resting against my skin. I kept my eyes and mouth closed like I was supposed to and tried not to think about my naked ass in the air. I nodded against the pillow.

'She'll tell you if she's not,' Miss Suzanne's voice came from the other side of me. 'Won't you, Cate?' I nodded again, the rasp of the pillow filling my ear. Miss Suzanne pressed her cool, slim fingers next to Andrew's, higher up on the inside of my thigh. The hot and cold of their hands made my ass break out in goose bumps. 'See, Andrew? She'll tell you. So stop stalling.'

Miss Suzanne's fingers left my skin. Her heels click-clicked away, presumably to another one of the six couples whose husband was also stalling.

Andrew's hands didn't move. I waited, head on my hands, belly and thighs resting on the prop-up pillow, ass in the air. My bare body was still in goose bumps, although the room was warm enough. Some of it was anticipation. But most of it was fear – Miss Suzanne's anal sex class was our last resort. If we couldn't get Andrew over his fear of anal sex here, I was afraid it was never going to happen.

It had been difficult enough to ask for it – the way I was brought up, girls aren't supposed to like any sex. And they definitely aren't supposed to like it the way I liked it. And poor Andrew – he wanted so badly to please me, but couldn't get over his fear of hurting me. No matter how many times I told him, no matter how much I begged for it. We'd tried videos and books. I'd even bought the smallest butt-plug at the store. Straw-sized, really, but still, he couldn't bring himself to put anything inside me. Not even just a little bit. Bad experience, was all he'd say. But this class had been his gift to me, and I knew he wanted to please me that way, even if he was too afraid. So, now, here we were, being taught anal sex by Miss Suzanne Saunders, southern belle turned sex therapist. Our first two classes had been lecture and book-learning. Today was hands-on. Today was our last chance.

I concentrated on letting my muscles go loose, on breathing in through my nose. We'd just spent ten minutes playing, getting warmed up. A little strange, to share foreplay with a dozen other people in the room, but every time I looked up, they were all concentrating on their own space, their own bodies. It was like a yoga class in the nude. And despite his fears about anal, Andrew didn't seem to have any fears about public sex. He just ran his tongue up and down between my thighs, reached up and ran his wet thumb over and over my nipple until I could only lean back and try to keep my moans quiet.

I wanted this so badly, I could already feel him inside me, the fullness of him, the weight. The way his balls would slap against me. Jesus, it had been so long, I could barely remember how it felt. I took a deep breath, tried to think of something else for a minute, to be calm so that Andrew would be calm.

Andrew's fingers held steady at the inside of my thigh, one second, two. Then he ran them up through the crack between my cheeks. With one hand, he spread my ass cheeks open. With the other, he circled the skin around my asshole. Part of our class had been learning the anatomy of the asshole, getting used to its pink pucker, its hairless expanse of skin. Knowing that Andrew was looking at me like that, that he was studying me, made my pussy ache for his fingers. My asshole too. I wanted to reach my fingers underneath me, to ease the ache in my clit, but we weren't supposed to move, so I squeezed my eyes tighter and tried to enjoy the ache. Maybe I could learn something too.

Andrew's finger went around and around, tighter and tighter circles toward my asshole until finally, the tip of his finger pressed against it and I could barely breath. I wanted him, any part of him inside me so bad. He held his finger there, not moving it in or out…just resting his finger against it like it was a button he was deciding whether or not to press.

Miss Suzanne's heels click-clicked toward the front of the room. 'Okay, boys, I want you to get your fingers really well lubricated, the way we talked about earlier. We're going in.'

The class broke into nervous giggles. I was glad to hear Andrew's snort, the same one he gave at the comic strips at home. But his finger at my ass didn't move. Against my legs, his thigh muscles tightened.

C'mon, baby. C'mon…mental telepathy, the only encouragement I could offer him. I hoped that on some kind of a subconscious level he could hear me begging, could hear how much I wanted him like this.

Miss Suzanne and her heels again, right at our table. 'Can I help, Andrew?' she asked. He must have said yes, because then her cool fingers were at my ass cheeks again, spreading them for him. My asshole puckered up against the cold. My tightening nipples crinkled the paper sheet beneath me.

Andrew's fingers left my body, coming back oiled and warm.

'It's like playing pool,' Miss Suzanne said, her thin fingers still in place. 'It's all about speed and angles.' Andrew's finger back against me, pressing, pressing. I fought the desire to lean back onto the tip of his finger, to force him inside me once and for all. But part of our class promise had been to let our partner do all the work, go at his own pace, let him do only what he was ready for.

He increased the pressure, opening my asshole, careful to use the flat of his fingertip. 'Go,' Miss Suzanne whispered, and then Andrew pushed his way inside me. Just a little, just the tip so I could barely feel it, but oh Jesus, there he was.

'More,' Miss Suzanne said. Andrew pushed his finger farther into my asshole. Farther, until I was sure he had to be at the first joint. Having him in there like that made my pussy ache with that special emptiness that I loved. Andrew entered me to the knuckle. I imagined what he looked like behind me – starting to sweat beneath his glasses out of fear and excitement, his finger disappearing into my asshole.

'All the way in,' Miss Suzanne said. And then he pushed and his finger was inside me, tearing through me with that certain pain that is mostly pleasure. I bit down on the pillow, but most of the moan came out anyway.

'See?' Miss Suzanne said. 'She likes it. You're doing a great job.'

'Jesus,' Andrew whispered. 'Oh fuck.' Awe and arousal deepened his voice to a husky whisper. Hearing that voice – no fear in there – almost made me come.

Miss Suzanne raised her voice. 'Okay, class, is everyone in? Foxes all in the holes?' I'm sure the class laughed, but I couldn't even concentrate to hear all the answers. All I could feel was Andrew's finger in my ass, the way he held it there, so still, the way it filled me and at the same time made me ache for something more, something bigger.

'Great,' she said. 'Now I just want you to wiggle your fingers in there a little bit. Not a lot, just enough to feel the room, to see what kind of reaction you get.'

This time, Andrew didn't hesitate. As soon as she said wiggle, his finger started moving, up and down, up and down, inside me.

'Okay?' Andrew asked. But this time he wasn't asking if I was okay. He was asking if it felt good, if he was doing the right thing in there.

My voice was all whisper and the pressure of not fucking his finger. 'Yes,' I said. 'Yes, please don't stop.'

Miss Suzanne click-clicked back to the front of the room, apparently trusting that Andrew had gotten the hang of things.

After a few minutes she said, 'Ladies, now it's your turn to help out. Gentlemen, your job is just to hold yourself still. Maybe for the first time ever, your ladies are going to fuck you.'

Andrew's finger stopped moving in my ass. Light-headed, I pushed myself backwards onto Andrew's finger, so far back his other curled knuckles rubbed against my skin. I let myself fuck him, showing him how much I wanted him like this, how much I wanted him inside me.

With each thrust, Andrew's breathing quickened. His finger burnt and rubbed the inside of me in pain and pleasure. I was so full back there that the rest of me ached, empty and untouched. With one hand, I reached beneath me and fingered my slippery clit, letting everything build inside me. The fullness and the emptiness. The sweet burn of Andrew's finger in my ass, the soft roll of pleasure through my clit. And the best part was Andrew behind me, bracing himself against the table, letting me fuck him, I hoped, without fear for the first time. Seeing there was no pain, that there was only pleasure.

I was close to coming, but I wasn't sure if we were supposed to, if we'd been given the go-ahead, or if there was more I was supposed to do. And then Andrew moved his finger inside me, up and down, just enough to hit that spot and it didn't matter if I was supposed to or not, it was happening. Everything sliding through me from Andrew's finger out to my toes, up into my head. I cried out, and heard Andrew do the same.

I pulled forward, off Andrew's finger, and let my head hang on the pillow. 'Holy shit,' I said. I had no idea where anyone else was in the room, or if there was even anyone else in the room any more. And then I heard Miss Suzanne's heels click-click up. 'Once you two have washed up, meet in the front room to debrief and get your assignments for next week.' She put her hand, still cool as ever, against my shoulder. 'Nice job, you two.'

When I sat up, Andrew's face was pink and flushed. But he had the biggest grin on his face. Just seeing him like that, aroused and confident, made me wet all over again. He leaned down and kissed the lobe of my ear. 'That,' he whispered, 'was awesome. I can't wait to see what our new assignment is.'

I thought of his cock, the tip of it entering me, the way it would feel when he finally pushed inside me. 'I can't either.'

Afterdeath
by Susan DiPlacido

Morning is the worst time of day. Whether the bleating alarm suddenly jolts me back to reality or I swim up from the quagmire of sleep on my own, it sucks.

It sucks because there's that moment. As I'm brushing the dreams from my eyelashes, I become oriented all over again. It happens in those first seconds, even before I know where I am, or what day it is. The hazy softness is gone, and even though I'm still buried deep in thick blankets and downy pillows, it's a nasty realization. It only takes a few stinging seconds. It starts with an off-kilter feeling of wrongness, and then it cracks with lightning dread before dissipating and mellowing down into the daily, draining, awful acceptance.

Mike is gone. Mike is gone and he's never coming back. I'm alone. I'm alone and Mike is dead.

And it sucks.

Thus begins my day. Sometimes there's someone next to me, sometimes I'm alone. Either way, I pad to the shower and slip into a few more minutes of solace. I stand there with the steam surrounding me, skin slicked by the warm water raining down upon my shoulder. Meandering drops trickle a crooked line down my legs, barely having time to pool at my feet before draining away. But as one droplet slides across the sloped tile and plummets down unseen dark pipes leading it far away, another is released to follow the same course. Out of the pipe above, falling onto my neck, washing down my back. It travels the curve of my butt, losing momentum, trickling down my hamstring. Imperceptible amounts of it gather along my skin while the rest of it rolls along. It is fulfilling its destiny down the back of my calf until it, too, reaches the tile under my bare feet and gets whisked even further by gravity to those unseen and seldom imagined places it will finally meet its rest.

One is lost, but another exactly the same takes its place. Until I choose to turn the faucet that controls it all and bring it to an end.

It's not a bad part of the day. Absorbed in my own thoughts, memories, and the calming cleansing of the water, I'm content. Sometimes the guy who's not Mike joins me, and I pretend. A finger touches me at the base of my hairline, dead in the centre of my neck. I sigh. It traces a line down my neck, breaking the flow of the water there. My spine tingles directly beneath it, a chasing shiver in anticipation of where it's going to land next. It doesn't disappoint. With steady pressure, the finger moves slowly downward, gracing tiny bumps of my vertebrae. I straighten my back involuntarily, reflexively, as it passes down further. Back arched, head and neck now thrown completely back, the water falls directly upon my chest as the finger comes to rest in the tiny hollow of my back at the base of my spine.

I sigh heavily as the whole hand is tangible there now. Human heat, bare skin pressing against me, rubbing and undulating, deciding where to move next. I'm happy.

It lasts until the water goes cold. Then the reverie is broken, and I reach up and turn the faucet, stopping the flow so that no more drops can fall.

Then I go to work. Or on days off I do other things. The details don't matter, because it's neither good or bad. It's just filler. Time spent waiting to catch up.

Sometimes, people get impatient with me. It doesn't last long. They go back to their families and their lives and I smile extra bright for a few days or gamely date some guy who's not Mike for a few weeks so they don't worry. So they'll stop saying things. Things like: you have to move on. Or: Mike is dead. Even after all this time, I'm still not quite sure how they expect me to respond when they say that. Once in a while, they'll say I drink too much. This is something they usually say after popping a nice Prozac/Paxil mixture. Then they tell me again that Mike is gone.

That's the reality, to everyone else.

It's what they perceive and know through their senses. What is seen, heard, touched, tasted, and smelled. Those things are real. Everything else is an illusion. Or crazy. If it isn't tangible, it can't be fully understood.

Or can it?

Time. We can't gather it in a box and label that box for later use. But it's very real, especially to someone like me. Love. What is love? It's not tangible. But it's real. And real love doesn't just fade away.

When it comes to time, Mike and I were out of synch a lot. We grew up together, but he was older than I was by a few years. So when he first noticed me I still thought boys were stupid. Then when I thought he was cool, he was ready to start fooling around, but I was still shy. Then when I was ready to start getting busy, he was away at college with a girlfriend. Then when he was done with that and ready to play again, I was away and getting my footing with boyfriends. Then he was ready to slow down and get serious, and I was ready to celebrate and play. I was always behind. Then, one day, I caught up.

Then we fell in love.

Then he jumped ahead of me again. He died. Now, I'm just waiting to catch up again.

They're right, I drink a lot. I drink nearly as much as I pretend. I don't drink to forget. I drink to get high. It makes me giddy and silly and horny. And that's a lot like being in love. And it makes them uncomfortable because that's not playing by the rules.

'Till death us do part.'

That's the rule I break. Vows are exchanges, promises made, and the rules are set. Rules for love. It's a loophole. Necessary, yes. Logical, yes. Merciful, yes. But still a loophole. Till death us do part. I don't need the loophole. We never took those vows or made those promises anyhow. He can't move on and meet someone new. Why should I?

For others, it's only human. Grieve, mourn, and then move on. Build a new life, allow yourself a new love. And what is that love? Why is it so important that I have to have a new one?

It can't be tasted, touched, smelled, heard, or seen. But we need it. I need it too. Sure, the nuances of our love can be felt in the sensual way. But is that all it is? Our love is predicated on our beloved looking like a fox and tasting like a warm spice? Mike was foxy and spicy.

But, no. Love is how they make us feel. It's what it does to us. Fluttering in the tummy, an insistent heartbeat, a feeling of happiness. The way they look at us, the way they touch us. The things they do, the words they say. But there's more. It can't be bottled, and it may sound crazy. It's their essence, it's their energy. Simple physics, or mystical magic. Energy. We all have it. Those who think we don't are the ones who are absurd. Molecular transfer creates it.

167

That's our basic building blocks. Beneath the skin, woven through our genetically granted dark, soulful eyes, smaller than the cells of blood that pump through our veins, we are made of molecules, and they create energy. Energy is never created or destroyed. Physics. But philosophy and religion will tell you the same. Buddhists say it. Energy is never destroyed, it merely changes and then re-groups. Nirvana.

Love is energy. Love is never created or destroyed. It's there. Waiting. Sometimes dormant. Sometimes hidden.

Mike died. My love didn't. So I go out and pass the time and have a few laughs and a few more drinks. Then someone catches my eye. Sometimes, it's the way he stands. Sometimes, it's his cologne. Sometimes it's his dark hair. But there's always a palpable similarity that reminds me of Mike. And that turns me on.

I'll be at least a little warmed up by rum. My mind blurry and easily confused. My body buzzing, prickling with the contagious excitement of flashing lights and pulsing bass. I stand close to him, the guy who's not Mike, and wait to see if there's a spark. There is. As he's talking to me, his forearm brushes across my breast. Already wired, my nipple reacts to the contact and hardens. I lick my lips and lean closer. He brushes again, this time with his hand. My breath catches in my throat and I lean, just slightly, into the touch.

He notices. He was flirting before. But now as my nipple pokes against the fabric of my shirt, he's looking at it along with the rise and fall of my breathing, and the amped vibrations come off him. He gets brave. He runs his thumb across my nipple, roughly. He sighs on my neck, hotly. I get wet, immediately. He'll fill the void, help me get where I want to be. Temporarily. And that's enough.

So I take him home. I fix us drinks and lead him to the bedroom.

I strip languidly, because even though I want this, I want it to last. We're kissing, his mouth on mine, warm lips and a hint of stubble, and when his tongue slips out the first time it sends a frisson up my spine. I lay him back on the bed and climb on top. I reach down and touch him. He's hard already, and he sighs as I take hold of him. Head fogged, my crotch pulsing, I want to rub his cock against my clit. But I know if I started that I'd catch fire too quickly and I wouldn't be able to stop. And I'm not really believing the lie yet, so it'd be an aggravating exercise in futility. I tease him, stroke him a few times. It's hot but dry so I'm careful.

The last vestiges of rationality tug at me, so I stop long enough to get a condom on him. Once that's done, I take another drink of rum. It's a slow, comforting heat, sliding down my throat, warming my belly, soothing my mind. Freeing me. I lay back and pull him on top of me, it's exactly what I wanted to feel. The reinforcing weight of him pressed against me. He kisses me again, deeper, more insistent. It's good. He works a hand down to my breast, rubbing it, teasing circles around the nipple I tempted him with. When he tugs on it, and slips me more tongue, I groan in approval. My eyes flutter open, and even in the dim light I pick out differences. His hair is lighter, his nose is smaller. So I take his free hand and place it over my eyes so I can't peek.

He obliges, this one. I reach down and stroke him again in appreciation. It makes him pant and squeeze my breast, sending a pulse right between my legs. Our breathing makes the air get dense and balmy. I flutter my eyes open and closed against the soft skin of his palm. Tickling, lashes grazing and teasing. Soft lips drop a kiss upon the side of my neck and my shoulders hunch up against the pleasing touch.

Thick and sultry, human scents taking over, sweat and flesh, the tang of my now dripping cunt. Salty, but warm, always warm. Then warmer, near my ear, a presence can be felt. Moist and hot, breath tingling, whispering softly as lips graze close, barely touching, moving to my mouth. His hand moves off my face, but I keep my eyes closed, the physical details are swirling and taking over anyhow; I'm getting lost in them.

Nipping, teasing with little kisses, our breath mixing, a line of kisses falls down my throat, a tongue licks my collarbone. I squirm and grab hold of him, start guiding him to me.

A hand moves across my chest, smooth, warm, lower. Down to my belly, rubbing back and forth across it while my neck is still being kissed. Sucking on my lips, teeth grazing pleasantly, the weight and warmth of another body pressed into mine. Heavy, not claustrophobic, I breathe deeply, blindly stroking him, and he finally does the same. His hand moves from my stomach and dives between my legs. Like a cat in heat I arch into it, he rubs a few times and then finds my hot spot. Strong fingers make slow, firm circles around my clit.

I writhe under him, using mental images of Mike doing these things to me to complete the illusion. The air is even heavier now, laden with humidity, soaked with lust, and vibrating with energy. It's charged. I'm charged, lit up. Heart racing, pulse coursing, spine tingling, I'm alive, present, we both are, I can feel it. Rushing, breathing heavy, muscles tensing everywhere that a hand brushes over them.

Nerves and sensors on edge, it's all good. I inhale roughly, the moisture, the heat, the salt of sex goes in, courses through my lungs, some of it absorbed, the rest forced right back out again with a sexual moan. He stops rubbing my clit and I could scream, but right away he places

170

his hand over mine on his cock and lines himself up. Sudden and deep, he thrusts inside me.

And it's intense.

I buck and moan, eyes still clamped shut, wrap my legs around his waist, move into him, and then we're fucking. I hope this one doesn't leap ahead of me. Mike, sometimes, he was faster than I was at this too. He usually made it up to me or finished me off so that we'd be even. But now, I've had enough of being left behind. From the way he's already sending silvery shivers down my spine, I doubt he'll come before I do. But he's panting and working, propped on his elbows, hips thrusting. Controlled power, but unrestrained passion. So as insurance I wiggle a hand down between us and start to stroke myself, conjuring images of my lover behind closed eyelids while my fingers rub away.

He groans in my ear and speaks with a hoarse voice, encouraging me. 'Yeah, work yourself up, baby.' I wish he wouldn't do that; talk. It's not the voice I'm imagining. My clit is responding and he feels so good inside, all that friction and heat, burying deep, hitting the spot. But it pulls me back off the edge. At least he's turned on by me and he feels so damn good and my eyes are still shut, picturing what I want. He talks again now. 'That's so hot, baby.'

I gently shush him, then pick up the pace on myself to get the spark back. He puts his hand on my wrist, feeling me working myself that way, and picks up his pace too. I'm burning up and rubbing furiously, he's driving into me, and I'm picturing everything that's going on in my mind with Mike's hand holding my wrist, Mike's cock deep inside me, Mike whispering to me, and then my skin flushed and sweaty, breath ragged, the tingles erupt and I'm right there. Intense pleasure that just can't last forever. I only hover on the edge for a short time, sucking in a deep breath, so good and so extreme I can't force myself to stop or pull away. Now, like a lighting crack, I come.

My whole body jolts, my breathing stops, every muscle contracts. I don't even try, I just think – Mike. He's still thrusting, sending shockwaves all through me and I grab him and pull him close and hold him tight. We're alive, it's exquisite. He stops thrusting and starts shaking, coming inside me as I shudder back into relaxation. Exhausted, we lay still now. Still panting, still warm, still coursing with energy, I sigh again, stroking his back, hazy but just cognizant enough to whisper a pre-emptive 'Shhhh.' I hover in that state for a time before dozing off.

It's the twilight time. Not asleep and dreaming. Not awake and acclimatised. Sated. Dazed. Warmth next to me. A pleasant buzz. I feel in love with Mike.

It's the best time of the day.

Am I crazy?

Love is energy.

Energy is never created or destroyed.

It just shifts and changes, but then it regroups. And until I catch up, I have this. Flowing through me, all around me. I can't just shut it off. Because I'm in love with Mike.

Titus Loves Flowers
by Jim Baker

Titus Andronicus is alive and well in County Cork, Southern Ireland. I know, I've met him.

It all begun with the annual family holiday meeting...

I live in London with my wife, Sheila, and the kids, Katie and young Steven. Every year we have a meeting about where we'll go on our summer holiday. Each year one member of the family has their turn to name the destination.

This year it was Katie's turn to decide and, according to the rules, the rest of us had to abide by her decision, as long as the budget allowed it.

Our sixteen-year-old daughter has three major interests: boys, the internet, and horses. Boys are, of course, inevitable, especially given the fact that she is exceptionally pretty. The internet is as much a part of a teenager's life as T.V. and mobile phones, but why on earth *horses*?

It's not something she's inherited from us. I don't mind small, friendly horses, but big ones, with steel plates on their feet, scare me. Sheila automatically shies away from any animal bigger than a gerbil.

Katie was bubbling with excitement when she put a computer printout on the table.

'Look everybody. Horse-drawn caravan holidays in Ireland!'

There was a muffled groan of despair from behind my wife's wine glass. I studied the document. At the bottom was a picture of a huge horse with great furry feet, pulling a decorated caravan.

'Well, I don't know, Katie,' I said. 'Your mother's not fond of horses. I don't think it's a good idea at all.'

'Oh, please, daddy. It's my turn to choose. You have to agree.'

Tears welled in her big blue eyes and Sheila's shoe contacted my shin, hard.

'No, Katie, not horses. Find something else.'

Sometimes you simply have to be firm.

Sheila was reading when I slid into bed beside her. She put her book down and looked across at me.

'You're not going to give in to her, are you?'

'What? Give in to who?'

'First commandment. Thou do not bullshit thy wife. To Katie of course. I saw the look on your face when she started howling and ran up to her room. She can twist you around her little finger three times.'

I opened my mouth to reply and she laughed.

'Don't even try. I am not going to Ireland and I am not going anywhere that involves a horse.'

A sly look settled on her face.

'Maybe a bribe would help you to decide?'

'What sort of bribe?'

Her hand stole down under the sheet.

I have to admit that I *had* given thought to allowing Katie's request. After all, we were a democratic household.

A more reasoned approach began to occur to me, though, when Sheila's lips engulfed the head of my cock.

Horses could be dangerous; I had to consider the family welfare.

She took the whole shaft down her throat, and as her lips moved slowly up and down, I realized she was almost certainly right.

I didn't do much thinking for a little while after that, but as she sucked the last drops from my throbbing cock, my mind was made up – I would be firm! It is important not to be manipulated by one's children.

I was enjoying the ferry trip across the Irish Sea when Sheila announced, sweetly, that she'd left her spectacles at home.

'Sorry, love,' she said. 'I won't be able to drive to Cork. I think I'll have a few glasses of wine at the bar.'

So much for my quiet snooze in the hire car.

We were staying overnight in Cork and I sighed with relief as we passed the town sign.

'OK, we're here.'

'Dad, aren't we going to Cork?'

'This is Cork, Steven.'

'Isn't.'

'We just passed the sign.'

'That said Cob-huh. C-O-B-H.' He spelled it out.

Katie sighed. She'd been quiet since her mother had discovered her in a dark corner of the deck behind the lifeboats, in a tight embrace with a boy. Their lips had been glued together, his hand was buried under her skirt and she was unzipping his jeans when Sheila spotted them. He had been sent packing and Katie was given a very sharp lecture on 'casual pick-ups'.

She muttered something about 'only snogging'.

'If you think that was only snogging, my girl,' her mother said, tight-lipped, 'we'd better have a long talk later.'

'What's snogging?' Steven asked. I made a mental note to have a talk with him later as well.

'That *is* Cork, stupid,' Katie said.

'What, C-O-B-H?'

'Yes, it's Gaelic.'

'What's Gaelic?'

'It's the Irish language.'

'Why don't they speak Irish?'

'Gaelic is Irish, dumbo.'

'Don't call me dumbo!'

'Shut up the pair of you!' Sheila snapped. 'John, aren't we staying at the Imperial?'

'Yes, why?'

'You drove past it five minutes ago.'

There was little further conversation until we were in the hotel bar, and the kids had been sent out for a walk.

'And no boys!' Sheila warned Katie.

'Come on, I'll tell you about snogging,' Katie said to Steven as they left.

I looked quizzically at Sheila. 'Just think, we haven't even got the horse yet.'

She groaned, downed her gin and tonic and ordered another.

At dinner, Steven wanted to know why pork wasn't spelled P-O-B-H on the menu.

Sex had been off my menu ever since I had agreed with Katie about the caravan holiday. Sheila had feigned sleep and claimed headaches for the past two weeks. I knew her appetite well, though, and I knew she was missing it as much as I was.

Sure enough the change of venue softened her, and she made no effort to resist when I rolled over in the huge bed and put my arm around her.

'Fancy your chances, do you?'

'Well, we're going to be cooped up with the kids in a caravan...'

I stopped abruptly as I realized the stupidity of what I was saying, but to my relief she laughed.

'And whose fault is that? Oh, come here, you of the small brain and big dick...'

We've been married for seventeen years, and Sheila still has the ability to give me an erection simply by looking at me. We met in the apartment of a mutual friend at a university party when I was nineteen and she was eighteen. The attraction was instant; we were screwing within the hour and ended up fucking all night in his spare bedroom. The result was Katie. Sheila and I got married, and produced Steven nine years later. Our hunger for each other's bodies hasn't lessened since.

'...and make me forget about horses and fucking caravans.'

She kissed me and stroked my cock, bit my ear lobes and licked my face.

'First of all, you can pay me back the bribe you took and didn't honour. Get down there and get busy!'

I brought her off twice with my lips and tongue, and then she tugged my hair and urged me back up the bed.

'That was gorgeous, sweetheart. Now for the main course.'

She put her lips close to my ear. 'Once with you on top. Then one doggy-style.'

Her voice got even lower. 'And after that, if you're man enough, I'm going to ride you. Like a fucking horse!'

The dawn light was creeping through the curtains when she rolled off me, after riding me to my third orgasm of the night. Every muscle in my body ached and my cock felt as if it was ready to drop off.

'That'll teach you to bring me on a horse-caravan holiday.'

The kids were sharing the room next door.

At breakfast, Katie gave me an impish smile.

'Sleep well, daddy?'

The taxi dropped us next morning at a ramshackle wooden building bearing the sign *O'Callaghan's Caravans* above the door. There were a couple of caravans in the cobbled front yard, resplendent in red, blue and yellow paintwork. The door opened and a small man emerged, bobbing, smiling and waving at the same time.

'Daniel O'Callaghan at your service,' he declared, bowing low. He took Sheila's hand in his, raised it to his lips and kissed it, then did the same with Katie, who giggled.

'And sure you'll be sisters.' he went on, 'Where's Mrs O'Neill, your lovely mother?'

I broke the ensuing silence. 'I'm John Andrews, Mr O'Callaghan.'

'No, you'll be Mr O'Neill.'

As I opened my mouth to argue he pulled a piece of paper from his pocket and squinted at it.

'To be sure, you're right,' he said. 'It's Tuesday. You are Mr Andrews. I'll get Titus.'

He vanished through the door. My relief at discovering I wasn't Mr O'Neill was short lived as a sound filled the air like stones being smashed with a sledgehammer. It got louder and louder and Mr O'Callaghan reappeared around the side of the building leading a huge brown and white horse, whose mighty hoofs crashed on the cobbles and sent sparks flying through the air.

'This,' he said proudly, 'is Titus Andronicus.' Steven and I backed off but Katie leapt forward with a squeal of joy, dragging her mother with her.

'Oh, isn't he beautiful!'

The enormous muzzle nodded up and down and the huge beast thrust it toward Sheila, who looked terrified.

'Stroke him, Mum!'

Sheila stretched forth a trembling hand, whereupon Titus tossed his head and, with a great snort, deposited a gallon of drool across her front.

'Ah,' said Mr O'Callaghan. 'He does that sometimes.'

'Not more than twice, he won't,' Sheila grated back as the viscous stream rolled down her designer shirt and jeans.

The remainder of the morning was taken up with lessons in harnessing, driving and feeding.

At last we were ready to go. As I climbed on board, Mr O'Callaghan took my arm.

'Two things you should know about Titus,' he said quietly.

'Yes?'

'He loves flowers. But he's not over fond of pulling caravans.'

I digested this somewhat disturbing information as we clopped off down the road.

For the first half hour we moved at walking pace. The tranquillity was broken only by occasional mutterings from inside the caravan, where Sheila was washing her be-drooled clothes in the tiny sink.

There was a distinctly rural smell in the air and I noticed Steven was pulling faces.

'What's that stink, Dad?'

Katie laughed. 'It's Titus, he's farting.'

'Katie!'

'But dad, horses do. All the time.'

I was contemplating the dubious pleasure of spending hours a day breathing poison gas when a particularly obnoxious wave spread about us. Steven gulped and threw himself back into the body of the van. Two seconds later there was a scream of, 'No! Not in there!' followed by the sound of retching.

We hung Sheila's clothes on the back of the van and straight away it started to rain, a relentless soaking drizzle.

After three hours we were in the middle of nowhere, drenched, with green meadows stretching all around.

Mr O'Callaghan had given us a list of farms whose owners would accommodate us, but he had assured us it wasn't really necessary.

'You can just pull into any meadow. Everyone around here knows me, you'll be fine.'

Spotting a gate I took him at his word.

We were soon settled; Katie and Steven unharnessed Titus and fed him, I brewed tea and Sheila opened the gin.

I was beginning to relax when I noticed a small man leaning on the gate, staring at the caravan.

'Good evening to you,' he said, as I approached beneath an umbrella. 'I was just wondering. Would there be a game on tonight?'

I gaped at him.

'This is the local hurling field, y'see,' he went on. 'Seeing your fine van, I thought there might be a game tonight.'

'No,' I stuttered. 'We're on a caravan holiday.'

'Oh, right.' He turned and walked away, then trudged back. 'It might be your horse then?'

'What horse?'

'The one I passed on the road. Big fella heading towards Cork.'

I gazed wildly round the empty field and tore back to the caravan.

'The horse has gone!'

'Praise the Lord,' said Sheila, raising her glass.

Katie and I found Titus plodding doggedly back along the road to Cork. We'd brought apples to bribe him and eventually he was back in the field, this time with both gates closed.

I've never played or seen hurling but I doubt the players appreciated the overnight offerings Titus spread about their playing area.

I won't go into the details of the next few days. Dwell on the words *equine hell*, use your imagination and you'll have some idea.

As an example, think about reversing a two-ton horse between the shafts of a caravan he doesn't want to pull. In the rain. Always in the bloody rain.

I had to admire Katie. She loved Titus.

She defended him when he ate all the flowers in the garden of the nice lady who let us stay in the meadow behind her house on the third night.

'He was hungry, daddy.'

'Titus loves flowers,' I muttered as I handed over fifty quid.

The fifth day was better. The rain stopped for a few hours and Sheila bought an expensive piece of Donegal tweed in a village store. It was a present for her mother.

Then, that evening, disaster struck.

Sheila was staring morosely over the top of her third glass of gin, across yet another soaking meadow, when her body stiffened.

'What's the horse got on its back?'

Katie looked up from her book. 'It's a blanket, Mum. He was cold.'

'Where did you get it?' Sheila's voice was dangerously soft.

'It was rolled up in the back of the caravan…'

Katie's voice wavered at the look on her mother's face.

'That's Donegal tweed for my mother! And you've put it on that stinking horse!'

'But…' Katie had no chance.

'Go and get it! Now! And take your brother with you! And don't come back for an hour!'

'What's wrong with Mum?' asked Steven as they went outside.

'Missing her nookie, probably,' Katie growled.

'What's nookie?'

'I'll explain when you're older.'

'Why not now?'

Their voices faded away. I buried my head in my hands, and then realized Sheila was giggling helplessly.

'What?'

Her giggles increased. 'It's Stevie. *What's nookie*? You have to talk to Steve.'

'Don't you think you should speak to Katie as well? She is only sixteen.'

She stopped giggling.

'Only sixteen? She's going on seventeen. I had a stiff dick in my hand when I was fourteen and my cherry popped on the back seat of a car three months later. Katie knows what she's about, don't worry. She knows exactly what we were up to in the hotel room.'

She stopped laughing.

'Right, mastermind, you got us into this shit, you get us out. But first, I'd like some of that nookie I've been missing.'

'What, now?'

'Now. Right now! And then you can organize something that means we don't spend another day in the company of that fucking horse!'

I was sitting on the one, semi-comfortable, chair in the caravan. She knelt in front of me.

'Still remember the first time?'

Remember? I was hardly likely to forget.

The party had been going for some time when I arrived with two other guys. We had stayed in the pub until it closed, and were all feeling a bit drunk and very horny.

The room was dark, lit only by two small table lamps set on the bar at one end. Music was playing quietly and a few couples were dancing, pressed tightly together. There were huddled shapes in the corners and very little conversation, just a bit of soft sighing and the occasional grunt of pleasure.

No available girls were in evidence, and I was about to suggest that we went elsewhere when an attractive redhead appeared behind the bar. She had a furious look on her face and I watched as she snatched up a glass, filled it with red wine and slurped it down. I arrived beside her as she lifted the second glass to her lips.

'Hey, slow down,' I said. 'Leave some for the poor and needy.'

For a second I thought she was going to throw her wine in my face, then she relaxed and smiled. I fell instantly in love.

'You're gorgeous.'

The words were out before I could stop myself.

'Thank you, kind sir.' She looked me up and down. 'You're not too bad yourself. Better than that prick I just got rid of, for sure.'

'Who?'

'Oh, some arrogant dickhead who tried to stick his hand up my skirt.'

'What happened?'

'I kneed him in the balls and poured a glass of beer over his head. He left. I'm Sheila, by the way.'

'John. I'll make a point of not putting my hand up your skirt.'

She grinned at me.

'It's not that I necessarily object to having a guy's hand under my skirt. It's just that I like to decide which guy's hand it's going to be.'

She took my hand, studied it and raised it to her lips.

'You've got nice hands,' she murmured and kissed the ends of my fingers. Goose bumps rose on my skin and my cock pressed hard against the front of my jeans.

She put her hand on the back of my neck.

'Will you dance with me?'

It took us five minutes to dance to the far corner of the room, which was in deep shadow. We stopped and she rubbed her lower body back and forth across mine.

My erection pressed into her and she chuckled.

'Someone's excited,' she murmured. 'Kiss me.'

The kiss lasted a long time and then she whispered in my ear.

'I'm excited too. Feel.' She took my hand under her skirt on to the front of her soaking wet panties.

'There's a chair just behind you. Move back.'

I edged slowly backwards until the backs of my legs bumped against something hard.

'Sit down.'

I lowered myself carefully and she came with me, looping her arms around my neck and straddling my knees. We kissed again and she moved her hand from my neck down to

184

my crotch. She kneaded my cock until it was standing like a pole in my jeans.

'Nice,' she said. 'Shall we let him out?'

I looked around nervously and she laughed.

'No one's watching us. It's dark and they're all too busy.'

As she spoke she worked down the zip, slid her hand inside and wriggled her fingers until they touched bare flesh. She played with my cock for a few moments and then gently tugged it out.

'Very nice,' she said. 'Now, I've got just the place for that.'

She hiked up her short skirt, lifted herself and moved forward until I felt the silky touch of her panties. She put her hand down between her thighs and eased the barrier to one side. Pubic hair tickled and I let out a long sigh of pleasure as she lowered herself, and my cock was sheathed in what felt like hot, damp velvet.

She wriggled her body to get comfortable and I gasped as her movements sent tingles of electricity through my body.

'Okay, John,' she said. 'Lie back and enjoy. I'll do the work.'

Her cunt muscles squeezed hard, she began to ride my cock and I did as I was told, letting the pleasure build up and up...

'Where have you gone?'

I started back into the present as Sheila settled on my knees, and found myself looking into the same blue eyes I had watched glaze over as we had climaxed together that night over seventeen years before.

'Wherever it was, it's given you one hell of a hard-on. You wouldn't have been thinking about a certain party, by any chance?'

She squeezed my rigid cock through my pants and I groaned.

She chuckled.

'Shall we let him out?'

'The kids…'

'The kids dumped the horse-blanket in the front of the van while you were day-dreaming. They've gone off for a walk.'

Her fingers were busy as she spoke and my cock jumped free of my pants.

'Hello,' she whispered, and played with it gently.

'I love you, John,' she said. 'And I'm in love with your cock.'

She took it between her lips and sucked it hard. I smoothed her red hair with my hand.

'Come on,' she said, standing up abruptly. 'I want you.'

She lay down on her back on the mattress, pulled up her skirt and spread her legs apart.

'Right here, sweetheart.'

I knelt down in front of her and she raised her knees.

'Take my panties off.'

I pulled them away, buried my face in the mass of red curly hair and went to work with lips and tongue until she shuddered and moaned.

She grabbed my hair and looked at me with wild eyes.

'Come inside me. Quickly!'

Her legs locked high around my back as I rammed into her and we slapped against each other in a mad frenzy of fucking until we together came in a gasping, moaning climax.

We lay stickily together, panting for breath, as my cock slowly softened and slid out.

'Christ, that was good.'

Her voice was husky and I smiled down at her.

'As good as the first time?'

'I think you've improved with age.'

I sat up and straddled her waist.

'Not so much about the age!'

I tickled her ribs and she squirmed and squealed.

I was unbuttoning her blouse when I heard the faint sound of voices.

'Christ, the kids!'

I leapt up, pulled her to her feet and stuffed my cock away. Sheila smoothed her skirt and ran her fingers through her hair. I'd just got my zipper closed when Katie stuck her head through the back door of the van.

'It started to rain so we came back...'

Her voice tailed off at the sight of her mother's flushed cheeks and her eyes flickered down to the bright blue panties lying in the middle of the mattress.

A broad grin spread across her face.

'Been doing a bit of snogging, have we?' she asked innocently, and ducked out of sight.

So here we are, me with my Guinness and Sheila with her gin, on the balcony of the Hotel Europe in Killarney.

I telephoned Mr O'Callaghan and we left Titus and the caravan with a farmer friend of his.

'But no refund for the rest of the week, mind,' Mr O'Callaghan said, sounding apologetic.

As if I cared.

'Titus is it?' the farmer said. 'He doesn't always get this far.'

187

Katie was upset but wisely didn't argue with her mother and brightened up when she found the hotel had a heated swimming pool. She bought a tiny bikini and on the second day she was holding court with three male admirers on the edge of the pool.

The hotel laundry sorted out the Donegal Tweed.

I'll just sup another Guinness before I have my talk with Steven. There's nothing like communing with nature to give a man a thirst.

Working Conditions
By Elizabeth Coldwell

When Leo took me to one side and told me the word on the grapevine was that I was being recommended for the vacant position at Wallace and Barker, I could barely believe it. Indeed, if it had been anyone other than Leo, I wouldn't have believed it. But we had been good friends, as well as work colleagues, for the best part of six years, and if he said the most prestigious law firm in the city were interested in me, they were interested in me.

'Of course,' he added, 'you'll want to think about it very carefully before you accept, Alison. You know the job has conditions attached.'

Of course I knew. Everyone knew about the conditions Wallace and Barker laid down when they offered a job to a female member of staff. It was just that no one knew exactly what those conditions actually were. It was not enough that even to be considered you had to possess an exceptional intellect and aptitude; you also had to possess certain qualities which were never openly defined, but were the subject of much speculation. And those women who worked – or had worked – for Wallace and Barker never offered the merest hint as to what was expected of them, or why such a large percentage of those who had attended the interview turned down the job outright.

'Don't worry,' I told him. 'It would take a lot to put me off.'

And so I continued to think, until the moment I found myself sitting in the oak-panelled boardroom, confronted by the firm's two senior partners, Mr Wallace and Mr Barker. I didn't learn their first names – not then, not for a long time afterwards. Mr Wallace was in his fifties, grey-haired and with the manner, I thought, of a rather remote and uninterested public school headmaster. Mr Barker was possibly ten years his junior, conspicuously overweight in his Savile Row suit, and with a cold intelligence glittering in his eyes. They made me feel uncomfortable, as though I was under-dressed and under-prepared for the interview, even though I had taken longer than usual with my hair and make-up that morning and had presented them with what was, even by their high, exacting standards, an impeccable CV.

I answered their questions as best I could, and gave careful thoughts to the tricky little points of law with which they tried to trip me up. Finally, Mr Walker cleared his throat and said, 'Well, Miss Mills, I have to say you really are everything we hoped. We would be delighted to accept you as a member of the firm. We are sure you will find the salary we are offering more than acceptable –' and he named an amount of money which was very nearly double what I was presently earning. Then, while I was still letting all that sink in, he continued, 'I'm sure you know that we expect certain standards of behaviour from our female members of staff. Firstly, Mr Barker and I must always be addressed as "sir".'

Not a problem, I thought to myself. Why all the fuss if that's what they want?

'Secondly,' he continued, 'your marital status. You describe yourself as "single". This is such an ambiguous term these days. Are you, in fact, co-habiting, or do you have a boyfriend?'

I hesitated for a moment, sure that this line of questioning had been outlawed by discrimination laws, along with enquiries as to whether I planned on becoming pregnant in the near future. Then, sensing that both men were waiting impatiently for an answer, I said, 'No – I mean, no, sir, I'm not seeing anyone at the moment.'

Mr Barker smiled. I noticed his teeth were sharp and pointed, like those of a wild animal. 'Good. Because throughout the time you are employed here, that is expected to be the case.'

That seemed like a little more of an imposition. I had never been one of those girls who considers herself incomplete without a man in her life, but I hoped they weren't demanding I should be entirely celibate for however long I worked for them.

'Thirdly,' said Mr Wallace, 'dress code. You are always to wear a skirt, never trousers. As you have particularly good legs, these skirts will be of mid-thigh length. You will wear stockings and suspenders with them, not tights. And the only knickers you are permitted to wear must be plain white cotton. No lace, no frills and definitely no thongs.'

I tried to keep my expression neutral. Was I sitting in front of two dirty old men, rather than the two most respected lawyers in the city? Was it turning them on to think of me in short skirts and stockings? And why the emphasis on white cotton panties? Still, for the money they were offering, I would have turned up in a bikini if they had requested it of me.

'Finally – and you will not be surprised to learn that this is the hurdle at which most of our applicants fall, even if, like you, Miss Mills, they have not uttered a word of objection so far – on the last working day of each month, you must submit to be beaten by Mr Barker or myself in front of all the male members of staff who are on the premises at the time.'

I looked at the two of them, trying to find any hint in their expressions to indicate that they were joking. I had never heard anything so outrageous. What did they mean, 'beaten'?

'You see now why we request that our female employees remain single, Miss Mills,' Mr Barker said. 'We never used to insist, but we lost a couple of highly valued employees because they had a husband or boyfriend who could not cope with seeing the nature and position of the marks these women returned home with once a month.'

'So what do you say, Miss Mills?' asked Mr Wallace. 'Are you prepared to work for us under those conditions?'

Part of me wanted to say no, to get up and go back to my secure, orthodox job, working alongside Leo and an office full of men who didn't want to watch me being beaten and marked in some unspecified fashion. But another part of me – a part which was no longer thinking about how far I might be prepared to go even for the ridiculous sum of money they were offering someone of my age and experience – was ready to rise to the challenge. And I was sure this was why these two self-satisfied lechers had hunted me out.

'Yes,' I said, meeting their greedy gaze. 'Yes, I accept – sir.'

And so I bid farewell to Leo and my other friends, and joined Wallace and Barker. At my leaving drink they all, as I had expected them to do, tried to worm the legendary 'special conditions' out of me, but I mumbled something about a 'confidentiality clause' and left it at that. If I had told them the truth, I expect they would have thought I was

192

having them on – after all, it sounded ludicrous even to my ears, and I was the one who had agreed to it.

Life at Wallace and Barker proved to be as challenging and exciting as I had hoped. The firm was preparing the prosecution case in a complicated fraud trial and I was set to work as part of that team. I quickly realised I was working with people of a much higher calibre than at my old firm – and that very few of them were female. In fact, apart from myself, there were only three women in the whole firm – Chloe, who was the PA for both Mr Wallace and Mr Barker, Suzanne, who doubled as the firm's receptionist and general secretary, and Catherine, who was a fairly senior lawyer within the hierarchy. For the first couple of weeks I was there, my path very rarely crossed with any of theirs, expect to speak to Suzanne briefly when I entered and left the building, and to pick up any messages from her. I suspected this was deliberate, to prevent me from asking any of them about what would happen on the last day of the month.

Of course, I found out soon enough. From the moment I walked into the end-of-terrace Regency building which housed the offices of Wallace and Barker on that Friday morning, I was aware of a completely different atmosphere in the place. I can only describe it as one of expectancy. When Suzanne pushed a couple of pieces of post across the desk to me, there was no cheery greeting. Chloe, who was quiet and nervy at the best of times, with her jet-black bobbed hair and small, wire-framed glasses, looked frankly terrified, even though I knew she must be a veteran of these occasions. Catherine was in court, but I was assured by one of my colleagues that she would be in the office by the end of the afternoon, even if it meant asking the judge for an adjournment.

I found it almost impossible to concentrate on my work. It was not so much the thought of what might be done to me, but the not knowing when or how. As usual, I slipped out to the café round the corner for lunch, but I left my sandwich after only a couple of bites, unable to eat for the sick, churning feeling in my stomach.

And then, at precisely half-past three, as if by some unspoken signal, all the men in the office stopped what they were doing. They closed and put away their files, logged off their PCs and trooped away from their desks. I waited a couple of moments, then I crept out to reception. As I suspected, Suzanne was nowhere to be seen. Wallace and Barker were nothing if not traditional in their concept of rank and superiority, and Suzanne was very much at the bottom of this particular food chain.

Left alone with Chloe, I tried to catch her eye, to find some indication that she sympathised with me in my imminent predicament. I was sure that however this nasty little game worked, she was next, and I wanted some reassurance before she disappeared that it wasn't going to be so bad. I didn't get it. She stubbornly refused to even acknowledge my presence and when, twenty minutes later, she took a hurried phone call and rushed out of the office, I could not even begin to imagine what might be about to happen to her – or to me.

For the next twenty-five minutes, I sat in a frenzy of such anticipation I thought about penning a resignation note, and then I decided against it. Whatever was going to be done to me, I was not about to run away once it was over. I had waited long enough for the opportunity to join Wallace and Barker; I was not going to jeopardise my career by being a wimp who buckled under their bizarre demands.

The phone rang, breaking the unnatural silence of the empty office. I answered it, only to hear Mr Barker's voice say, 'We're ready for you in the boardroom, Miss Mills.'

I stood up on legs which no longer felt like my own, and tottered out into the corridor. As I climbed the stairs to the boardroom, I met Chloe coming the other way. She was clutching a number of files to her chest protectively, her normally neat bob was dishevelled and she looked as though she had been crying. All she said was, 'I'll see you on Monday, Alison,' in a voice which was little more than a squeak.

And that was it. No wishing me good luck, no kind words to help stem the anxiety which was tying my insides in knots, just a muttered farewell and she was gone.

I stood in front of the boardroom door, telling myself that, if I really wanted to, I still had time to turn and run. But if timid, mousy Chloe could take whatever punishment had been handed out to her, then so could I. I smoothed my skirt and hair, knocked on the door and entered.

Nine pairs of eyes burned into me as I walked into the room. Mr Wallace and Mr Barker were sitting at the big mahogany boardroom table, and all the other men in the building that Friday were seated in a semi-circle which started and ended at the edge of the table. I recognised them all, spotting Michael and Neil, who were compiling material on the fraud case, and Scott from the post room, who couldn't have been more than eighteen. But though, outwardly, they were the same men I had been chatting with and working alongside until an hour or so ago, something within every one of them had changed.

As had been requested at my interview, I had complied with the dress code. That day, I was wearing a slate grey suit with a short skirt which, as Mr Wallace had suggested it would, made the most of my long legs, and a white blouse. My underwear also fitted their requirements precisely, even though I still found it hard to get used to the functionality of my plain cotton knickers when contrasted with the innate sexiness of my stockings and suspenders. As I stood there, however, I felt naked before all of them. I could feel them mentally stripping me with their gaze, could sense them imagining what it would be like to rip the blouse from my back so their hands could maul my breasts, or pull down my knickers and ram their hard cocks into me without ceremony. To be the focus of so much raw, feral lust frightened me – though I could not deny that a small, deeply hidden part of me found it strangely arousing.

But they did not fall on me as a pack and ravage me. That would have been too quick, too easy. This was no wild, undisciplined orgy; it was a ritual, something which followed a set pattern. Everyone in the room understood it and so, instinctively, did I. Without really being sure of why I was doing it, I went to stand close to the boardroom table, within the ring of seated men. I clasped my hands behind my back, and waited.

'Welcome, Miss Mills,' Mr Barker began, baring his pointed little teeth again. I thought again of small woodland creatures who dispatch their prey with a single bite. 'I must admit, we did think you might not keep this appointment. You would not be the first, after all.'

'I was informed of the usual working conditions when I joined the firm, sir,' I said, trying to sound more self-assured than I felt. 'And I would not wish to be in breach of my contract.'

'Very good, Miss Mills, very good,' Mr Wallace said. 'It's so nice to see you are fully aware of your responsibilities. So, shall we begin?' He paused for a moment, then continued, 'Remove your skirt, please, Miss Mills, and bend over the edge of the table.' His tone made it clear that I was expected to comply without question or hesitation.

A sick, primitive thrill ran through me as I reached for the zip of my neat little grey skirt and pulled it down. I could sense the expectations of the watching men as I stepped out of my skirt. They had seen whatever Suzanne and Chloe had to offer on many previous occasions; this was new flesh, being bared to them for the first time.

As I had been ordered, I bent over the edge of the boardroom table, resting on my folded arms and breathing in the scent of beeswax polish. I heard soft footsteps approaching me, and then I felt a hand resting lightly on my bottom, caressing me gently through my panties.

'Yes, I thought we had chosen well,' Mr Wallace murmured. He gave my bottom a proprietorial pat, as owners often do to the flanks of a prize racehorse. 'This will be a pleasure. Mr Barker, if you would…'

I raised my head as I caught a glimpse of something being passed over the table. It was a ruler, the wood so old that the measurements were faded away almost to nothing.

'This ruler, Miss Mills,' Mr Wallace said, in the tones of one who has delivered this particular lecture many times before, 'belonged to my father and his father before him. It has always been used for one purpose and one purpose only. When my grandfather was finally persuaded that he could no longer turn away prospective female employees from this firm, he did so with the stipulation that any woman who worked for him submitted to be beaten with this ruler, so that she would always know her place. Of course, it was only much later that he realised there were some women who would actively welcome this treatment.'

He rested his hand on my bottom again, and this time his touch moved lower, down between my legs, where he must have registered the heat, the tell-tale dampness.

'Shall we continue, Miss Mills?' When I gave a small nod, not knowing how else to respond, he said, 'Good, now spread your legs wider apart.'

I did as he asked. I was pleased I couldn't see the reactions of the watching men, as they stared at my rear view, the white panties stretched taut across my cheeks.

There was a long moment when nothing happened, and I even thought briefly that Mr Wallace and the others might break out laughing, tell me I had passed the initiation and let me dress and go on my embarrassed way. Then I felt a couple of gentle taps with the ruler, one on each cheek, as though Mr Wallace was finding his range. There was a low, excited rumbling of male voices, and some shifting in chairs. Almost unconsciously, I stiffened up as I waited.

The first blow fell, hard across my bottom. I stifled a yelp. This was no joke; Mr Wallace had said he was going to beat me, and he meant it.

The ruler landed again, and again. Mr Wallace was placing it with care, covering every inch of my cheeks. Occasionally, he would aim lower, catching the tops of my thighs. Those blows were particularly painful, and it was all I could do not to cry out, or reach behind me and rub my burning flesh. Both were powerful temptations and both, I was sure, would merit further punishments.

After perhaps a dozen blows, I felt Mr Wallace gather up the material of my panties and arrange it so that it was pushed firmly into the crack of my arse. Not only did this expose most of my cheeks to the blade of his ruler, it also enabled him to slip a finger into the gusset to check on the wetness there. Almost as if by accident, he brushed that finger along my unfurling lips, chuckling to himself as I stifled a whimper of longing.

He cracked the ruler briskly across my bum a few more times – he had not asked me to keep count, and I doubt I would have been able to, given the overwrought state I was in – then announced, 'The final half-dozen on the bare, I think.'

Even as I was registering the impact of those words, I felt him grab the waistband of my panties and pull them firmly down around my knees. There were grunts of approval from around the room. I wanted to turn my head and see the effect I was having on my audience; I hoped that cocks were being rubbed through suit trousers, or even brought out into the open to be brazenly wanked. I wanted the sight of my wet pussy, seen from behind and framed by suspender straps, to drive them mad with wanting. I wanted them to be aware that I knew my place – at the centre of a crowd of fiercely aroused men who all desired to punish and possess me. No wonder Mr Wallace had tried to keep women out of his firm; he knew the power they owned, even when they were half-stripped and their arses striped with welts.

When Mr Wallace placed the final blows, he made sure a couple landed on the pout of my pussy lips. This time I did let out a moan, but even as the tears filled my eyes I knew it was not only pain which was causing the tender flesh between my legs to throb. My nipples were hard points, aching to be rubbed and twisted by fingers other than my own; indeed, my whole body craved a man's touch – any man's – but although I had somehow known how this dark ritual began, I had no idea if that was how it ended.

And then my unspoken question was answered, as I felt hands gripping my ravaged cheeks, pulling them further apart so that wet lips and a pointed tongue could nuzzle deep into my cleft. I glanced behind me and realised it was Scott from the post room whose face was buried in my cunt. He was too young for me, with a crop of pimples around his mouth and doused in too much aftershave, but as he licked and snuffled at my clit, his clumsy attentions were enough to push me over the edge. I howled as I came, my body shuddering against Scott's tongue and the cheers and crude comments of the other men ringing in my ears.

That was the first time. Since then, I have gone back there on the last working day of every month and submitted to all manner of indignities. I have been stripped naked before my beating takes place, I have lain on the floor while every man in the room has wanked himself over my breasts, belly or face. I have had my hands tied and clamps attached to my aching nipples. And I have been fucked – repeatedly and gloriously. The week after we won the fraud case, Michael and Neil were rewarded for all their hard work by being allowed to have me simultaneously, Michael's cock in my throat and Neil's buried deep in my cunt.

Mr Wallace and Mr Barker called me in for a special meeting yesterday. They told me Catherine is leaving the firm to take up a post in New York and they would like to offer me her position. They made me completely aware that with the higher salary and the extra responsibility comes more severe punishment. I will be required to take cocks in my arse, I may have to be placed in more complicated restraints and every one of the sessions will be filmed so copies can be taken away and watched by my male colleagues at their leisure. They have given me forty-eight hours to make up my mind, but even before I left the boardroom at the end of the meeting, I already knew that my answer will be yes.

More great stories from the Xcite Books range

 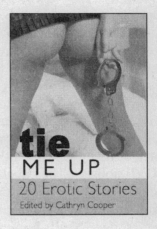

THE FIVE A[ND THE]
STATELY HO[MES GANG]

THE FIVE are Julia[n, Dick,]
George (Georgina by [right), A]nne
and Timmy the dog.

Julian, Dick, George, Anne and
Timmy are all back at Kirren
Cottage for the holidays. There
have been a series of daring
robberies in the area, and
George is certain that they
can solve the case. However,
when the Five get caught in a
storm and have to shelter in
some caves, they become more
involved in the mystery than
any of them expected.

Cover illustration by Peter Mennim

The Five and the Stately Homes Gang

Claude Voilier
translated by Anthea Bell

Hodder
Children's
Books

a division of Hodder Headline plc

A Catalogue record for this book is available from the British
Library

ISBN 0 340 59834 3

Typeset by
Hewer Text Composition Services, Edinburgh

Printed and bound in Great Britain by
Cox & Wyman Ltd, Reading, Berkshire

Hodder Children's Books
A Division of Hodder Headline plc
338 Euston Road
London NW1 3BH

Contents

— 1 —

New bicycles

'Throw the ball over this way, Julian! Oh, Timmy, do stop jumping around like that. Can't you see you're getting in my way and being a nuisance?'

'How dare you speak to Timmy like that?'

And George flung herself at her cousin Dick. She was quite red with anger!

'Oh, please, you two!' cried Anne, Dick and Julian's younger sister, trying to make peace between her brother and her cousin. 'Surely you're not going to start quarrelling at the very beginning of the holidays, are you? We all know you prefer looking like a boy, George – but if you start fighting like one too your father won't be very pleased!'

'Anne's right,' said Julian cheerfully. 'Why don't we just enjoy the fine weather and being on holiday? What luck to be back at Kirrin Cottage for the hols again this year!'

George calmed down at once. She was a quick-tempered girl, but good natured, and she adored her three cousins – who felt just the same about her!

George's parents had invited Julian, Dick and Anne to spend the summer holidays with them, as they often did. Uncle Quentin was a famous scientist. He needed peace and quiet for his work, and he couldn't stand being disturbed by the sound of children playing, so George and her cousins had to make as little noise as possible.

George, whose real name was Georgina, was not afraid of anything. Her boldness was quite proverbial in the family! All the same, she did feel scared of her father when he got angry with her, and she usually kept quiet and was well-behaved at home.

With her dark hair cut very short, George looked exactly like a boy. She was lively and full of energy, and she was generally the ringleader of the Five when they had adventures. Dick was dark-haired too, and the same age as his cousin – eleven. They were very much alike. Julian was thirteen and Anne was ten. They were both fair-haired.

'Let's take the ball somewhere further away from the house,' George suggested. 'You know how Father hates it if we disturb him while he's buried in his work. He wouldn't be a bit pleased if we broke one of his study windows with our ball!'

The children ran off, with Timmy, George's

beloved dog, bounding along in front of them. The pair of them were inseparable companions!

George and her three cousins got on very well indeed together. They all had one thing in common – they loved mysteries and exciting adventures, even if Anne was inclined to feel frightened at times. They had already solved many problems which had baffled the police, and they were so pleased with their success that they had christened themselves the 'Famous Five'. The fifth was Timmy, of course!

Kirrin Cottage stood near the sea, close to Kirrin village. It was the home of George, Uncle Quentin and Aunt Fanny. The cousins were never bored staying at Kirrin. Aunt Fanny was kind, and tended to spoil the children a bit, but she did insist that they must be in punctually for mealtimes. Apart from that, however, she let them do as they wanted.

The Five really enjoyed being so free. They had so much fun in the country near Kirrin Cottage – they could go for outings, and picnics, and all sorts of things.

After they had finished their ball game, the five of them piled into George's rowing boat.

'Let's row over to Kirrin Island and have a game of hide-and-seek,' Dick suggested.

'What, in this heat?' Julian protested. 'No, if you ask me, a bathe in the little cove on the island would be a better idea. We can have a diving competition.'

'Right!' agreed George, seizing the oars.

Kirrin Island belonged to George. She was very proud of it, and wouldn't let anyone land there without her permission.

The Five had a fine time for the rest of the day, though Julian, who was very sensible and grown-up for his age, had to call George to order several times! Her vivid imagination was always suggesting new and daring ideas to her – and it must be admitted that they didn't always work. When that happened, Julian often had to step in to prevent disaster. At other times, however, 'George's brainwaves', as Dick called them, really *were* brilliant, and her cousins admired her for being able to think them up.

'Well,' said George, as they pulled the boat up on the beach near Kirrin Cottage, after they had rowed home, 'we still have a bit of time before supper. Why don't we go for a bike ride?'

Dick made a face. 'I'm sick and tired of my old bike!' he said. 'It's a real boneshaker! Almost falling to bits, and so slow and uncomfortable to ride. You remember how Uncle Quentin promised us all brand new bikes if we did well at school this term? Well, *I* haven't seen any sign of them so far!'

'We did work hard, too, all four of us!' sighed Julian.

'You can trust my father,' said George firmly. 'He

may be terribly absent-minded, but he *never* forgets his promises!'

And George turned out to be right. After breakfast next day, Aunt Fanny told the children, with a smile, 'There's a surprise waiting for you out in the shed. Why don't you go and look?'

The Five ran to the little ivy-covered shed which stood at the end of the garden. George flung open the door, and their faces all lit up at once.

'Hurrah!' cried George. 'Father has kept his promise! Four beautiful, shiny new bikes to replace our old ones! Oh, look, they all have three-speed gears too! We'll be able to cycle along the roads much faster now – and it won't be nearly such hard work going up hills.'

'I think we'd better wait till lunch time to say thank you to Uncle Quentin,' Julian said. 'We don't want to disturb him at work.'

'Look at that!' exclaimed George, jumping for joy. 'There's a special basket fixed to the carrier of my bike, so that Timmy can have a ride too if he wants. Timmy, old fellow, you won't have to wear your paws out running along beside me any more!'

'Woof!' said Timmy. He seemed to understand everything George said.

'Let's try our new bikes at once,' suggested Dick. 'You've ridden a three-speed bike before, Ju – you can tell us when to change gear until we get the hang of it!'

The children spent all morning getting used to their beautiful new bikes. At lunch time they thanked Uncle Quentin for his splendid present, and directly after the meal they set out for a ride.

'Just think how easily we'll be able to whizz around the countryside now!' said George to her cousins. 'Off we go to the wide open spaces!'

— 2 —

Visiting the castle

The children spent most of the next two days riding their new bikes. They had never been able to go so far in a single day on their old ones!

On the morning of the third day, they met in the garden to decide where to go for their next expedition.

'Why don't we ride north for a change?' said Julian. 'There are all sorts of interesting places on that road.'

'There are interesting places on the road south too!' Dick said.

'Well, we can't ride in two directions at once!' George pointed out. 'I vote we go north, myself.'

'I'll go wherever the rest of you decide,' said Anne, who was always perfectly happy to fit in with other people's plans.

Timmy made it quite clear that he would rather

stretch his legs than ride in the basket on George's bike today.

'I can see your point, old fellow!' said Dick. 'Since we've had these fine new bikes, *we've* hardly done any walking or running ourselves!'

'And our brains aren't getting much exercise at the moment, either!' said George, pulling a face. 'Not the tiniest little mystery on the horizon! I shouldn't wonder if our grey matter didn't go rusty like our old bikes – they aren't good for anything but the scrap heap now. I wouldn't like that to happen to *us*!'

'I agree,' said Julian. 'It's ages since we had any problems to solve. It looks as if we shan't have any adventures these hols.'

'Well, let's start off on our bikes, and who knows, we may find one!' said George, mounting her bicycle. 'Come on, Timmy – you can run if you like and then have a ride when you get tired. We're planning to go a really long way today!'

The Five had cycled farther than they could go on an outing with their old bikes when they saw an old castle ahead, with a sign pointing to it telling them it was 'Open to the Public'.

'Shall we go and look over that castle?' suggested Dick.

'Oh yes, let's!' replied the others in chorus.

The children left their bikes in some bicycle stands inside the castle courtyard itself. Then they went in through the big arched doorway of the main entrance. How cool it was inside! Anne strained her eyes in the dim light.

'What is there to see here?' she whispered.

A man selling tickets inside a kind of lodge with perspex walls smiled at her.

'This castle dates from the sixteenth century,' he explained. 'Besides its architecture, and some beautiful old pieces of furniture, you can see items of interest exhibited in glass cases – pretty snuff-boxes, valuable vases, old weapons, brooches and buckles and other pieces of gold and silver jewellery which the ladies of the Castle wore when they went to court, and so on.'

Anne loved jewellery and knick-knacks, and she was delighted at the thought of seeing all these pretty things. Julian bought tickets for them all. However, just as George was about to follow her cousins on into the castle, with Timmy at her heels, the man selling tickets called her back.

'Hi, laddie!' he shouted. Like so many other people, he thought George was a boy! 'Dogs aren't allowed in. Tie him up here – you can collect him on your way out.'

George immediately bristled angrily.

'My dog is *extremely* well behaved!' she said, in a very dignified voice. 'He doesn't bark, and he never does anything naughty – and I'm quite willing to pay for him to go in. There you are!'

And with what she hoped was a lordly gesture, she put a couple of coins down in front of the astonished ticket seller.

'Come on, Tim, what are you waiting for?' she said.

She joined her cousins, who were already gathering round a long, low show-case with a glass top.

Dick was looking disappointed.

'Are these supposed to be the valuable jewels and things?' he asked. 'Well, I must say! They're obviously all fakes – why, they're just like stage jewellery in a play!'

Julian frowned. As usual, he felt responsible for the younger children's behaviour. 'Dick, it isn't very polite to say so inside the castle,' he told his brother. 'Though I must admit you're right! None of these things can be worth any money to speak of – that man selling tickets wasn't telling us the truth. *I* can't see any precious jewellery at all.'

'Let's go a bit further,' suggested Anne.

But the other glass cases held things which were just as obviously imitations as the jewellery in the first case.

'How odd,' said George, under her breath. 'And there's something rather strange about the empty cases under the window over there, too. Hullo,' she added, going over to them, 'just look! The locks have been forced – and the top of this one's broken.'

At the same moment another visitor looking over the castle, like the children, turned round.

'It's hardly surprising those cases are empty,' he told George. 'This castle was burgled only last week. The story was in all the newspapers. I was wondering just what the burglars had left here in the castle museum. Well, now I know – practically nothing! They ought to warn people on their way in. I call it disgraceful making us pay the full price just to look at bare walls and empty cases. That's theft too, only in a different way!'

The man went off, muttering crossly to himself.

'Did you hear that?' George asked her cousins. 'There was a burglary here at the castle only a few days ago.'

'I hope they caught the thieves!' said Dick. 'Let's go and ask the man who sells the tickets.'

The Five went back to the ticket seller, who glared sternly at Timmy, but when the children asked him if there had really been a burglary he was quite ready to tell them all about it.

'Oh, yes, it's true enough,' he said. 'We had a visit from some thieves who must have been very well informed. They broke open the cases containing the most precious jewellery and other objects in our museum. All they left were a few things which either aren't worth anything much, or would be difficult for them to sell. I have to admit they were clever.

They worked fast, and they knew just what they were doing!'

'I suppose the police have caught them by now?' asked Dick, hoping that justice had been done.

'No such luck,' said the man, shaking his head. 'The thieves are still at large. And they've made the headlines again this week – I suppose you're too young to read the papers, or you'd know that two other big houses and a private museum in this part of the country have been raided too, and the police are sure it was the same gang. They certainly are cool customers!'

Julian looked rather annoyed. 'We're certainly not too young to read the papers!' he said. 'It just so happens we're on holiday, so we haven't been taking much notice of the news. But I *do* seem to remember hearing something about those burglars on the radio yesterday evening – yes, it's coming back to me now!'

'The police are hard at work at the moment, trying to track the thieves down,' said the man. 'They really had a nerve, coming here! I wonder where they'll be heard of next!'

The Five set off back to Kirrin Cottage, leaning forward into the wind as they rode along. On the way home they discussed the burglary. It had interested the children at once. When they were back at Kirrin Cottage George went to find all that week's old newspapers. Then the four children read through the papers to pick out the news reports about the burgled houses. The series of thefts seemed to be the work of an organised gang with inside knowledge of the stately homes in that area, and it looked as if they intended to make a clean sweep of the countryside. Yes, thought the children, these burglars were certainly a daring gang!

A mysterious gorse bush

Next day the weather was really lovely; so warm and sunny that Aunt Fanny asked the children, 'How about taking a nice picnic out on a fine day like this? You could have lunch out of doors somewhere, and bathe in Kirrin Bay on the way back. It's well sheltered from the wind and strong currents.'

George and her cousins thought that was a grand idea. They loved eating out of doors, without any grown-ups to tell them about table manners!

They went off to the kitchen to help Aunt Fanny make sardine and cheese and tomato sandwiches, and fill thermos flasks with cool drinks of orange and lemon squash. Dick had put his little radio down on the kitchen table beside him. He had it tuned to the local radio station. Suddenly the music was interrupted.

'This is a news flash,' said an announcer's voice on the radio. 'We have just heard that Pendleton

Place, six miles from Kirrin village, was raided last night by the daring gang of thieves who have been systematically burgling the stately homes in this area over the last three weeks. Paintings by old masters hanging in the picture gallery of Pendleton Place, showing local landscapes and sea scenes, were stolen. The police say that the thieves worked as if they were very confident, taking no precautions against being disturbed or caught in the act. They left no clues behind. The police are continuing their inquiries, and say they hope that they will soon be on the track of the thieves.'

'Did you hear that?' cried George. 'The gang raiding the stately homes has struck again! At this rate, they'll soon have stolen all the treasures to be found in these parts. If *I* were in the police force I'd – I'd *do* something!'

'You might not find that so easy!' Aunt Fanny told her daughter, smiling.

George shrugged her shoulders. 'Well, you must admit that the police aren't getting anywhere, Mother! How the thieves must be laughing at them! If you ask me – '

'I'm quite sure the police know what they're doing,' Aunt Fanny interrupted. 'And I'm sure you wouldn't do any better, either! These burglars must be very clever people. The police have been keeping a watch on all the roads and ports and airfields ever since the first theft, but they haven't found a trace of the thieves – or their haul. The valuables must be well hidden, and I expect they'll stay hidden until the hue and cry over the burglaries has died down.'

Soon afterwards, the children and Timmy were starting off down the road on their bicycles. They rode past Kirrin Bay, and after a while they came within sight of a small hill covered with green grass. Some trees and gorse bushes grew on it here and there. Dick suggested climbing part of the way up the hill to have their picnic. Once they had found a good picnic place half-way up, they happily unwrapped their sandwiches, while Timmy chased about barking wildly at butterflies and dragonflies.

'Help me to spread the cloth out, Anne!' said George. 'Julian, will you open this packet of chocolate biscuits? Oh, do watch out, Dick, you'll knock those bottles of squash over! Timmy – stop fooling about like that!'

'Yes, your Royal Highness!'

'Just as you say, ma'am!'

'At your service, my lady!'

'Woof! Woof!'

George flicked a teacloth at Dick, and aimed a mock blow at Anne. Julian pretended to be squaring up to her for a fight, and Timmy, entering into the spirit of the game, made out that he was going to leap to his young mistress's aid. The mock quarrel turned into a friendly scuffle on the grass, with everyone shouting and laughing.

What fun they were having!

When the Five had eaten their picnic, they looked at the delicious remains and sighed – what a shame they couldn't finish them all! After eating so hungrily, the children felt a little sleepy, and they lay down in the shade of the trees for a rest.

At their feet, below the slope of the grassy hill, the road they had come along was like a curving ribbon running parallel to the cliff top. They could see the sea shining in the sun beyond the cliffs. The water was almost completely flat and calm, and there wasn't a cloud in the blue sky. It was wonderfully fine weather.

Anne had eaten several of the little strawberry tarts Aunt Fanny had packed, and she was beginning to wish she hadn't had quite so many! She did feel terribly drowsy. She had to make a real effort to keep her eyes open – and in spite of her efforts, they closed for several seconds.

Suddenly she woke up, rather ashamed of herself for giving in to her drowsy feeling – though she was sure she could not have been asleep for long. Had the others noticed? They were sitting there beside her, laughing and talking. Anne sat up too. Then she let out a cry.

Julian jumped. 'What's the matter?' he asked.

'That bush over there! I've just seen it move!'

Dick roared with laughter.

'Well, fancy! *What* a surprise!' he said. 'Hear that, everyone? Isn't it amazing – the wind actually made that gorse bush move when it blew!'

'But that's just the point – there isn't a breath of wind!' said Anne. 'That's what surprised me. Anyway, the bush didn't move at all as if the wind was shaking its branches. It was – as if an invisible hand was shaking it!'

George burst out laughing too. 'Well, people say *I've* got a vivid imagination, but yours runs it pretty close!' she told her cousin, patting Timmy, who was stretched out beside her. 'Did you hear her, Timmy? She was fast asleep, dreaming she was in some mysterious place where an invisible man walks about among the heather and gorse bushes – and then she gives us all a fright by shouting out like that!'

Anne protested indignantly.

'I wasn't dreaming! I *did* see the bush move – it's one of that big clump of gorse bushes over there. Oh, look! It's moving again, though not so much this time. All the same, I *wasn't* seeing things – '

Timmy's loud barking interrupted her. He had dashed over to the bushes Anne was talking about, and was racing round and round them, barking frantically. George called him to heel.

'Tim! Heel, Timmy – heel! Come here, you bad dog! What on earth is the matter with you?'

'That dog's gone completely potty!' said Dick.

'Just trying to get a bit of attention, that's all,' said Julian.

'No, I think he's picked up the scent of a wild rabbit,' George told them. 'If I felt energetic enough to move,' she added, yawning, 'I'd go and explore your clump of bushes, Anne, and I dare say I'd find a rabbit hole there!'

Anne was not convinced.

'A rabbit couldn't have shaken a big bush like that so much,' she insisted. 'It was almost as if – '

'Yes, we know, you've already told us!' Dick interrupted. 'You saw someone – only it was an invisible someone, of course! – going down the rabbit hole on his tummy. What fun it must be seeing invisible things, Anne! Have you developed second sight or something? We'd know about it if you were the seventh child of a seventh child, so *that* can't be it!'

— 4 —

Riddington Hall

Julian got to his feet. 'That's enough of sitting about talking!' he said. 'We don't want to stay here for ever if we're going to see over Riddington Hall.'

George, Dick and Anne looked at him in surprise.

'See over where?'

'Riddington Hall! I was keeping my plan a surprise for you. I read a tourist leaflet before we started out today – and someone in the village told me the Hall is one of the few big houses in these parts which *hasn't* had a visit from that gang of burglars yet. I thought we might take a look at it before they go off with all the stuff from there too!'

'Do you really think they'll be planning to burgle it?' said Dick, his eyes bright with interest.

'What does it have that's so valuable?' asked George.

'Watches, that's what!' Looking at the bewildered

expressions on the others' faces, Julian burst out laughing. 'I ought to mention that they're gold watches,' he added. 'Sir Donald Riddington, the owner of the Hall, has made this wonderful collection of priceless watches. Some of them are of great historical interest. He's very proud of his collection, and quite rightly.'

'Yes, I remember hearing about Sir Donald's watches,' said George, getting on her bicycle. 'But I don't think Riddington Hall is open to the public – and I live in these parts, so I ought to know!'

'It's only been opened quite recently,' Julian told her. 'Apparently Sir Donald lost all his money, and though he hated the thought of having his house open for people to look round, he made up his mind to do it, because he knew so many people interested in his collection would want to come and see it.'

'But if he's short of money, why doesn't he sell the gold watches?' asked Dick, puzzled. 'That would get him out of his financial difficulties!'

Julian shook his head.

'The watches are all that's left of the Riddington family fortune. I was told that the mere idea of parting with them horrified Sir Donald – he'd rather starve to death than get rid of them! Each of the watches has its own history. One of them was given to an ancestor of Sir Donald's by King James II, and – '

'You seem to know an awful lot about it, old

fellow! said Dick, laughing. 'Where on earth did you pick all that up?'

'From my leaflet and the man I met in the village, of course! Ah, here we are!'

Coming round a bend in the road, the children saw a big old stone house, with very thick walls. It had a real moat all round it, too.

'Why, it's quite a fortress!' cried George. 'You could sit out a siege in there!'

The Five cycled on, and got off their new bikes when they reached the Hall. Pushing the bikes, they crossed the bridge over the moat. There was a notice on one of the big iron gates at the end of the bridge, saying what times Riddington Hall was open.

Dick read the notice. 'Good,' he said. 'It looks as if we've come at the very best time of day. It's too early for any big crowds yet – so we'll be able to take our time seeing over the place. Come on, let's go in!'

The other children followed him. There was a gravel drive up to the Hall, ending in a paved forecourt, which looked rather neglected. Grass grew up between the broken flagstones, and the house itself seemed to be in need of repair.

'Brr!' said Anne, shivering. 'This is a sinister sort of place. I can *quite* see why the thieves decided not to come here! *I* wouldn't like to visit this house at night, either – I should think it must be chock-full of ghosts!'

Riddington Hall, which really was rather dilapidated, didn't look as if it would be a very grand place to visit, from the outside. But once indoors, the children saw a wonderful collection of engraved gold watches shining behind the glass doors of show-cases with carved wooden frames.

'Goodness, those watches must be worth a fortune!' George exclaimed. 'And they aren't even guarded!'

'You're wrong there, young man,' said a voice behind them. 'They're very well guarded indeed – I guard them myself! I am Sir Donald Riddington.'

Julian shook hands with the owner of the Hall, and introduced himself and the others. Sir Donald, smiling, said he was sorry he had mistaken George for a boy. But George didn't mind that a bit – she smiled back at him.

'I do hope your beautiful collection is insured,' she said.

'I'm afraid not! Unfortunately I simply can't afford to insure a collection which is worth as much as this. That's why I guard the watches myself, with the help of my faithful old servant Andrews.'

Dick couldn't help saying, 'But isn't it awfully unwise to – ' Then he stopped, biting the words back. He didn't want to seem impertinent.

'Awfully unwise to do what?' asked Sir Donald.

'Well, to leave this wonderful collection of watches out on show, with only the two of you to guard

them? Of course, I know you're keeping your eyes
open for thieves, sir, but you and your servant can't
be on guard here day and night! There must be times
when you're having a meal or going for a walk or
something!'

Sir Donald laughed. 'You're quite right, of course
there are! No, we stay on guard during visiting
hours, but the rest of the time we have nothing to
worry about. My collection can look after itself!'

Sir Donald pointed to the thick walls of the house,
and the moat outside the window. 'This building is
a huge safe in itself,' he explained. 'It was built in
the days when they made walls immensely thick and
solid – it would take dynamite to blow up the walls
or force the locks of the doors. And the only way
out is over the moat. No, once all the doors are
locked, I can sleep soundly, with nothing to fear
from thieves!'

'All the same,' said Anne timidly, 'they do say
that the gang of thieves going about at the moment,
burgling all the stately homes, is a very clever one.
I expect you've heard about it, Sir Donald?'

Sir Donald nodded.

'Yes, of course,' he said. 'But I don't think there's
any danger that the burglars will raid the Hall. As
I was saying, it's too difficult to get in or out of
the place – our friends would really be in trouble if
they tried breaking in, let alone making a getaway
afterwards.'

George was not convinced. 'I wouldn't be so sure if I were you,' she said.

Sir Donald started to laugh.

'Don't worry about me, my dear young lady,' he said. George made a face – she didn't like being called anyone's dear young lady! 'As it happens, I'm not just trusting to my thick walls and good strong doors. The fact is, there are burglar alarms fitted to all the doors and windows of the Hall, *and* to all the show-cases for the exhibits too. The alarms would go off the moment anyone tried interfering with them. So you need have no fear for my watches, children! Now, do let me show you round the place.'

The four cousins decided that they liked Sir Donald, and they really enjoyed looking at the watches, which were very rare and valuable. They had plenty of time to admire them. Sir Donald was very interesting and amusing when he talked about his collection, telling them exciting stories about the watches, and when the Five at last said goodbye to him, they agreed that they had really enjoyed their visit to Riddington Hall.

On the way home, the children bathed in Kirrin Bay. The water was nice and cool, and George did some daring dives from the top of a big rock.

Julian seemed rather thoughtful.

'I can't help it,' he told the others, 'but I just can't stop thinking about those watches. I'm afraid of some harm coming to them.'

'Do you think the gang of burglars might really try to steal them?' asked Dick, splashing about in the water.

'They're quite capable of it,' said Anne. 'I know I'd be worried, if I were Sir Donald.'

'Well, *he* seems very sure of himself,' said George.

— 5 —

Another burglary!

The Five slept very soundly that night, tired out after their long and interesting day. Bright sunlight woke them up in the morning. George jumped briskly out of bed and shook Anne – her cousin was very sleepy, and didn't seem to want to open her eyes.

'Come on, lazybones, get up!' said George. 'And hurry up about it – it's quite late already.'

The girls heard Dick and Julian's voices out in the garden, calling to them.

'Time to get out of bed, you two!'

'We've got some news!'

George ran to the window. 'News?' she repeated. 'What is it?'

'Come downstairs and you'll find out!'

George and Anne were soon dressed, and they hurried downstairs. Dick came to meet them, obviously very excited.

'We've just been listening to the regional news on the radio,' he told the girls, 'and what do you think the main news item of the day was?'

'The main news item of the night, you mean,' Julian corrected him.

'I can guess!' cried George excitedly. 'Riddington Hall has been burgled, and Sir Donald's gold watches have disappeared! Well, am I right?'

'Perfectly right!' said Julian, laughing at the disappointed look on Dick's face. 'However did you know? You must be telepathic or something!'

'But how did it happen?' asked Anne, sitting down to breakfast with the others.

'That's just what the police would like to know,' said Dick, helping himself to a big slice of toast and spreading plenty of home-made marmalade on it. 'The thieves were even cleverer than before! This time, no one has any idea how they managed it. It's a real mystery!'

'What do you mean?' George looked very surprised. 'They must have had to force the locks of the show-cases, or else break the glass to get at the watches.'

'Oh yes, they did that all right,' replied Dick. 'And the gold watches have certainly disappeared. But what no one can make out is how the gang got inside the Hall in the first place. It's a mystery, because the place does seem to have been quite burglar-proof.'

'How do you mean?' asked Anne, interested.

'Well – imagine the room with Sir Donald's collection in it, the way you saw it yesterday,' said Julian. 'All the windows had steel shutters over them, remember – and none of those shutters had been forced open. Besides which, the room has only two doors, and the locks of those doors hadn't been picked, *or* the doors forced open either!'

'What about the chimney?' asked George.

'Sir Donald had it blocked up twenty years ago! There hasn't been a fire in the hearth of that room for ages, and Sir Donald thought he'd block the chimney up to avoid draughts – you easily get draughts in an old house like that.'

'How queer!' said George. 'I suppose the burglar alarms on the show-cases didn't work?'

'You've guessed right yet again! No, it looks as though the gang cut the electric cables of the alarm bells.'

'So no one went into the exhibition room at all – or it *looks* as if no one went in! And the thieves didn't leave anything behind to show they'd ever been there at all – but we know they were, because the watches weren't left behind either!'

'That's right! And if you can make head or tail of it, well, good for you, George!'

The children spent the rest of that morning discussing the mystery of Riddington Hall. How on earth had the thieves managed to ransack the glass show-cases without leaving any other clue to show that they had been there? The puzzle of their latest robbery really did show how audacious this gang was!

George and her cousins felt so intrigued by the mystery that they went back to Riddington Hall that very afternoon. They didn't see Sir Donald, but Julian asked one of the plain-clothes policemen carrying out inquiries some polite questions, and the policeman confirmed what the boys had heard on the radio news. The gang of thieves which was raiding all the stately homes in that part of the country had brought off yet another amazingly successful burglary.

'What's more,' the policeman told the children, 'we've been keeping a discreet watch on this place for several days. We were on the alert all right. But as you can see, it didn't do anyone much good!'

The Five set off for home again feeling that they had got nowhere.

— 6 —

The shipwreck

Three days later the police inquiries were still making no headway. Dick was getting sick and tired of hearing the newsreader on the radio announce that there were 'no new developments in the search for the daring gang of thieves at large in this area'.

It was all very well for George to suggest that the Five could start making inquiries of their own – the weather was so hot that the others did not welcome her idea with any enthusiasm.

'What d'you expect *we'd* find, when even the police aren't getting anywhere?' Julian had said, yawning.

The heat was certainly oppressive, so the children decided to go out in the boat that day.

'We'll row over to Kirrin Island,' said George, 'and then we'll decide what to do next.'

The children and Timmy got into George's boat and rowed away from the shore. There was a

pleasant little breeze. The sky was cloudless –
except for two very black little clouds just coming
up on the horizon.

Generally speaking, George knew a lot about the
sea and everything to do with it. If she had taken the
trouble to stop and think what the sky and the wind
meant – or even to look at the barometer before they
left, which would have been easier still! – she would
have known they should be on their guard. But she
didn't stop to think. She was just enjoying being out
on the sea, where the air was a little bit cooler.

Anne was the first to realise that the sea had
suddenly changed.

'Look!' she cried, pointing at the waves with
their crests of foam lapping round the boat. White
horses! The whole sea was the colour of ink. The
wind had risen, too, and was suddenly blowing
quite hard.

'My goodness, Anne's right!' Julian realised.
'Looks as if there's a storm brewing up.'

The sky was quickly covering over with clouds
now.

A moment later, a strong squall of wind hit the
boat. It scared even George.

'We'd better turn back,' she said. 'It's dangerous
to go on in this sort of weather. There's no point in
running unnecessary risky when – '

She broke off as the boat lurched again. Keeping her head, George immediately shouted, 'Dick!

Anne! Lean over the other way to balance the boat! Julian, help me to row.'

George's cousins always did just as she said when they were out in the boat. They trusted her to know what to do. So there was no argument. Dick and Anne tried to balance the boat. Anne was terribly frightened, but she was a brave girl at heart and tried her best not to show it. She sat as near as she dared to the edge of the boat which was rising out of the water. With some difficulty, Julian and George managed to get the boat under control and pointing towards the shore.

Just then Dick let out a cry.

'Anne! Anne! Oh, quickly, she's fallen in!'

George rushed to help. Tossed about by the waves, the boat was swaying up and down and turning round and round – and all the time it was getting farther from Anne, who had taken an unintentional header into the waves and was now struggling frantically among the white horses. They were very wild white horses too. George cupped her hands round her mouth.

'Anne! Swim over this way and we'll come to meet you!' she shouted.

The boys had already seized the oars and were pulling away at them, trying to row in Anne's direction – but in vain. In spite of their efforts and her own, the girl was getting farther and farther away from the boat every minute. George did not hesitate. She dived into the sea herself, followed by Timmy! It was a crazy thing to do, but George was ready to take any risk, however great. At all costs she must try to save her cousin!

Dick let go of the oars and jumped to his feet.

'George, no! Wait! Come back!'

He was so worked up that he had begun waving his arms about. The boat was already unbalanced, and a particularly strong wave caught it sideways on and capsized it. Before they even realised what had happened, Julian and Dick found themselves in the water too.

Now the Five were struggling against the rough sea. It was difficult to stay afloat without getting a mouthful of water. Anne, who was not such a strong swimmer as the others, swallowed enormous gulps of salt water in spite of all her attempts to keep her mouth closed. She was getting weaker all the time.

Suddenly she saw Timmy not far away from her, and she heard her cousin's voice.

'Keep going, Anne!' George shouted.

Then Anne fainted – but good old Timmy, faithful as ever, was there! At the very moment when Anne lost consciousness, he seized her fair hair in his mouth, preventing her from sinking to the bottom. Unfortunately his hold on her wasn't a very strong one. A dog's jaws could not keep a good grip on Anne's smooth, fine hair for long, and it kept slipping out. But Timmy was a very intelligent animal, and he thought of a better idea. Letting go of the little girl's hair, he tried to grip her clothes in his mouth instead. However, Anne was only wearing a thin cardigan over her bathing suit. The material ripped, and it was in danger of tearing away from her completely. Tim was very careful not to tug at it too hard, and in that way he managed to keep the unconscious girl afloat in the water for several moments longer.

George swam up, panting for breath.

'Well done, Timmy!' she gasped. 'Just keep holding on!'

She got hold of the unconscious Anne, and started swimming towards the shore – with difficulty, because she was tired herself by now. How far away the land looked!

The two girls, one supporting the other, were soon joined by Julian. Anne came round from her faint.

'Here!' her brother told her. 'Hang on to my shoulder!'

She did as she was told. Clinging to Julian and George, she made herself as light as possible, and with so much of Anne's weight taken off her, George found she could swim faster. Timmy followed them, and Dick joined the others.

'Make straight for the shore!' he shouted into the wind. 'We must swim that way as hard as we can!'

But George did not agree.

'No!' she yelled back. 'The current's too strong – we shouldn't be able to swim against it! We must go *with* the current and approach the shore sideways on!' She added silently to herself, 'And let's just hope we make it that far! Oh, bother! The storm's really breaking now.'

Sure enough, the sea was getting very rough indeed. Lightning flashed through the sky, and there were deafening crashes of thunder. The rain had been falling for several minutes, and was simply pelting down. It was dense, warm rain, and it made a sound like hailstones falling on the water.

Though they were fit and athletic, Julian and George had to summon up all their strength to get Anne safely ashore. Dick took over from George for a while so that she could have a short rest.

Anne's teeth were chattering. She was terrified. At last the shore looked as if it were gradually coming closer.

'Well done, everyone! We're nearly there,' cried Dick.

And then, at last, they reached land.

— 7 —

The cave

Timmy was the first to set foot – or rather paw! – on solid land again. At least, if it wasn't exactly land, he was the first to clamber up on one of the big rocks scattered at the foot of a sheer cliff. This would be a pebbly beach at low tide, but just now the beach itself was covered by the waves. So was the footpath climbing up the cliffside. The children would not be able to reach that path for at least another hour, as they soon realised when they had joined Timmy, feeling quite worn out.

'Well, we can't just stay sitting here in this wind, wet through,' said Dick, once he had got his breath back. 'We'll catch our deaths of cold!'

'But what else can we do?' asked Julian, looking glum. 'It's no good trying to get to that cliff path – the water's too deep at the foot of it.'

'Don't let's sit here freezing, anyway!' said George.

'We'd better move around a bit. Splashing about in the breakers may warm us up!'

Anne was too tired to move yet, so she stayed on her rock to rest for a little longer, while the others made for the cliff where the water was not so deep. They spotted a cave which they could reach. And soon George, Dick and Julian found themselves at the entrance to the cave.

From a distance they had thought it was not a very large one and did not go far back into the rock. Seen close to, the cave looked very different. There was a strange green light coming from it, possibly produced by phosphorescent seaweed or lichens. The light showed up the inside of the cave and made it look rather mysterious. The children could see rock pools on the cave floor – altogether it seemed like a magical kind of place.

'Let's explore this cave!' George suggested straight away. 'It will give us something to do while we wait for low tide.'

Julian nodded. 'At least we'll have shelter from the wind and the rain in there,' he said.

Dick called his sister. 'Come on, Anne! Quick! We're going to explore the cave here!'

Anne rejoined the others, and the Five went into the cave, taking care not to slip on the wet rocks. It was still raining outside, but oddly enough it was quite warm inside the cave, and the children were glad they had ventured in.

Julian, who was always very sensible and practical, organised the expedition and set the others a good example. 'We'd better hurry up and take our wet things off,' he told them. 'We don't need to keep anything on but our bathing suits, and it may help us to avoid catching cold.'

George, Dick and Anne did as he said.

'Right!' Dick began. 'Now let's – '

But Timmy interrupted him. 'Woof! Woof!'

'Why, anyone would think Timmy had discovered something!' said George. 'Let's have a look.'

They were to the far end of the cave.

Timmy was still barking, and when George came up to him he bounded towards her, and then seemed to be showing her something just in front of her.

The other children all joined George, and they saw an opening going right on into the cliff, half hidden behind an upright spur of rock. The opening was a tall and narrow one.

'An underground passage!' said Dick, excited. 'Let's go along it! It may even bring us out into the open at the top of the cliff, and that would save us having to wait for low tide!'

'Hm,' said Julian, peering cautiously into the opening. 'We haven't got any torches to give us light.'

'That doesn't matter. There's just enough light for us to see our way,' said George. 'Come on, do let's explore this passage!'

'I don't think I want to very much,' said Anne,
shivering. 'Goodness knows what we might meet in
there! The roof of the passage may cave in on top of
us, we might run into – '

'Spiders and rats and robbers and ghosts and mur-
derers and werewolves and witches!' Dick finished
the sentence, imitating his sister's scared little voice.
'Honestly, Anne, how soppy can you be!'

'Dick, don't be unkind to Anne!' Julian snapped
at his brother.

'Well, are you coming or aren't you?' George said
impatiently.

Dick followed his cousin into the passage. Julian
and Anne came after them, more slowly. The
passage was wide and there was plenty of air, so
it was quite easy to walk along it. But it forked after
only a few yards. Then the children had to choose
which way to go. On their right, one branch of the
passage went farther down into the ground, and on
their left the other one sloped gently uphill.

The four cousins stopped to discuss the best
way to go.

'It's perfectly obvious, if you ask me,' said George.
'I mean, we want to come out at the top of the cliff,
don't we? So let's take the left-hand passage, and
we'll be climbing up!'

'It looks quite a bit narrower than the passage on
the right,' Julian pointed out. 'It'll be more difficult
to get along it.'

'But if the other one takes us right down to the earth's core, a fat lot of good that's going to do us!' said Dick sarcastically.

'Oh, why don't we just wait for low tide?' suggested Anne.

'No fear!' said George. 'I'm beginning to get the shivers – it's high time I went home for a change of clothes. What's more, I must tell the coastguards about our shipwreck, so that they can rescue my poor little boat. Oh, look! You see? Timmy feels just the same as me! He's starting along the left-hand passage. Hi, Tim, wait for us!'

Sure enough, Timmy was off along the passage which sloped uphill. Julian decided that it would be sensible to trust the dog's instincts after all.

'All right,' he said. 'Let's follow Timmy!'

The Five started to go along the narrow passage in single file. It was not such easy going as the first part of the passage, leading from the cave. Loose stones rolled around under their feet. Several times, Anne let out a squeak of alarm. It was difficult to see anything much, and the dim, greenish light coming from the walls was not nearly bright enough to get rid of the shadows.

George, leading the way, suddenly stopped because Timmy, who was just in front of her, had stopped too. She was rather worried.

'Hello, Tim – what's the matter, old boy?'

Timmy replied with a 'Woof!' in a special tone – one which George understood straight away.

'Watch out!' she told her cousins, who were just catching up with them. 'Timmy says there's danger ahead.'

Dick craned his neck. 'Well, *I* don't see anything,' he said, staring hard into the darkness.

George leaned forward. Putting out a cautious foot, she felt the ground ahead with the toe of her sandal. Then she said, 'Timmy was quite right! He stopped us just in time. There's a hole in the ground here, right in front of us. If we'd gone on walking straight along the passage we'd have fallen down it!'

'Oh, do let's go back!' begged Anne.

'Not likely! There must be some way of getting round this wretched hole – wait a minute!'

And keeping close to one of the rocky walls of the passage, George started inching her way forward, standing sideways with her back to the rock and testing the ground with her foot. She soon discovered that though the hole was in the very middle of the passage, there was plenty of room to get round the edge – and the Five did so at once, without any accidents!

After that the passage went on climbing upwards. The slope became steeper and steeper, and now the roof of the passage was so low that the Five had to bend right over and sometimes went on all fours. Timmy was the only one who felt comfortable in *that* position!

Suddenly George called out, 'Hurrah! We're coming to the end of the passage!'

Julian, Dick and Anne, too, were all exclaiming at once.

'Good! I can see daylight ahead!'

'We'll be coming out any moment now!'

'If the opening's big enough to let us out!'

Suddenly the passage grew wider. The Five found themselves emerging into a little round room hewn out of the rock. Daylight came in through a hole just above their heads! Julian only had to raise his arms and pull himself up to the hole to get out into the open air.

'Go carefully!' he warned the others. 'I've landed in the middle of a gorse bush! Ow – it hurts!'

George, Dick and Anne, in their turn, hauled themselves up out of the hole.

'Phew!' said Dick. 'It's much nicer out in the open.'

'And it's stopped raining too,' said Anne, pleased.

George didn't say anything. Frowning, she looked round her. Suddenly she asked, 'Doesn't this place remind you of anything?'

The cousins looked round in surprise. Julian was the first to realise what she meant.

'Yes, it does! We're a little way from the clifftop

– we're on that hillside where we had our picnic the other day. I remember it very well!'

'So do I,' said Anne. 'I even recognise the gorse bush – the one I saw moving. It's part of this clump of bushes hiding the hole we've just come out of!'

'That's right!' said George. All of a sudden she was quite pink with excitement. 'So you weren't seeing things after all, Anne! Or rather, you *were* – and when you saw the bush moving, it must have been because there was someone hiding in this clump. Someone who wanted to get out of the underground passage. But when he saw us so close, he had to stay hidden in his hole.'

Anne looked very surprised.

'You mean other people have used this passage before?' she asked.

Dick roared with laughter. 'What a question! You really are silly sometimes, Anne! Did you honestly think we were the first who ever went along it and came here?'

Anne shook her head. 'No, of course not,' she said. 'But there *is* one funny thing, isn't there? Why did whoever it was here the other day stay in hiding, when I called out to you and said I'd seen the bush moving?'

'Oh, Anne, do we have to explain every single thing to you?' sighed George. 'If the person in the bushes stayed hidden, it was because he didn't want to be seen!'

'And when people hide because they don't want to be seen,' Dick added gravely, 'it's usually because they have something on their consciences. *Now* are you starting to get the idea?'

Anne shuddered.

'You mean that – that this person might have been planning something bad? He might have been a thief, or – '

'Or a murderer, or a spook, or a werewolf!' Dick went on. 'Oh, for goodness' sake, Anne, *don't* start on again about all those scary things you're so afraid of! Put another record on, for a change! I've never known anyone who was such a coward, I really haven't!'

Julian interrupted to make peace between them.

'*I* think it was probably just a poacher who didn't want anyone to spot him,' he said, putting his shorts on over his bathing trunks, though they were still rather wet. 'Well, now let's get home as fast as we can. I'm not too keen on risking pneumonia any longer – so hurry up and get dressed, everyone!'

The Five all realised it was only sensible to go home to Kirrin Cottage as quickly as they could. However, that didn't stop them planning to come back and explore the mysterious underground passage again another day. They were full of curiosity about it.

— 8 —

Down the other passage

The next day started with a stroke of luck. The coastguard vessel had salvaged George's boat. The coastguards brought it back to Kirrin Cottage and returned it to its owner. George was delighted.

'Oh, I'm so glad! My poor boat! I thought it might be gone for good. Thank goodness I've got it back again. And what luck – it's hardly suffered any damage in the storm at all!'

'You'd better let it dry out,' Julian advised her. 'And then we'll repaint it if you like, since it'll be out of the water anyway.'

George happily accepted his offer. The sun had come out again, now that the fierce storm was over, so the children decided to go back to the cave that very morning – going down the underground passage the other way this time, starting from the top of the cliff. They mounted their new bikes and set off.

They rode along as fast as they could. On the way, George said, 'I really do want to find out what it's all about. If someone's been using that underground passage for something shady – well, we must try and discover just what!'

'The passage links the beach to the top of the cliff,' Dick said, 'so perhaps smugglers use it.'

'That's rather a melodramatic idea, Dick!' said Julian. 'Your imagination's running away with you!'

'Couldn't the passage just be a short cut used by the local people?' asked Anne.

'But in that case, why would whoever was in there the other day want to hide?' George pointed out. 'And don't forget there's another passage too – one going *down* instead of up! I'd love to find out where that one leads.'

The Five soon arrived at the foot of the grassy hill, wheeled their bikes part of the way up the slope and left them in a little spinney. Then they made for the big clump of prickly gorse bushes which concealed the mouth of the mysterious underground passage.

There was nothing moving. The children had all brought torches with them, because they wanted to explore the place properly. George was the first to start towards the way into the passage. She was putting out her hand to push the branches of the gorse bushes aside when she suddenly stopped dead.

Timmy stopped too and began to growl.

'Ssh!' George hissed to her cousins. 'Don't come

any closer! I can hear a noise. There's someone coming!'

Julian, Dick and Anne stood perfectly still too. Their hearts were thumping hard.

What would happen now?

Who was going to come out of the underground passage?

Suddenly Timmy leaped forward! At the same moment, a large ball of fur shot out of the bushes and hared off – which wasn't surprising, because it really *was* a hare! A great big one, too! George called Timmy off at once.

'Timmy!' she shouted. 'Heel! Come back this minute! You should be ashamed of yourself, frightening that poor animal!'

Pleased to have had a little run, Timmy obediently came back, wagging his tail, while the hare disappeared into the distance.

A false alarm! Anne started to laugh rather nervously. 'I was really frightened!' she admitted.

'Well, never mind,' said George, feeling cross with herself for making such a silly mistake. 'We've wasted enough time. Got the torches, Dick? Come on, then – follow me!'

The four children and Timmy made their way into the underground passage. Julian switched his torch on, and the other three kept theirs in reserve. They started off in single file again. This time, the light of the torch showed up the hole George would have fallen down the day before, if Timmy hadn't warned her. The ground had caved in at that spot, and as far as they could see the hole was a deep one. Dick picked up a stone and dropped it in. He counted seven quite slowly before he heard it hit the bottom.

'Gosh!' he said, whistling through his teeth. 'It must go a really long way down. This cliff seems to be simply riddled with holes!'

The children went round the edge of the hole, and quite soon they reached the place where the other underground passage branched off.

'We've come to the fork in the path!' said George triumphantly. 'There's the other passage! It looks as if it goes right down into the ground, doesn't it?'

Julian took over command of the expedition. 'Let me go first,' he said. 'I'm the eldest, so it's up to me to take the risks – if there are any!'

'*I* think this passage will come to a dead end,' muttered Anne, 'and I don't mind if it does either! I don't like this sort of exploration much.'

'Cowardly custard!' Dick told her. 'Go on, then, Julian – shine your torch along the passage ahead of you. We'll follow.'

Julian started along the tunnel. They could see nothing but dark shadows beyond the beam of light from the torch. There was none of the phosphorescent green light which lit the other passage up faintly.

The Five walked on in single file, feeling as if they were going right down into the depths of the earth. Anne was starting to get really scared. The atmosphere was so strange that she had difficulty breathing properly.

Even George, who usually talked a lot, was quiet. Timmy was following her, his nose close to her heels. Suddenly, making the others jump, Julian exclaimed, 'Oh, good! The passage is widening out.'

He was quite right. Until now the walls of the underground passage had been so close together that the young explorers could only squeeze through. But now the passage suddenly got wider, and they emerged into a low-roofed but quite large cave.

Anne heaved a sigh of relief – but the next moment she had another fright. Almost at once, the little girl let out a shriek of alarm.

'Oh, help! Someone's hand has just touched my hair – oh, there it is again! Julian – Dick! Help!'

There was a faint sound like wings flapping above her head. George and Dick leaped forward, while Julian shone his torch at his sister. Then George burst out laughing! In the torchlight, they saw Anne looking panic-stricken, while a harmless little bat was circling round her head. It was quite as frightened as she was.

'You silly thing, Anne! It's only a poor little bat. Do stop kicking up such a fuss!'

Anne shut her mouth, feeling rather silly. Her life wasn't in danger after all! The bat brushed past Julian's torch and then shot up to the roof. As if it had given a signal, dozens of other bats, roused from their sleep, dropped from the rocky roof of the cave and began fluttering around in a strange, silent dance.

This time Anne couldn't help screaming again, and Timmy began to bark in surprise. George scolded him and Dick shouted at the bats. What a terrible noise! But it was Julian who sorted out the confusion. He was a sensible, intelligent boy, and he had seen that the underground passage went on again, the other side of the bats' cave, so he started off along it – and as he was holding the torch which showed them the way, the other children naturally followed him. The bats calmed down at once.

As for the children, they hurried along the narrow passage. Anne, who had not quite got over her fright yet, was breathing fast. No, she really wasn't enjoying this expedition one little bit! Julian was rather worried about her. He stopped for a moment to ask, 'Are you all right, Anne? Not feeling any the worse for your fright? You don't look too good to me.'

The little girl smiled.

'I'm feeling quite all right, Ju – but – well, I'm *not* perfectly happy about this,' she admitted. 'It's all very well for Dick to make fun of me, but I do feel as though we're walking into trouble!'

'TROUBLE, *trouble*, trouble!' a hollow voice in front of her repeated.

'Oh!' screamed Anne.

'OH! *Oh*! Oh!' the voice repeated, as if mocking her.

The Five stopped dead, rooted to the spot, right on the threshold of another cave, larger than the first. They couldn't see anyone at all.

'Whatever is it?' whispered Dick.

'An echo!' said George, bursting into laughter. 'Only an echo – nothing to be afraid of. Ha, ha, ha!'

'HA! *Ha*! Ha!' said the echo, making her laughter boom around the cave in an alarming way.

Quite bewildered, Timmy looked all round him, trying to find the invisible enemy whose voice he thought he could hear. Since there was no one in sight he began to bark.

'Woof! Woof!'

And of course the echo answered him. There was such a deafening noise in the cave that even George was almost frightened.

Julian was quick to march on again, and the others followed him. Crossing the echo cave was quite a noisy business, what with Anne screaming with fright and Timmy barking – and the echo ringing in the young explorers' ears the whole time. The row was tremendous! But at last they were out of the cave on the other side, and the echoes died away.

— 9 —

The underground river

By way of a contrast to the echo cave, the Five found themselves walking along the passage again in complete silence. They were still going downhill. Julian was slightly uneasy.

'I wonder where this is leading us?' he said. 'I'm not sure it wouldn't be a good idea to turn round and go back again.'

'Oh no!' George protested. 'Hello – what's that funny roaring sound? Can you hear it? It sounds like – ' She stopped, interrupting herself, and then cried, 'Oh, look!'

George had taken over the lead from Julian when they left the echo cave, and so she was the first to make a fascinating discovery. For the third time the passage widened and the children emerged into a cave – a really huge one this time. And before their startled eyes ran an underground river! It flowed fast between its rocky banks, one of them forming a kind of landing stage.

'Gosh!' said Julian.

'I say!' exclaimed Dick. 'Doesn't it look dramatic? Like something out of a film!'

'Oh, do let's explore!' cried George.

The children hurried on into the cave. Its arched roof was high, and there was plenty of room for them to move about. Anne was breathing more easily now. She felt better!

All the children stood staring at the river.

'You know,' said Julian, thinking out loud, 'it looks as if this river is making straight for the sea.'

'Well, of course it is!' said George. 'That's what rivers usually do! If we jumped into the water here, we'd come out in the creek where we landed after being shipwrecked.'

'We might *not* come out,' said Dick. 'The roof may suddenly come low down. If it does, we'd be drowned before we ever got out into the open.'

'Look here, couldn't we talk about something a bit more cheerful?' protested Anne.

George did not reply. She seemed to be rooted to the spot, staring at the ground. At last she said quietly, 'Look at that! An iron ring!'

She was quite right. There *was* an iron ring, sunk into the rock of the river bank and almost level with the water.

'It looks brand new, too!' said Dick. 'That proves

that someone's been mooring a boat here quite recently.'

'Just what I was thinking myself.'

'Quick! We must look for more clues!'

George had switched her own torch on, and she was already swinging its beam from right to left, searching the cave. Suddenly she gave a shout of triumph. She had just found a wooden chest, well hidden in a hollow in the ground behind a jutting rock.

Her cousins gathered round and helped her drag the chest out of its hiding place.

'Let's see what's in it,' said Julian, raising the lid.

George, Dick and Anne leaned over to look.

There were three big bags inside the chest! Full of curiosity, the children craned further forward. What could be in those bags? Did they have the right to open them? George settled the question.

'We're not on anyone's private property – and I suspect there's something shady behind all this. So let's see what's in the bags, Julian!'

Julian always carried a useful scout knife on him. He hesitated for a moment, and then took it out and cut the cord tying up one of the bags. He tipped the contents out on the ground. And then the four children stood there open-mouthed, so surprised they couldn't say a word.

A whole heap of gold coins, precious stones,

jewellery and old medals had rolled out at their feet!

'Treasure!' stammered Anne in amazement.

'It certainly looks like it,' said Julian.

'I should just about think it is treasure!' cried Dick. 'Why, there must be thousands and thousands of pounds' worth there – I'm sure there is!'

In silence, George bent down to pick up a magnificent rose made of gold, with delicately engraved petals. There were little diamonds set on them to look like dewdrops, and the leaves were made of splendid emeralds with gold veins.

Anne gasped with admiration. 'But – why – ' she stammered, 'why, this is the famous gold rose they were talking about on the radio! The one that was stolen from the first of the stately homes to be burgled, over a fortnight ago!'

'You're right!' said Julian, taking the jewel from George to examine it himself. 'Which shows that at this very moment we're – '

'Right in the robbers' den!' said George. 'This must be the gang's headquarters!'

Anne gave a little scream. Things were happening much too fast for her liking!

Dick calmly emptied out the other two bags. One contained some rolls of canvas. They were not very large, but at first glance Julian and George saw that they were valuable paintings by old masters – and photographs of these very paintings had been in the newspapers after the burglary at Pendleton Place!

'There's no doubt about it,' said Julian, gazing at one of the pictures.

'No,' George agreed. 'We really hit the bull's eye when we came down here. It's like finding the cave where the Forty Thieves stored their treasure!'

Anne had pulled herself together a bit. She was such a neat, tidy little girl that she couldn't help saying, 'Those burglars must be real vandals! They've rolled up the canvases the wrong way round, with the pictures on the outside!'

Julian smiled. 'But that's just what you're supposed to do, Anne! You have to, if you aren't going to ruin the paintings!'

Dick shook the last bag upside down – and out fell a pile of magnificent gold watches which rolled away in all directions.

'Good gracious me!' cried George. 'Why, those are the watches from Riddington Hall – the ones we saw when we visited it! Sir Donald was so proud of them. How glad he'll be that we've found his property!'

'I suppose,' said Julian slowly, 'the burglars are using this cave as a kind of store-room. This is where they're keeping their haul while they wait for a chance to dispose of it abroad – after they've taken the jewels out of their settings and camouflaged the pictures to look like something

else. They may even be going to melt down the
gold watches!'

'In fact, we've solved the mystery just in time!'
George added. 'A little longer, and all the things
the thieves stole from the stately homes would have
disappeared for ever. I think we can congratulate
ourselves, don't you?'

Anne had turned rather pale.

'*I* think we can congratulate ourselves on having
turned up in the robbers' den when they didn't
happen to be there!' she said. 'Let's hurry up and
go away!'

'Don't be silly!' said Dick. 'The first thing to do
is put all this stuff back into the bags, put the bags
inside the chest, and get the chest back to its hiding
place, so there's no sign that we've been here.'

'You're right,' Julian agreed. 'We can't take away
all the thieves' loot – there must be more of it
somewhere, too, perhaps hidden in other chests
like this one.'

'Yes,' said George. 'Let's put everything back
where it was and then go and tell the police. That's
the most sensible thing to do!'

They all hurried to drag the chest back to the
place where they had found it. No, they certainly
didn't want to put the thieves on their guard before
the police had come to take the stolen valuables into
custody and set a trap for the burglars themselves!

Once they were sure they had left no trace of

their presence in the cave behind them, George and her cousins turned to start back the way they had come.

'Well, we can really say our expedition has been successful!' said George, pleased. 'You have to admit we've been lucky! We'd hardly started making any inquiries about the burglaries, and we were working in the dark too – and here we are already. The police weren't getting anywhere, but thanks to us the gang will soon be behind bars. Good for the Famous Five, I say!'

A growl from Timmy stopped her short.

— 10 —

The gang

The children had earlier switched on all four torches and put them down on the ground or wedged them into cracks in the rock, so as to get everything back in its place as quickly as possible. The torches had given them quite a bright light to work by.

'Quick, we'd better put out the torches, just in case,' said George. 'Timmy never growls unless there's some reason.'

Julian, Dick and Anne did as she said. In the dim light, George put a soothing hand on her dog's neck. She could feel his hair standing on end.

'Ssh, Timmy! Don't make any noise!'

The intelligent animal understood her, and kept quiet. But he was on the alert, his head turned towards the water of the underground river running downstream. The four children looked that way too, straining their eyes as they tried to peer through the darkness. They could just make out the shapes of the rocks around them.

Timmy had not moved! He was still looking in the same direction. Holding their breath, the four children listened hard.

At first they could not hear anything. Then George caught a faint splashing sound.

'I can hear oars!' she whispered.

Who could be rowing along in the dark like that?

'The thieves, of course,' Anne told herself, answering the question in all their minds. She put her hand over her mouth. It took her all her courage not to cry out, she was so frightened!

Julian guessed that his little sister was terrified, and silently he put his arm round her shoulders. He could feel her trembling with fright, and he was ready to defend her if necessary. All of a sudden a faint flicker of light appeared on the surface of the water downstream.

As soon as George saw the light she acted. 'We must hide!' she whispered urgently. 'We don't want them to find us here!'

As she spoke, she was silently making for a big spur of rock. It was big enough for them all to hide behind it. Timmy went with her, and Dick followed them. Anne went through one of the worst moments of her life. She was so terrified she simply couldn't move, and seeing what a state she was in, Julian took her arm and pulled her away. 'Come on!' he told her under his breath.

Anne did not resist. She let him lead her to the hiding place. Hidden in the shadows behind the rock, the Five cautiously peered out, straining their eyes to see all they could.

The light was getting better all the time – and suddenly a boat appeared round the bend of the river, with a big headlight fastened to its bows. There were three very disreputable-looking men in the boat. The one who was rowing was tall and fair-haired. The other two were dark and thin, and one of them had a short beard.

A murmur of voices reached the children, who were all thinking the same thing. 'These men seem very sure of themselves,' they thought, 'so they must know this place well. Yes, there's no doubt about it – these must be the men who have been burgling all the stately homes, and they're just laughing at the efforts of the police to catch them!'

For once, even George didn't feel too happy about the situation they were in – and as for poor Anne, the less said the better!

The boat came closer, and soon drew up beside the river bank. The big fair man shipped his oars and jumped ashore. Then he pulled the boat in. Taking his time, he tied it up to the big iron ring.

Meanwhile, his companions were unloading a sack. It seemed to be very heavy.

'Here, Eric!' grumbled one of them, speaking to the big fair man. 'Hurry up and lend us a hand, can't you? If it's not too tiring for you, that is!'

The fair-haired man called Eric smiled, showing a lot of white teeth in a big smile. 'And just where would you little runts be without me, I wonder?' he asked.

'Doing very well!' snapped one of the dark men. 'You may be the brawn of this outfit, but we're the brains, eh, Manuel?'

'You bet we are, Joe!' said his companion.

'Well, don't let's argue,' said Eric. 'It's good to see our takings piling up like this!'

'Just one or two more stately homes left in this neighbourhood – and we should get good pickings from them,' said Joe, sounding satisfied. 'Then we'll be off out of the country!'

'Yes – so let's get last night's haul safely stowed away!'

The children were terrified of being discovered. If the criminals came their way, they really would be in trouble! Judging by the sinister appearance of the three men, they couldn't expect any mercy from this gang. Julian squeezed Anne's hand as if to try and give her strength, because he could feel her trembling. As for George, she signed to Timmy to keep still – he was getting ready to leap at the men.

The children need not have worried. Instead of

coming in their direction, the thieves turned their
backs on them. Carrying the big sack, they went
over to the hiding place where the children had
discovered the chest, went past it and dragged
another chest out of hiding a little farther away.
From behind their rock, George and her cousins
saw them tip the sack into the chest.

They heard Joe's voice. 'Good!' he said. 'That last
job'll bring in even more than the others. There'll
be plenty for all of us when we come to divide out
the loot!'

'And well earned too,' said Manuel.

Eric started to laugh. 'I can't help laughing when
I think of all those coppers chasing about trying
to pull us in – we're too clever to get caught.
They're nowhere near finding out how we got into
Riddington Hall, for instance! Ha, ha, ha!'

In her hiding place, George clenched her fists.
She was longing to tell them out loud, 'Don't count
your chickens before they're hatched! Just wait till
we get out of here and you'll have quite a surprise.
So enjoy gloating over your loot while there's still
time, because you won't be feeling nearly so cheerful
tomorrow!'

Julian was too sensible to feel tempted to give the
gang a piece of his mind – he was just hoping the
burglars wouldn't realise the Five were anywhere
near them. Dick and Anne, too, were crossing their
fingers and hoping the men would leave again in

their boat as soon as they had finished their work here. They were anxiously watching every move the gang made. And sure enough, after putting their haul safely away, the thieves went back to the landing stage.

'Good! They're off!' thought George.

At that moment, something brushed her ankle and darted between Timmy's paws. It was a rat!

This time George wasn't quick enough to foresee her dog's reactions and stop him in time. Forgetting that he had been told to sit perfectly still, Timmy gave way to his hunting instincts. With a' huge bound, he dashed out in pursuit of the rat, barking, 'Woof! Woof! Woof!'

Of course the thieves heard him. They were about to get into their boat again, but they turned round in surprise to see Timmy chasing his rat!

'A dog!' exclaimed Eric. 'Where on earth did *he* spring from?'

Well, blow me down!' muttered Joe, unable to believe his eyes.

'Catch him!' said Manuel, making for Timmy.

But the dog didn't wait to be caught – his rat had just darted into the tunnel the children had come along, and Timmy didn't intend to let it get away! Taking no notice of the thieves, who were running after him, shouting and waving their arms, he disappeared along the underground passage too. The children could hear the sound of his barking.

— 11 —

Escape!

The strange hunt dashed off, with the rat in front. Then came Timmy, then Eric, whose long legs carried him very fast, and Joe and Manuel followed a little way behind. Suddenly the four children in their hiding place heard a tremendous noise in the distance. They exchanged glances of alarm.

'They've reached the echo cave, that's what it is!' said Dick in a whisper. 'That must be why the shouts and Timmy's barking sound so loud.'

'Oh, how dreadful!' stammered Anne, almost in tears. She was badly upset.

Julian came to a quick decision.

'We can't just hang about here doing nothing,' he said. 'Those men will be back in a moment, and then they'll start looking for us.'

'But they don't know we're here!' murmured Anne, choking back a sob.

'Oh, don't be so silly!' said Dick impatiently.

'Surely you can see that the men will soon realise Timmy didn't come down here on his own?
They chased him on the spur of the moment, but
they'll soon realise that there must be someone else
down here.'

'Timmy won't let them catch him,' said George.
'He'll lead them a real chase.'

'Whether they catch him or not they'll come back
here to ferret around. They'll search the whole
place, and when they find us they'll – '

'That'll do,' said Julian, cutting him short. 'We'd
better start off straight away – come on!'

He took Anne's arm and made her follow him.
Dick came out of the hiding place behind the rock
too, followed more slowly by George. He went up
to his brother.

'Ju, don't you realise we can't go back the same
way we came?' he said. 'The men are somewhere
along that passage, and they'll cut us off.'

'That's exactly why I *don't* intend to go along the
passage,' said Julian calmly. 'I have another idea.
Follow me!'

Julian's idea was both simple and ingenious. He
explained it to Dick, George and Anne.

'I was thinking along these lines,' he said. 'Since
Eric and his accomplices came here by boat, it must
be possible to get along the river and out to sea.
All things considered, that's the only way *we* can
get out, since we can't go along the underground

passage. And as for our means of transport down the river – here it is! The gang's boat! They've been kind enough to leave it here for us to use ourselves. They didn't *mean* to let us have it, but we'd be silly not to take advantage of their kindness!'

Dick hurried after Julian. He had absolute faith in his brother. Julian's idea seemed a good one. It was a pity that things had gone wrong just when everything had seemed to be working so well. If only they could have got away and reached the police before the men had come back!

Still leading Anne, Julian stopped on the landing stage. He pointed to the boat and told the others, 'Quick, jump in! It's our only chance of getting away safely! The current of the river will soon carry us down to the sea – and, at the same time, we'll be taking the gang's only means of transport. If we're lucky, we may be able to warn the police and get back here before the criminals have had time to move all their loot. It'll take them several journeys along the tunnel and back to get it out of its hiding place. And anyway, I imagine they'll be putting their own safety first. So let's hurry!'

Dick did not hesitate for a moment. He jumped into the boat. It was a good, solid little craft, lying well balanced in the water, and it hardly rocked at all as he got in. Julian gave Anne a gentle push.

'Jump, Anne! Catch her, Dick!'

And Anne jumped into the boat too. Julian turned

to George, who was standing perfectly still a little way off. He was surprised to see her looking so sullen and almost hostile – his cousin was usually such an active, live-wire of a girl!

'Come on, George!' he said. 'Trying to make your mind up? We haven't got much time, you know! Come on, jump in and hurry up about it!'

George didn't budge. 'You three go,' she said, looking obstinate. 'I'm staying here.'

The others stared at her in astonishment.

'You're mad!' said Dick. 'What's come over you all of a sudden? Do you *want* those men to catch you, or what?'

'I don't want to go without Timmy, that's all. If *you* can bring yourselves to leave the poor thing with those brutes – well, I can't!'

'You needn't worry about old Tim!' said Julian. 'He won't let them catch him. You said so yourself. He'll probably shoot straight out of the other end of the passage and make for Kirrin Cottage!'

'That's what you think! He won't – he'll come back here to look for me! And if I go with you he won't find anyone here. I'll never abandon Timmy.'

'But – but if you stay here you may be risking your life!' Anne pleaded with her cousin, terrified.

'What does that matter? Timmy would never

run off without *me*! It would be disloyal of me to leave *him*!'

'Look here, George, your feelings do you credit and all that,' said Julian drily. 'But there's no time to stand here arguing! You've *got* to do as I say.' And seizing his cousin's shoulders, he repeated, 'Go on, jump into that boat.'

Since George resisted, he decided he would have to use force. Picking her up round the waist, he almost threw her into the boat.

'Catch her, Dick!' he called.

George struggled, but with Anne's help Dick clung on to her and stopped her climbing out of the boat again. Julian hastily cast off and jumped into the boat himself.

It was high time, too! The boat moved away, and it was just beginning to get up speed, carried by the fast current, when Eric, Joe and Manuel, arguing in loud voices, emerged from the underground passage.

Joe spotted the children first. He yelled, at the top of his voice, 'Look at that! So I was right! That dog wasn't on his own.'

'Kids!' Manuel exclaimed. 'It's a bunch of kids!'

Eric's big chest swelled as he took a deep breath, cupped his hands round his mouth and shouted, in a voice like thunder, 'Hi – you there! Come back! And hurry up about it!'

'No thanks!' Dick shouted back. 'We'd only come

back if we felt like it – and as it happens we *don't* feel like it, so there!'

'Oh, keep your mouth shut and row, Dick!' Julian told him.

George, who was very pale, did not say a word. As for Anne, she was frightened out of her wits. She couldn't stop her teeth chattering.

'Bring our boat back and we won't hurt you!' Eric called. But the boat and the children were already disappearing from sight!

Dick began to laugh. 'They thought themselves so clever, but they couldn't do anything to stop us!' he said. 'That was a really good trick we played on them – ha, ha, ha!'

Julian had taken the tiller and left Dick to do the rowing. He steered the boat expertly along, taking advantage of the swift current. He didn't join in his brother's roars of laughter – he was thoughtful and frowning.

'You don't look very happy, Ju!' said Dick, amused.

'I've got more sense than you have, old chap. Honestly, you're acting like a little boy who's just played a practical joke on someone, without thinking what may come of it!'

'Well, if you ask me, we've got ourselves out of a nasty hole very neatly.'

'Yes, of course, that's the main thing! But it doesn't alter the fact that those criminals have seen us. Now they'll know that *we* know where they're hiding out, and you can bet they'll be off as fast as they can.'

'Listen, I thought of that myself, Ju. But then I thought, after all, the men don't know that we've found the stolen valuables, so why should they suspect we know they're up to no good? I should think they'll just take us for children who aren't very scrupulous about borrowing other people's property – they'll work out that we were having fun exploring this system of underground caves and passages, and we happened to find their boat and pinch it.'

'I don't know – criminals aren't usually very trusting folk! I'd be rather surprised if they don't guess the truth and realise that they must have been overheard. They'll be in a hurry to move their loot and then disappear. All we can do is hope that we can act faster!'

Dick had stopped laughing, seeing that things were more serious than he had realised. George did not say anything. She was sitting quite still on her seat in the boat.

Anne gently put a hand on her cousin's. 'Oh, George,' she said timidly, 'you do look angry!'

'I *am* angry!' said George, shaking Anne's hand off roughly. 'My goodness, I don't think you have any decent feelings, any of you! Cowards, that's what you are! Are we the Famous *Five* or aren't we? I'd have thought every single one of us would be loyal to all the rest. I call it sheer treachery, deserting poor Timmy. And I shall never, never forgive you for dragging me away by force!'

Julian frowned. 'Oh, George, don't make such a fuss about it,' he said. 'After all, our lives matter more than Timmy – and what's more, he isn't in any danger!'

'How do you know?' asked George furiously. 'Those horrible men may quite well have killed him by now!'

'Take it easy, George,' said Dick, trying to calm her down. 'I'm sure they won't even have caught him.'

'George, I do think Dick is right,' Anne agreed. 'Didn't you notice that the men were on their own when they came out of the underground passage?'

George was still scowling. 'What does that prove?' she said. 'If they'd killed Timmy they wouldn't have bothered to bring him back to the cave. And what good could he have done them alive?'

'But what good would it have done them to kill him?' argued sensible Anne. 'Do listen, George – I'm convinced Timmy must have been able to look after himself perfectly well. He's so clever!'

Anne's praise of Timmy did help to reassure George. Yes, he really was an unusually intelligent dog! Perhaps she shouldn't worry too much about him after all.

— 12 —

A trap for the thieves

With Anne to cheer her up, George perked up a bit and started to look on the bright side. As for Julian and Dick, they were still feeling cross because of the bad luck they felt they'd had, and Anne was only hoping they would reach the end of their voyage underground without running into any more problems.

Meanwhile, the boat was going along at a good pace. It was as if the river itself was in a hurry.

'I can't make it out,' muttered Dick, after a while. 'Surely the underground river shouldn't be flowing so fast, since it ought to be about level with the sea by my calculations!'

'No,' said George. 'You probably didn't notice, but though the passage we went along did go downwards at first, later on it climbed up again for quite a way. So I should think we're sloping down to the sea again now, and that explains why we're going so fast.'

'You're right, the passage did climb uphill – specially in between the bats' cave and the echo cave,' sighed Anne. 'I got quite out of breath going up the slope!'

Suddenly Julian called, in a warning voice, 'Watch out! I think I can see a patch of light ahead.'

Dick turned to look, without letting go of the oars.

'Hurrah!' he cried. 'Daylight!'

George and Anne shouted for joy too. They could all see the end of the narrow underground passage along which the river ran, standing out like a circle of light at the end of the long dark tunnel.

'We're safe!' sighed Anne, squeezing George's hand.

'I wonder where we shall come out, though?' said George, frowning. 'Because what we have to do is get back to the spot where we left our bikes, as fast as we possibly can. There's no time to lose!'

'Here we are! We're really out now!' shouted Dick.

Sure enough, the boat was floating out of the tunnel. It was high tide, and everything went perfectly smoothly. As soon as the boat was out on the open sea, it paused for just a moment and then started to drift with the tide. Dick picked up the oars and asked his brother, 'Now what, Ju? Where are we going?'

Julian looked round.

'Well, I can see the cave entrance at the foot of the cliff,' he said. 'But we can't use the cliff path leading up to the road at the minute, because it's high tide, just as it was when we were shipwrecked. Now, what shall we do?'

George was never at a loss in a crisis.

'The first thing is to get in touch with the police,' she said. 'That's urgent. And then we must make sure we know what the thieves do next, which means following them when they come out of their hiding place. So for a start, let's put Anne and Dick ashore in the little cove just beyond the cave. The rocks there look quite easy to climb. Anne, you must get to your bike as fast as you can, and then it's all up to you! Go to the police station in the nearest village, tell the policemen what's been happening, and come back here with them. And mind you tell them to hurry! Every moment counts. As for you, Dick, you'd better watch the other entrance to the underground passage – the one in the gorse bushes!'

'But what about you and Julian?' asked Dick and Anne in chorus.

'Julian can stay on watch at the cave entrance, and I'll take the boat back to the mouth of the underground river and watch that, just in case the

gang decide to make their getaway by swimming
out. Then we'll be sure of either being able to
follow them – or if we're lucky, cornering them!
Understand?'

There was no time to lose. Julian thought George's
plan was a good one – and at least his young sister
Anne would be safe!

Dick started rowing again, and made straight for
the little cove George had mentioned. She had been
quite right. It was a miniature bay, with a fine sandy
beach which the tide hardly ever reached, and it was
surrounded by scattered rocks which wouldn't be
very difficult even for Anne to climb.

As soon as the boat had grounded Dick shipped
his oars and helped Anne to jump out on to the
beach. Then they both started climbing up to the
road which ran along the cliff-top overhead.

George did not waste any time. She took over
Dick's place in the boat, seized the oars, and set
off again, making for the cave this time. Once
she had reached it, she stopped to let Julian out
in his turn.

'You and Dick probably have the best chance of
seeing the men come out,' she said. 'So keep your
eyes open, Julian!'

'You bet I will! And mind you take care yourself.'

'You bet *I* will!'

Julian nodded, but he didn't look very happy.

'This is a heavy boat for one person to manage,' he said, 'and I don't much like the idea of leaving you on your own.'

'Well, we're all running a bit of a risk,' said George in a matter-of-fact tone, starting to row again. 'Good luck, Julian!'

And off she went, rowing like a real old salt. Watching her, Julian couldn't help admiring his cousin.

Now, thanks to George's clever imagination and quick thinking, they all had separate jobs to do, and a few minutes later they were getting down to them.

Dick and Anne, knowing how important their part in the whole operation was, scrambled up to the top of the cliff as fast as they could. They both used their hands and feet to get a good grip and clamber from rock to rock. At first the climb seemed a fairly easy one, but then the slope became steeper, and Dick had to help his sister several times. However, at last they were up.

Now there was no time to be lost!

Dick made for the clump of prickly gorse bushes and hid behind a nearby tree, so that he could keep watch on the way out of the underground passage without being seen himself.

As for Anne, she hurried to fetch her bicycle, and once she had mounted it she rode off to Dunsham, the nearest village.

'I only hope the police believe me!' she thought as she rode along, with her hair blowing in the wind. 'And most of all, I hope we get back in time to prevent anything awful happening! Julian, Dick and George aren't nearly big and strong enough to stand up to those men, especially when they're all separated.'

Dick watched his sister until she had disappeared round the bend in the road.

'Good!' he thought. 'Now, I must keep my eye on those bushes. The only thing is, what shall I *do* if the men come out that way? I think it would be best to follow them without letting them see me. I could find out where they're going and then come back as fast as possible to tell the others. Or I could telephone the police. Or then again, I could . . .'

He was still wondering exactly what he should do when Anne arrived in Dunsham. She went straight to the police station, and told the policeman there such a convincing story that he believed her at once.

'We must act fast,' he told her. 'I want to set a nice little trap for these men!'

He rang through to the nearest town to summon more police help and then told Anne to get into his car. He loaded her bicycle on the roof, and immediately set off along the cliff-top road. He was obviously impatient to go into action. It would be a grand thing for him if he could help to capture this notorious gang of thieves and recover the valuables they had stolen from the stately homes!

They did the drive in record time, and Dick was very relieved to see the police car arrive. He ran out of his hiding place as soon as it had stopped.

'Gosh, I'm glad to see you!' he told the policeman. 'Look – one of the ways out of the underground passage is here, in among these bushes. But I haven't seen any of the men come out of it yet.'

Just at that moment another police car screeched round the corner and came to a halt. The reinforcements had arrived just in time. The policeman explained the situation briefly.

'Right!' said the sergeant, who had just arrived, taking control. Turning to one of his men, he said, 'Okay, Fred, you take over from this young man! And blow your whistle if you see anything happening.'

'Yes, Sergeant.'

Following by the other policemen, the sergeant started clambering down to the foot of the cliff. Dick and Anne followed him.

Julian saw them coming. 'No one's come out of this cave yet,' he told the police, just as Dick had done. 'I'm sure of that!'

Anne turned quite pale.

'Oh, my goodness!' she murmured. 'Then – then that means George must have had to face the criminals all on her own!'

Julian cupped his hands round his mouth, turned towards the sea and shouted, 'George! Come back here, George!'

In a minute George appeared, rowing back round the rocky promontory which had hidden her from view. 'Have you seen the thieves yet?' she shouted when she saw the policemen. 'No? Well, I haven't either! So that means they must still be down there in the underground caves and passages!'

'Let's go and take a look,' said the sergeant.

He would rather not have taken the four cousins too, but he and his men needed someone to guide them. Julian said he would go – and as Dick, George and Anne all insisted on accompanying him, the sergeant ended up by saying they could all four come.

'After all,' he told them, 'I doubt if there'll be any danger. The men thought they were quite safe, so it's not very likely they'll be armed.'

He left one policeman on guard outside in the boat, to watch the mouth of the underground river, and then went into the cave, along with the children and the other two police constables.

— 13 —

Where has the gang gone?

They all went along the passage in silence. When they reached the place where the path forked, Julian unhesitatingly chose the passage going downwards. Before they went through the bats' cave, George advised them to put their torches out so as not to rouse the creatures clinging to the rock, and when they came to the echo cave, she said it would be a good idea to walk as quietly as possible, so that the gang wouldn't know they were coming. At last, keeping on the alert the whole time, the little party came out on the banks of the underground river.

They had not seen a sign of the thieves yet. Had they really stayed down here by the river all this time? No – to the dismay of the four children, there was no sign of them in the huge cave with the river running through it either!

The men had just disappeared in a most mysterious way – it was like a conjuring trick. The police sergeant frowned.

'I hope you kids haven't been amusing yourselves by trying to fool us,' he said. 'Are you quite sure of what you saw?'

'Absolutely positive!' cried Julian. He gave them a rapid description of the thieves.

'And their haul's hidden just over there, too!' said Dick. 'Go and look at it!'

But there was yet another disappointment in store for the children. The chests containing the valuables had disappeared from their hiding places.

'All the same,' Dick told the policemen, 'I can swear to it that the pictures and jewellery and so on stolen from the stately homes *were* there!'

The sergeant bent down to pick something up.

'Oh yes, I believe you all right,' he said, heaving a deep sigh. 'Look – they left a gold watch behind. That's evidence, and no mistake! I'm afraid our friends have left, taking their haul with them!'

'But they can't have done!' Julian protested. 'There were three of us watching the three ways out the whole time! The men simply *must* be hiding somewhere near here!'

At that moment he was interrupted by joyous barking.

'Woof! Woof!'

George's face lit up at once. 'Timmy!' she cried.

She would have recognised her own dog's bark among a thousand.

Sure enough, it really was Timmy, racing up as if he had come out of thin air! He leaped into his little mistress's arms and licked her face enthusiastically with his big wet tongue.

George didn't have the heart to scold him for going after that rat earlier in the day – she was so pleased to see him safe and sound again! She had been afraid some harm might have come to him, and then, all the time they were going down the underground passage with the police, she had been wondering if they would find him. Now, just as she was beginning to give up hope again, here he was – her own dear old Timmy, quite beside himself with delight at being back with her.

She patted his hairy head. 'Timmy! Good old Timmy! Where *have* you been?' she asked.

The clever dog seemed to understand. Turning round at once, he made for the shadows from which he had emerged.

'Woof! Woof!'

'Let's follow him!' said George. 'I'm sure he wants to show us something.'

Julian, Dick, Anne and the policemen followed George. Suddenly she gave an exclamation of surprise. 'Look, *another* passage, one we haven't found before. Timmy was hiding there! I wonder where he's taking us? I bet this is the way the gang got out. Oh, my goodness, what bad luck we didn't know about this branch of the passage before!'

She was already starting along it when the sergeant stopped her.

'Hold on, miss! It's my job to go first, along with my men. You can never be too careful.'

And like it or not, the children had to let the policemen take the lead this time.

The way into this new passage was so narrow that it was difficult to spot it, but the passage itself was big and well ventilated. They could walk along it quite easily. They went along underground for so long that the sergeant began to get worried.

'Why, we must have come nearly a mile by now!' he said.

Suddenly the passage turned a corner – and they saw that Timmy had stopped in front of what looked like a dead end. He was standing on his back legs, with his front paws up against the rock.

'Woof! Woof!'

Spotting a ring set in the stone, the sergeant tugged it – and the rock moved on a pivot, showing them a secret staircase climbing quite steeply upwards. The policemen and the children climbed it in silence.

What would they find at the top of the stairs?

George counted twenty steps. When they reached the top, the sergeant and his men stopped.

'Seems we can't get any farther!' said the sergeant,

sounding annoyed. 'I can't see anything ahead but a smooth wall. However, there must *be* a way out somewhere, if only we can find it!'

Dick joined the sergeant.

'Can I have a go?' he asked. 'I've got an idea.'

And he ran his fingers nimbly along an almost invisible line. There was a sudden click – and a square panel swung round on another pivot, showing them a faint light beyond. The sergeant immediately pushed Dick aside.

'Let us go first,' he told the boy. 'It may be dangerous.'

Taking careful precautions, the three men slipped in through the opening. The children followed them without asking permission first.

'Why – we're in the big exhibition room in Riddington Hall!' whispered Anne.

Sure enough, the policemen and the children had come out in the room with the glass showcases, where Sir Donald Riddington had shown the four cousins his valuable collection only a few days before. Looking round, the children saw that the entrance to the secret staircase and the underground passage they had just come along was hidden by the back wall of the huge fireplace.

After all, they could see just what had happened.

The gang had come along the secret passage to burgle the Hall, and taken Sir Donald's gold watches back with them the same way. That solved the mystery of how they had got into the Hall without tampering with the doors and windows. And only a little while ago, they must have made their escape from the underground cave the same way, taking their haul with them!

'That explains it!' said one of the policemen. 'Our birds flew this way – along with the jewels, the money, the watches and the paintings. They knew about that passage and they made use of it when they wanted a secret way out. But I wonder just how they managed it – in broad daylight, without being stopped by Sir Donald or his man Andrews, let alone the visitors to the house!'

'That's easy,' said the sergeant, looking crest-fallen. 'As it happens, the house isn't open to visitors at all today – and I can't see old Sir Donald and Andrews standing up to three desperate criminals for long.'

'Oh, gosh!' said Julian, feeling worried. 'Do you think those men may have hurt Sir Donald and his servant?'

'We'd better go and look for them,' said the sergeant, and turning to his men he added, 'Search the whole place!'

The children went with the policemen, who paused in the doorway of every room before going in to make sure there was no danger lurking there. That was just police routine, because they knew the criminals must be far away by now.

There was no one at all on the ground floor of the Hall, but up on the first floor the policemen and the children heard faint grunting sounds. They all made for the room where the noises seemed to be coming from. It was obviously Sir Donald's bedroom. The little party stopped in the doorway, listening hard.

'Over there!' cried George, pointing to a big wardrobe.

The sergeant turned the key in the lock of the wardrobe door and opened it. There were Sir Donald and his servant, lying side by side in the huge cupboard, tightly bound and gagged.

'Sir Donald!' cried Julian. 'Quick, we must get him out of here!'

No sooner said than done, because Julian was already kneeling beside Sir Donald. He removed the gag and cut the ropes with his scout knife. Meanwhile, the sergeant was setting Andrews free.

'Have you been wounded?' he asked the two men.

'No,' said Sir Donald. 'But those villains didn't spare our feelings! All the time they were tying us up, they boasted about stealing my watches. What impudence! They actually laughed as they told us they were about to walk out through the front door, and they weren't at all worried about the police – they said they were cleverer than the police force anyway, and they didn't intend to leave this part of the country until they'd made a clean sweep of all the treasures in its stately homes!'

The sergeant was red with anger. 'Well, their boastfulness may be their undoing!' he grunted.

'Meanwhile, however,' said Sir Donald bitterly, 'the rascals are still at large – with my precious watches! And to think they aren't even insured! The money that opening the house to tourists brought in was my only means of support – I'm a ruined man now!'

Anne felt tears come to her eyes. She went over to poor old Sir Donald and gently took his hand.

'You must trust the police, Sir Donald,' she said in her gentle voice. 'And the five of us will do all we can to get your collection back, too.'

Julian smiled.

'You're taking on rather a job there, Anne. We're not quite fully fledged detectives yet!'

'But we *will* do our very best to track down the gang!' George assured Sir Donald firmly. 'Just as Anne says.'

George's bright idea

Over the next two days, George and her cousins spent most of their time finding out how the police were getting on with their inquiries. They even went back to Riddington Hall to talk to Sir Donald again – and even more important, to talk to the policemen working on the case.

Sir Donald could not tell them anything new. Poor old man – he was terribly upset. Anne in particular, being very tender-hearted, felt really sorry for him.

They met the policeman they had seen at the Hall before, just after it was burgled, when he told them what was going on. He was rather chilly in his manner to them this time – obviously he didn't like having to admit that all his work was getting him nowhere. The Five soon left the Hall.

That afternoon, the children discussed their findings in the garden of Kirrin Cottage. It turned

out that Julian, for one, was feeling rather pes-
simistic.

'The gang hasn't been heard of again,' he said
gloomily. 'If you ask me, they've taken fright and
probably left the area, in spite of their boasting to
Sir Donald.'

'I'm not so sure of that,' said George. 'They could
quite well be lying low for a while, before bringing
off another big burglary!'

'And meanwhile we've lost track of them,' sighed
Dick. 'We haven't the faintest idea where to look
for Eric and Co. – not to mention all that stolen
property!'

'I suppose all we can do is wait and hope for a
stroke of luck,' was Anne's suggestion.

Next day the news bulletin on the local radio station seemed to prove George right. The newsreader
announced that an old house called Dangerfield
Abbey, about twenty miles from Kirrin, had been
ransacked the previous night. This time, the audacious thieves had stolen some valuable gold and
silver plate, some priceless miniatures, and jewellery
worth thousands of pounds.

'There!' said George. 'That shows that Eric, Joe
and Manuel are still in these parts.'

'Unless there's a rival gang at work,' Julian
suggested.

'That's not likely – one gang of criminals wouldn't
poach on another gang's territory, would they? No,

the men who burgled Riddington Hall are doing just what they said they'd do – making a clean sweep of the treasures of all the stately homes in this part of the country. Well, we must make sure we catch them before they carry out their threat!'

'But how?' asked Dick. 'The police are on their mettle, and they've searched all the caves along the coast. *And* they've combed any rocky areas for hiding places, and investigated all the woods and wild stretches of moorland in this part of the country, and they haven't found a thing. You must admit our gang of thieves is very clever!'

Julian scratched his head.

'What I'd like to know,' he said, 'is where they've hidden their haul. They must have done it in a hurry, because they didn't have very much time. So their new hiding place can't be far from Riddington Hall.'

'What's more,' added Anne, 'they must have chosen somewhere quite large. Those chests were pretty big.'

Dick agreed. 'In fact, I should think it must be somewhere big enough for *them* to hide in, too, until the police have finished searching the countryside,' he said.

'Well, the police inquiries aren't getting anywhere,' Julian went on, 'and I can only see one explanation. If you ask me, this gang knows the lie of the land very well indeed – better than we do, *or* the police.'

'What do you think, George?' asked Anne, seeing that her cousin was obviously thinking hard, but was not saying anything.

'What do I think?' said George slowly. 'Well, the other day the thieves got to their hideout in the cave by boat. A boat is a quiet means of transport, and a common one in these parts too, with so many fishermen. It meant they could move around without being noticed more easily than in a car, for instance. Now they haven't got their boat any more – and they needed to find a hiding place big enough to take them *and* their haul. They had to find it very quickly, too. So they can only have hidden – '

'Where?' asked the other three in suspense.

'Why, back in the cave where we first came across them, of course!'

Dick looked staggered.

'You mean they could have gone back to their old den again?'

'Why not? It's the very last place where anyone would think of looking for them!'

The theory George had worked out and explained to her cousins struck them as a very bright idea. Julian was the first to recover from his surprise.

'My word, you could well be right!' he said. 'That cave really *is* the only place the police haven't thought of. As they didn't find the gang there when they first hoped to corner them, they very soon lost interest in that part of the network of underground passages.'

'If the gang really did go back to their old cave, you have to admit they're very daring criminals!' added Anne.

'They've already proved that,' Dick pointed out. 'In fact, *I* think they've got more nerve than intelligence! The police were watching the ports to make sure they didn't get out of the country – and all the time the gang was stealing more and more treasures and storing them very close to the actual houses they'd been stolen from! Everyone thought the thieves would try to get away as fast as possible, but they just went on calmly burgling more stately homes – and taking their time about it. The police put up road blocks, so they got about in that boat of theirs, rowing round the coast! Why, it really *wouldn't* be surprising if they went back to their old haunts, as George suggests. In fact, they're probably feeling quite safe there!'

George, who had been perched on a little wall, jumped down.

'Well, all we have to do is go and see!' she said calmly. 'I suggest we go back to the cave with the underground river running through it tonight.'

'You're crazy!' cried Anne, in horror. 'It'd be putting out heads into the lion's mouth!'

'Not at all! The thieves must have to go out sometimes, to get stocks of provisions. And they can't leave their hiding place except at night, under cover of dark. So we can go along the passage to their cave at night, and get the treasures out again the same way!'

'George,' said Julian very firmly, 'I entirely agree with Anne! It *would* be crazy to go back to that cave! What we ought to do is tell the police, and then if they think you're right – '

George interrupted her cousin.

'But if they think I'm wrong, we'll have lost precious time! No, Ju, that won't do! We must take action ourselves. After all, the Five have already proved they *can* take daring action on their own, and very effectively too – haven't they?'

'It really isn't very sensible,' objected Julian.

'Listen, everyone,' said Dick, 'why don't we go there, as George suggests – but leaving a note of explanation behind for your parents, George? That would be daring *and* sensible. And then, if we get into any kind of trouble, at least Uncle Quentin will know where we are. Well, what do you think?'

It took George quite long time to persuade Julian that Dick's idea was a good one – and much less time to scribble a note for her father! The children spent the rest of the day impatiently waiting for evening, and working out their expedition in detail. They must take as few risks as possible, so they tried to think of everything.

'If you ask me, the safest way to get into the cave is upstream along the river itself,' said Dick. 'The men have lost their own boat – and George's boat is mended now. If we go that way we won't risk meeting the thieves in the passage on their way out of their den. And if we see them still inside the cave as we get near, all we have to do is turn round and go back. They won't be able to follow us!'

'No, they won't,' said Julian. 'But you're forgetting that it will take us an awfully long time to get to the cave if we go by boat! It would be much quicker to ride our bikes to the opening of the tunnel among the gorse bushes.'

'Yes,' said George. 'And if we all strap carriers and baskets to the backs and fronts of our bikes, we ought to be able to get the stolen valuables away. We'll take the biggest bicycle baskets we can find in the shed – better safe than sorry!'

'Safe?' said Julian. 'I don't see anything very *safe* about this expedition at all! Still, since we seem to have settled the details, let's start as soon as it's dark.'

'But how shall we explain to Aunt Fanny and Uncle Quentin that we want to go out on our bikes?' Anne wondered.

'Oh, we'll just say we feel like going for a little ride after supper for the good of our health! We shan't be lying, either. The fresh air *will* do us good – I feel all on edge!' said George.

It was one of George's principles that she absolutely never told lies. On the very few occasions when she really couldn't allow herself the luxury of telling the whole truth, at least she didn't say anything that was actualy *un*true. When the Five set off that evening, however, she did have a rather guilty conscience. She knew they would never have gone out 'for the good of their health' if they hadn't decided to explore the cave!

Aunt Fanny did not suspect anything as she watched the children leave. She didn't even think it was odd that they all had both carriers and baskets on their bicycles, just to go for a little evening ride!

— 15 —

Disaster strikes

Once they were on the road which would bring them to the gorse bushes above the underground passage, the children rode along fast, because it was some way to go. None of them talked much, and even Timmy was quiet. It was almost as if some secret threat were hovering over the four children and the dog.

It was bright moonlight when the Five reached the top of the cliff. They were very familiar with the landscape here by now!

After hiding their bicycles in the nearby spinney, they cautiously approached the big clump of bushes hiding the entrance to the underground passage. Julian stood and listened for quite a long time before he would let George, Dick and Anne follow him into the passage itself. Timmy would never leave George unless he positively had to, so of course he was sticking close to her as usual.

'Aren't we going to leave someone on guard outside?' asked Anne.

'No,' said Julian. 'I don't see what real use that would be. I think we ought to keep together. But we must be on the alert the whole time, and at the first sign of danger we must turn round straight away and come back!'

The children made their way slowly and cautiously as far as the echo cave. They all held their breath as they crossed the cave. Yes, everything was going smoothly so far! They hadn't met anyone, and to judge by the silence round them, there really *wasn't* anyone in the network of underground caves and passages.

Just before they were near the entrance to what they had christened 'the gang's cave', Julian ordered them to stop, while he went on ahead scouting. He soon came back, with a broad smile on his face.

'All clear!' he told them. 'I even took a look at the places where the chests were hidden before – and George's guess was quite right! The burglars really *have* brought their haul back to their old den. And they're not in the cave themselves at the moment either!'

The others were delighted to hear these two bits of good news, though they kept quiet about it. So George had been right when she worked out her theory!

All they had to do now was put their plan into action!

Feeling very pleased with themselves, the Five went on again. All the children felt their hearts beating fast. This time, at last, they were really going to reap the reward of their efforts! They had found the stolen property once before, only to lose it again. However, it looked as if they were going to have another chance to retrieve it, and they certainly didn't intend to let that chance slip by. This was almost more than they could have hoped for!

George was quietly congratulating herself on their success – because she already felt sure that the expedition *would* be a success! Dick was thinking happily of the police and how impressed they would be by the courage and intelligence of the Five. They really would be the 'Famous Five' now! For once Anne forgot her own fears as she realised that victory was very close. Even Julian, usually so down-to-earth and sensible, felt they had as good as done what they set out to do already.

Perhaps Timmy was the only one who wasn't absolutely happy. Now and then he raised his head and sniffed the strange smells around him, but George didn't take any special notice of that. After all, she knew the thieves must be coming and going in the passage quite often, so of course he would pick up their scent.

When the children and Timmy arrived on the

bank of the underground river, the children ran to the gang's old hiding places. Sure enough, the chests of stolen goods were back where they had been before!

'This is fantastic,' George exclaimed.

'Look!' said Dick. 'There's a little handcart here – the thieves must have used it to move their haul about the passages. Well, we can use it for *our* furniture removals too – getting the treasures back up to our bikes!'

He roared with laughter. And it was at that very moment that Julian noticed how oddly Timmy was behaving.

Timmy had stopped at the spot where the hidden passage began – the one leading to Riddington Hall. He was sniffing the air very hard, looking in the direction of the passage, with one forepaw raised.

'George – look at Timmy!' said Julian. 'He seems to be worried about something, doesn't he?'

'Oh, never mind him!' said George. She was helping Dick to put one of the chests into the little handcart. 'I expect he's picked up the scent of a rat or something! Here, come and lend a hand, Ju! This chest is terribly heavy. Mind your feet, Anne!'

Feeling rather uneasy, though he couldn't quite have said why, Julian rejoined the others. With some difficulty, the four cousins got the chest in place on the little handcart. Suddenly, a loud bark from Tim made them all jump.

This time, now that their hard work was not absorbing all their attention, George, Dick and Anne turned their heads to look. Julian, who was already on his guard, jumped. He was very pale.

'The men!' he whispered. 'Quick – we'd better get out of here!'

But there was no time for the Five to escape. The three men they had thought were safely out of the way had just emerged from the passage joining the cave to Riddington Hall!

Eric, who was leading them, made straight for Julian. In a moment he had seized the boy and tied his hands together with a length of thin cord. Next, the big man grabbed Dick.

Meanwhile Manuel had thrown his jacket over Timmy's head to keep him quiet. Joe had his work cut out to overpower Geroge! She hit and scratched and kicked like mad – but of course Joe was stronger than a young girl, however brave.

When at last, the Five found themselves powerless, Eric roared with laughter.

'Well, kiddies, so you thought you could run rings round us, the way we're running rings round the police? You certainly didn't know who you were dealing with! You may have managed to pinch our boat the other day, but you're in our power now – you and that flea-bitten mongrel of yours!'

'Shut up, Eric!' said Joe, scowling. 'This is a rotten time for these kids to come interfering –

just as we were going to make off with our haul! I'm wondering what we'd better do with them.' He gave George a furious look, and added, 'If I had *my* way I'd wring all their necks! That lad bit me like a wild thing – and that's what he is, too.'

This time, George didn't even notice that she'd been mistaken for a boy! She was seething with anger.

'I'm only sorry I didn't manage to bite you harder!' she said. 'But mark my words, the police will catch up with you sooner or later!'

'Oh, better gag the lot of 'em, Eric!' said Joe.

While the big man gagged the children, Manuel was saying, 'I can always dispose of the dog – shall I do it?'

George was shaking all over with terror, but Joe shook his head.

'No,' he said. 'Better avoid violence if we can. The trouble is, if we leave these kids here they could starve to death. And if they don't starve to death, and they're found – well, they won't waste any time before they start off after us again. You know, it may sound funny, but I feel they're almost as dangerous to us as the police! So the only thing we can do is take them along with us!'

A car journey by night

Forcing their prisoners to go ahead of them, the gang of thieves set off along the underground passage, the way that the children had come. Manuel brought up the rear. He had stuffed poor Timmy into a sack which he was carrying over his shoulder. Timmy kicked frantically, trying to escape, but he couldn't – the sack was too tightly tied up, and he didn't have room to struggle very well.

George was still furious. Julian was horrified by the way their adventure had turned out, and Dick hadn't got over his surprise yet. Poor Anne was almost fainting with terror. Her knees felt as if they might give way any moment.

'I wonder where these ruffians are taking us?' thought George.

She was wondering, too, which way the criminals would choose to bring them all out into the open. If they had got hold of another boat somehow or other, they would most likely come out in the cave beside the sea. But if they were using a car or a van, they would go up to the clifftop road. And that was just what happened. It was hard work even for a man as strong as Eric to haul the little handcart with the chests of treasures up the slope of the underground passage to the clump of gorse bushes.

Once they were at the end of the passage, the burglars hauled the children out into the open with them. The moonlight was very bright.

'This way!' was all Joe said.

They had to follow him towards a group of trees where there were two cars waiting in the shadows.

'A good thing we brought two cars, the way all this has turned out!' muttered Manuel.

'Well, you know Joe and his premonitions!' laughed Eric. 'He's very far-sighted, is Joe! Go on, you kids, get in!' he added, giving his prisoners a push.

Julian and Dick were pushed into one car with Eric at the wheel, while George and Anne found themselves on the back seat of the other with Joe driving. The two cars set off with Joe leading the way. It was not light enough for the children to be able to see the countryside around them, and after a few miles Anne fell asleep. She was quite exhausted with weariness and crying.

Manuel, who was sitting next to Joe, turned round from time to time.

'Hullo, the little girl's dropped off to sleep,' he said, seeing that Anne had closed her eyes. Like the other men, he thought Anne was the only girl in the party, and George was a boy!

His remark gave George an idea. After a while she let her own head nod, and pretended to be falling asleep herself. Soon afterwards Manuel turned round again.

'The boy's snoring too now,' he told his companion. 'And good riddance! That one's worse than all the other three put together!'

'I shan't feel happy till we've arrived and these kids are under lock and key,' said Joe.

He didn't seem to want to continue the conversation, so Manuel stopped talking.

As carefully as possible, taking advantage of every bump in the road, George wriggled her hands around until she had one of them free. Once she had done that, she got her handkerchief out of her pocket – that wasn't easy to do without being noticed. With even more difficulty, she started trying to work the square of white cotton through the car window, which was wound half-way down, until she could throw it out on to the road.

'If I can drop it out, it will at least be some sort of clue for anyone searching for us,' she thought. 'And when we've gone a little farther I'll throw out the identity bracelet Father gave me last Christmas – and then my wallet.'

But unfortunately, Manuel didn't give George a chance to put her clever plan into action.

'You young schemer, you! Trying to leave a trail, eh? We're not having any of that, my lad!'

He had taken hold of George's wrist and was shaking her roughly. Frightened, Anne woke up with a start. Manuel watched the two girls like a hawk for the rest of the journey, and George felt angrier than ever.

At last the car ride ended, and the children were dragged out. They looked round. In the moonlight, they saw a long white building. There was no other house in sight anywhere near. Joe and his accomplices must have chosen this lonely place on purpose, so that no one would notice them coming and going.

Eric shoved the children forward.

'Hurry up and get inside! We've got no time to waste!'

He made them cross a kind of paved hall, and then ordered them to climb a staircase. On the first floor they saw another, very steep flight of steps leading to an attic, and Eric made the children climb this staircase too. Then, with Manuel's help, he took off their gags and untied them.

'Right – you can shout to your hearts' content in here, and no one will hear you!' he said. 'Sweet dreams!'

Manuel threw the sack with Timmy inside it down

at George's feet. Then the two men disappeared, closing and locking the attic door after them. George quickly set poor Timmy free.

Julian had a quick look round the attic at once.

'There doesn't seem to be any way at all to get out,' he said gloomily. 'Well, we'd better try to get some sleep, and then we'll take stock of things tomorrow.'

Quite worn out, the Five lay down on the attic floor and closed their eyes.

— 17 —

The alarm is raised

At home in Kirrin Cottage, Aunt Fanny and Uncle Quentin had no idea what risks the four children were running!

When they left in the evening, Aunt Fanny had a slight headache, so she went to bed early. Her husband, on the other hand, worked very late in the peace and quiet of his study on a very difficult experiment he was doing.

Before she went to sleep, Aunt Fanny told herself that the children were very sensible young people, and she was sure they wouldn't stay out too late. As for Uncle Quentin, he didn't even know that the Five had gone out at all!

So it was not until next morning that the scientist and his wife found the note George had left for them. Feeling surprised that the children had not come down for breakfast yet – and it was well past breakfast time! – Aunt Fanny went up to the room

which Anne shared with George. She saw at once
that the beds had not been slept in, and there was
an envelope on one of the bedspreads, placed so
that she would be sure to see it. She read the
note inside.

'Oh, Quentin!' she called. Her voice was quite
hoarse. 'Oh dear – this is terrible! Something
dreadful must have happened to the children.'

Her husband ran upstairs and found her – she
had collapsed into an armchair. She held out the
note to him in a trembling hand. 'Read that,
Quentin!'

Uncle Quentin did as she asked.

'They must be out of their minds!' he said angrily.
'Why on earth didn't they tell us? I'd have warned
the police!'

'Oh, Quentin – quick! We must do something to
help them!'

'Just keep calm, my dear. I'll see about it straight
away.'

He ran downstairs like the wind, dashed into his
study and picked up the telephone. A few moments
later, all the police in the Kirrin area had been
alerted.

It was quite a little army which set off to the
cliff-top. Uncle Quentin, who was frantic with
worry, kept urging the children's rescuers to make
haste, and it was not long before they arrived. The
weather was beautiful again today, and the sun was

shining brightly in a blue sky, just as if no one could be in any kind of trouble.

Once they had reached the cliff-top, the police took all the correct precautions for going into the underground passages to capture the gang and rescue the children. Some of the men went down to the beach to block the entrance to the cave. A coastguard vessel had been alerted too, and it was already watching the mouth of the underground river. The rest of the policemen went down into the passage which came out in the middle of the gorse bushes.

Uncle Quentin insisted on going with the rescue party.

'My daughter and my niece and nephews are inside these caves!' he told the policemen. 'I really can't be expected to wait quietly outside to see what happens!'

The police inspector in charge of the rescuers had no alternative but to agree to let Uncle Quentin come with them.

'Very well, then,' he said. 'But be sure you don't make any noise. We must take these criminals by surprise – the children's safety is at stake.'

Unfortunately, however, careful as the policemen had been, it was no use. When they and Uncle Quentin finally came out on the banks of the underground river, they did not find anyone.

The whole gang had disappeared, taking the

children with them! The police searched all the passages, exploring every nook and cranny of the underground network of caves, but they did not find anything – except the pretty ribbon Anne had worn to tie her hair back the day before, lying in one corner of the gang's cave.

Poor Uncle Quentin was in despair – and he had to go home and tell Aunt Fanny the bad news too.

— 18 —

Prisoners in the attic

Tired, worn-out and upset, the children slept surprisingly soundly on the hard boards of their prison floor until dawn.

Dick was the first to open his eyes. He looked round him, puzzled, not knowing where he was at first. Then his memory came back, and he shook the others awake.

'Come on, time to get up! Whatever we do, we *must* get out of here!'

Easier said than done!

'Let's have a really thorough look around,' suggested Julian. That didn't take long! When the four cousins inspected their attic prison they found that there were only two possible ways out – the door, which was locked, and very solid, and a skylight in the ceiling opening on to the slope of the roof.

'We're in a real mess now!' sighed Julian.

'What – what will they do to us?' stammered Anne. Her teeth were chattering with fright.

'Oh, Anne, for goodness' sake don't start weeping and wailing again!' said George. 'You know, I'm *furious* with myself for dragging you all into this adventure. It's my fault – I acted without thinking! I should have listened to Julian and been more careful.'

'You mustn't blame yourself,' Julian told her kindly. 'It was really up to me, as the eldest to stop you, so it's quite as much my fault as yours! Here, Dick – give me a leg up, old fellow! I want to try looking out of that skylight. The window in it seems to open, and I think I can get up to it with some help from you. It's lucky the ceiling is quite low, because we haven't even got a table or chair in here to stand on!'

Dick gave his brother a leg up as Julian had asked, and Julian clung to the sill of the skylight with both hands and craned his neck to see out.

'Blow!' he said. 'All I can see is fields – and they're absolutely deserted!'

As they had no idea just where they were, the children settled down to try listening for any noises inside the house, in case they could pick up clues from that. George knelt on the floor and took Timmy by the scruff of the neck.

'Listen, Tim!' she told him. 'Listen!'

The dog obediently pricked up his ears, but that was all.

'Oh dear – I don't think there's anyone here at all!' sighed George. 'The house seems to be perfectly silent. The gang must have left.'

'Perhaps this isn't their real hideout?' said Anne in a low voice. 'Perhaps they just left us here on their way to somewhere else?'

'No, I should guess this is their den all right!'

'But why have they gone off, then?' asked Anne.

'They could be taking their loot abroad to dispose of it,' suggested Julian.

'Yes, you're probably right,' George agreed.

Suddenly Timmy growled, and the children froze.

'Someone's coming!' Dick whispered.

The steps of the attic staircase creaked as footsteps came up them, and the key turned in the lock. An unfriendly-looking woman appeared in the doorway.

'Here you are,' she said in a cross voice, putting a basket down on the floor. 'Food enough to last you till tomorrow.'

And she disappeared as abruptly as she had come, locking the door again behind her. George clenched her fists.

'Oh, how stupid we are!' she cried. 'We ought all to have jumped on her at once! There are five of us – we could have overpowered her!'

The dull sound of the front door closing echoed

through the house. With Julian's help, Dick hoisted himself up to look out of the skylight this time.

'Yes, our jailer's just gone out,' he told the others. 'She's walking along the road towards a village – I can just see it in the distance.'

He slid to the ground again, scratching his head thoughtfully. 'What can we do?' he asked, baffled. 'This house seems to be empty, and here we are shut up in the attic!'

'We can only wait,' said Anne sadly. 'By now Uncle Quentin and Aunt Fanny must have found the note George left for them, and they'll go and tell the police.'

'Yes,' said Julian. 'And the police will go straight to the cave – and they won't find anyone there. A fat lot of good *that* will do us!'

'Why don't you stop talking and do something instead?' grumbled George. 'Obviously we've got to stand on our own feet – so first of all, we'd better get out of this attic.'

Her cousins stared at her as if they thought she was mad. 'But how?' they asked.

'Julian, you're good with your hands – and I've just noticed that that woman left the key in the lock. On the other side of the door, of course, but a little thing like that isn't going to stop you, is it?'

Julian let out a shout of glee.

'You're right, George, it certainly isn't! This won't be the first time I've retrieved a key with the

help of – oh, but I haven't got a sheet of newspaper!
Or a pencil either.'

'No,' said Dick, 'but look! Here's a flat piece of
cardboard, and a bit of wire.'

He had just found both objects among the odds
and ends of rubbish in one corner of the attic.
Julian did not waste any time. He knelt down by
the door and got to work. To start with, he slipped
the cardboard under the door, making sure that he
left enough of it on his side for him to be able to
pull it back again. Then he worked the wire round
in the keyhole until he had pushed the key out of the
lock. It fell on the cardboard on the other side of the
door. Now Julian should be able to pull the piece of
cardboard back inside the attic, with the key on it!

Breathless with excitement, George, Dick, Anne
– and even Timmy, who seemed to understand what
was going on – gathered round him.

Gently, the boy pulled the cardboard towards
him. It ought to have had the key on it – but
the key must have been bigger than the children
had expected, and, after all, it turned out to be too
thick to slip through the gap between the bottom of
the door and the floorboards themselves!

Julian stood up, looking rather pale and holding
the useless piece of cardboard.

'Sorry,' he said. 'No good.'

There was a dismayed silence. Dick was the first
to recover.

'Well, we're not done for yet!' he said, tapping his forehead. 'I've just had a brainwave – a brilliant, marvellous, amazing, fantastic idea, in fact, an idea worthy only of a genius like me!'

'Yes, yes, all right, you're a genius, Dick!' said George. 'But what's your idea exactly?'

'We escape over the rooftop! See?'

Julian and Anne did not reply, but George was enthusiastic.

'Wonderful!' she cried. 'You really *are* a genius after all, Dick! You're quite right, there's no other solution.'

'Here, take it easy!' said Julian. 'Do you want us all to break our necks, or what?'

'Certainly not!' said George. 'I have a very good head for heights, and I'm sure-footed too. So is Dick! You give him a leg up, Julian, and then *I'll* go up, and once we're out on the roof there must be some way we can get down to the ground. Then we'll come upstairs and let you and Anne out too.'

Dick and George insisted on trying to climb out, and Julian ended by giving in. As for Anne, she was so terrified and wanted to get away so badly that, just for once, she didn't object to the risks of Dick and George's daring plan!

Julian helped his brother and his cousin to haul themselves up through the window in the skylight and out on the roof. 'See you soon!' said George, before she disappeared.

Then she and Dick were making their way along the ridge of the roof, bent low and going almost on all fours. They took great care not to slip. One badly judged movement, and they would tumble off into space.

'George,' whispered Dick, after a few moments, 'how do you think we can get down?'

'Come on – oh, go carefully along this sloping bit! There should be a drainpipe somewhere over here!'

George was right, but it was dangerous climbing down it. If the two cousins lost their grip, it was more than likely they might break an arm or leg as they fell to the ground.

'Well, too bad!' said George under her breath. 'Whatever happens, we *must* get down!'

It took all the strength, skill and courage George and Dick could summon up to manage the risky climb down. Clinging to the drainpipe which ran to the ground from the guttering along the edge of the roof, they tried to get a series of good grips with their hands and feet, but every now and then their fingers or heels slipped, and they only just stopped themselves falling. Luckily they kept their heads the whole time.

And at last they were safe on the ground! George felt very proud of their success. Julian would have been a little too heavy and Anne quite a lot too frightened to manage the climb down as she and Dick had done! As for Timmy, the poor dog could

never have followed his little mistress down the
drainpipe.

'And now to find a way to get back into the house,
Dick!' she said.

That was easier than they might have expected.
The doors and windows were tightly closed and
locked, but there was a trapdoor into the coal
cellar, which was not fastened properly. Thanks
to this oversight, Dick and George were able to
get into the basement of the house quite easily –
and they didn't even get dirty, because it was a long
time since anyone had kept coal in the coal cellar!
Skirting the central heating boiler which stood in
the middle of the cellar, the two cousins found a
small flight of steps leading up to a door.

'I only hope this door isn't bolted on the other
side,' said George, suddenly feeling worried.

But luckily her fears were needless. The door
was only closed with a simple latch. Dick lifted
the latch, and the two children found themselves
in a huge kitchen with flagstones on the floor. The
kitchen opened straight into the front hall.

They grinned at each other. They had done it!

19

Hitching a lift

After that, George and Dick didn't waste any time.
They made for the stairs and ran up them four steps
at once.

When they reached the attic door, Dick picked
up the key from where it had fallen on the floor,
and let Julian, Anne and Timmy out.

Anne was crying with relief, Tim was barking,
and Julian clapped his brother and his cousin on
the shoulder.

'Well done indeed!' he said. 'Congratulations!
Now, we must hurry! Let's explore the house before
we escape. But we must be quick.'

It had to be a rapid inspection of the place,
because they knew they didn't have much time.
It seemed to be a big farmhouse – a very modern
one. No doubt Joe, Eric and Manuel had chosen it
because it was so isolated, and they were planning

to lie down here and wait for a chance to get out of the country.

'We saw them bring their loot out of the cave – if it's here, it must be well hidden somewhere,' said Julian thoughtfully. 'They wouldn't want to lug those chests with them everywhere they went.'

The rooms on the first floor and ground floor did not reveal anything odd. The young friends searched them, but they saw nothing suspicious. However, down in the basement a room next to the coal cellar did look promising. Its huge door was fitted with no less than three enormous brand new locks. The steel of the locks shone brightly in the dim light.

'Hm,' said George. 'Those locks look as if they were put on quite recently – and why would they be there except to lock up some kind of treasure?'

'You're right,' said Julian. 'I bet the stolen property is hidden in there for the time being, until the gang can get it out of the country!'

'Oh, do let's be quick and go and tell the police!' whispered Anne, who hated hanging around in such a dangerous place.

They went back to the coal cellar, climbed out through the trapdoor, and found themselves out in the open.

'Whew! Free at last!' said Julian happily. 'I say, it's really good to get your lungs full of fresh country air again!'

'Oh, Ju, don't stand there talking about fresh air!'

Anne begged him. 'Let's hurry! I can't wait to get well away from here. Just suppose the gang come back – or that woman!'

'Don't worry, Anne,' said Dick. 'The provisions she brought us were supposed to last till tomorrow, or so she said. That must mean she won't be back before then!'

'I'm not so sure of that,' said George. She was already setting off along the road. 'She went off on foot, didn't she? So she probably hasn't gone far. In any case, I think we should keep our eyes well open. If we see anyone suspicious coming towards us, we must get off the road and hide. I don't want to be locked up again, thank you very much!'

The children walked on in silence. They did not recognise the countryside round them at all. They were going along a minor road, and it seemed to stretch on for ever and ever. They could only just make out a church tower in the distance, to show them that the village Dick had seen from the skylight lay in that direction.

The sun was quite high in the sky now. The children were perspiring, and Timmy was panting.

'At this rate, we'll be exhausted before we get to the village!' said George. 'Why don't we hitch a lift?'

'Too risky,' Julian told her. 'Just suppose we stopped one of the thieves' cars! Anyway, there isn't a car in sight!'

As if to contradict him, they suddenly heard the sound of a car's engine.

The Five turned to look. Yes – a long, low sports car was coming in their direction. They were sure it was not a bit like the cars the thieves had been driving.

George didn't hesitate for a moment. She stood right in the middle of the road and waved her arms. The sports car came up to her, braked and stopped. There was a young man at the wheel.

'Hullo there, kids!' he said cheerfully. 'What's up? Missed your bus?'

'No, sir,' said Julian politely, stepping forward. 'Something much more serious. Could you possibly give us a lift to the nearest village? We must go to a police station.'

'A police station?' said the driver in surprise. 'All right! So long as you're not running away from home, or anything like that!'

On the way, the children quickly explained what it was all about. Their new friend was very interested, and he went to the police station with them to tell the police just where he had met them, so as to back up their statement.

The quiet little country police station had never known such excitement before!

Of course Uncle Quentin and the Kirrin police had made sure that a nation-wide alert had gone out for the missing children, so the policemen here knew

all about the Five and the gang of thieves. The first
thing they did was to telephone Kirrin police station,
so that George's parents could have their minds set
at rest as soon as possible.

Then, after sending for some reinforcements to
come quickly, they organised an expedition to go
and trap the gang.

'We shall need you to come along and show us
just where the farmhouse is, so that we can surround
it,' the inspector in charge of the party of policemen
told the children. Of course, they were delighted
to help.

Soon they were all ready to leave. Patrick Bartlett,
the young man with the sports car who had been
so helpful to the Five, asked if he could join the
expedition too.

'And if you like,' he suggested to the inspector,
'I could give these young people a lift in my car
again. That would leave you more room for your
own men.'

The inspector was happy to accept this kind offer.
'Thank you very much, sir!' he said.

George and her cousins couldn't have asked for
anything better than another ride in their new
friend's beautiful car. Timmy curled up as small
as he could at George's feet. He had made it very
clear that he had no intention of staying behind!
So the white sports car started off, with three
police cars following it. It was very important for

them to reach the farm before the gang and their woman accomplice got back, so as to set a police trap for them.

20

Sir Donald to the rescue!

Everything went smoothly. The children showed the policemen the house where they had been kept prisoner, and the inspector and two of his men made sure that no one had returned there since the children left. Then he gave orders for the police cars to be hidden behind a big farm building. Finally, he stationed half of his men outside the house, hidden in the shelter of trees and bushes.

'And now for us!' he told the children. 'We'd better get inside quickly. I sent an expert to pick the lock of the front door as soon as we arrived. You young people are to go up to the first floor with Mr Bartlett here – you'll be quite safe there. The rest of us will set the trap for those villains indoors. So come along! We'll close the front door behind us, so that it will look as if nothing's wrong.'

Soon the Five and Patrick, up on the first-floor landing, were peering with interest through the bars

of the banisters. None of the people inside the house
moved.

'There are policemen posted all round the hall,
ready to jump out when the gang come through the
door!' Julian whispered.

'*I* think this is silly!' Anne whispered back. 'I
mean, Eric and the others may easily not come back
here till tomorrow – or even later!'

'Yes, but that woman will be back before then!'
said George. 'She left the house on foot, remember,
and without any luggage. So as I said before, she
can't have gone very far. The police will be counting
on that.'

'Sssh!' said Patrick quietly. 'Listen!'

Down below, the silence in the hall had just been
broken by one of the policemen. 'Watch out, sir!'
he said to the inspector, in a low voice. 'I can see a
woman coming along the road. Yes – she's coming
this way sure enough!'

The inspector hurried to join the policeman, who
was on watch with a pair of binoculars at a window
beside the front door. He passed the binoculars to
the inspector.

'See for yourself, sir!'

The inspector raised the binoculars and looked
out of the window. He smiled. Then he beckoned
to George, who ran downstairs.

'Here!' he told her. 'You have a look, Miss Kirrin,
and tell me if you recognise her.'

'Yes!' said George. 'Oh, yes – that's the woman who was acting as our jailer!'

'Right – you nip back upstairs to the others, then, and whatever you do, keep quiet and don't move. She'll be here in a minute or so.'

George did as the inspector said, and the Five waited, pressed close together, their hearts beating fast, to see what would happen next.

Feeling rather worried, Anne squeezed her big brother's arm. 'Julian, I'm frightened!' she whispered.

'Sssh, Anne! Keep quiet!'

'What's going to happen?'

'The police will arrest that woman, that's all. She's an accomplice of the gang who burgled all those stately homes, so she jolly well deserves what she gets!'

Up on the landing, the children stopped whispering, and down below in the hall the police stood absolutely still and quiet, ready to spring.

In the silence, they heard footsteps approaching outside. A key was turned in the lock, and from where they were standing the children saw the door open. Golden sunlight flooded in on the paved floor.

Not suspecting anything, the woman who had visited the Five in their attic prison came in.

Then everything happened very fast. Two police-men emerged from the shadows in the hall, took hold of the woman's arms and overpowered her, although she struggled with them.

'Who are you? What do you want?' she shouted.

'I'd have thought you could tell who we are from our uniforms, ma'am,' said one of the policemen. 'As for what we want – we want to know who *you* are!'

'I'm not saying anything!' yelped the woman furiously. 'Not a word! You have no right to do this!'

'Oh, so you don't think we have any right to do it?' said the inspector, coming out of hiding and walking up to her. 'Be careful what you say, ma'am! I should warn you that it may be taken down and used in evidence against you. I'm arresting you for aiding and abetting the gang that burgled Riddington Hall and a number of other stately homes in the neighbourhood of Kirrin. For all I know, you may be an active member of the gang yourself.'

'I don't know what you're talking about!' cried the woman. 'I deny everything!'

'Including keeping these children prisoners in your attic?' asked the inspector, pointing to the Five on the first-floor landing.

The woman looked up and glared at the children, full of hatred. Then she said, shrugging her shoulders, 'I don't even know who they are!'

'Witnesses for the prosecution, ma'am – that's who they are!'

At that moment they all heard a car's engine in

the distance. The policeman with the binoculars, who had taken up his post at the window again, told the inspector, 'There's a car coming now, sir, with three men in it. One tall fair man, and a couple of smaller dark men, one of them with a beard.'

'That's them!' cried George. 'Those are the men who kidnapped us!'

'We'll be asking you and your cousins to identify them officially in a minute, Miss Kirrin. Just stay up there a little longer! As for you, ma'am – not a word out of you to warn your accomplices, or you'll be sorry!'

Down in the hall, the inspector drew the woman into the background. There was silence again, and the children and Patrick waited with bated breath. The showdown was coming any moment now! Would everything work out the way they hoped?

They heard the car stop quite close to the house, and then Eric's loud voice.

'Hullo there, Miriam!' he called. 'Are you in? We've got news! We shall be off tomorrow!'

As he spoke, Eric pushed the door open – and the woman called Miriam suddenly wrenched herself free of the inspector and shouted, 'Watch out, Eric! Run for it! The police are on to us!'

There was a moment's silence, and then the men could be heard running away from the front door. The inspector, looking furious, raised a whistle to his lips. He blew it – the sound was intended to give warning to the policemen stationed outside the house. But by the time they had come round to the front door the gang could easily have made their getaway, so the inspector and the men inside the house gave chase themselves.

The Five and Patrick were already on their way downstairs, and they ran out of the doorway too.

They stopped dead for a moment at the sight before them! The three criminals were running towards their car, parked among the trees a little way off. And George immediately realised that they were going to escape their pursuers – the police cars were still round at the other side of the house, hidden by the farm building.

She did not hesitate for a moment.

'Go on, Timmy – get them! Good dog! *Bite* them, Tim!'

Timmy didn't wait to be told twice. In three bounds, he was after the men.

Eric heard him coming and turned round, raising an arm to defend himself – just in time to protect his throat. Timmy's jaws had been about to close on it!

'Clear off – get away, will you!' yelled Eric, making faces and trying to get his arm away from the dog. Timmy was holding it in a firm and painful grip. And Timmy was not going to let him go! In a moment the police arrived.

As soon as they had arrested Eric and taken him

into custody, Timmy lost interest in the man, and raced off after the other two criminals. He had a particular grudge against Manuel, for tying him up in that sack!

When Manuel turned round to see the dog's threatening jaws and gleaming eyes so close to him, he felt so terrified that Timmy had no trouble at all in overpowering him. As the dog jumped at him, Manuel fainted with terror and fell flat on the ground.

That meant there was only Joe left. Joe had actually reached the car – he wasn't stopping to bother about his companions. He jumped into the driving seat. The engine was still warm. It started at once, and the car moved away.

The policemen gave exclamations of annoyance. Patrick, Julian, Dick and Anne were watching in dismay – but George wasn't beaten yet!

'Go on, Timmy, get him!' she shouted to her dog.

Timmy had almost reached the car when it drove past him, and he might have given up the attempt but for that last shout from his little mistress. Her voice spurred him on to make a final effort!

Suddenly he gathered speed, and with one powerful spring he leaped right into the car. It was not going very fast yet, and Joe had been in such a hurry to start off that he had not closed the door. He had to let go of the steering wheel to defend himself from the dog. Then everything seemed to happen all at once. Out of control, the car crashed into a tree! Joe staggered out, half stunned, and still struggling with brave old Timmy. The inspector and his men arrived on the scene, rather breathless, and now all they had to do was arrest Joe, the gang-leader. He didn't seem to be in very good shape when Timmy left the police to deal with him!

A few moments later, the inspector was looking at Eric, Joe, Manuel and Miriam with satisfaction. They cut a sorry figure in handcuffs!

'Well now,' he said, after congratulating George warmly and patting Timmy, 'well now, my young friends, I'm going to take you back to the village. I should think your father will have arrived to collect you by now, Georgina. But first we'll just have a little look at this den of thieves!'

The children had been quite right. The three stout locks on the cellar door didn't stand up to the policemen for long, and when they had broken down the door and explored the room beyond it, they found all the valuables stolen from the stately homes near Kirrin by Joe and his gang.

'And here are Sir Donald's gold watches, too!' said George happily. 'How pleased he'll be to get them back!'

A little later, after saying goodbye to Patrick Bartlett, the Five and the police – and their prisoners too, of course – got back to the village and the police station. Uncle Quentin, who had just arrived, looked very angry when he saw the children.

'Well, if you're expecting praise from *me*, you're in for a disappointment!' he said. 'Your mother was quite ill with worry over your escapade, Georgina. As for you, Julian – you're the eldest, I should have expected you to show a little more sense! I shall find it very hard to forgive you for the fright you gave your poor Aunt Fanny.'

The children looked very upset – and it was no good for the inspector, who was surprised to find that Uncle Quentin could be so stern, to try calming him down. Uncle Quentin refused to listen.

'You will be punished,' he told the children as he drove them home to Kirrin Cottage in his car. 'To begin with, I'm confiscating your new bicycles – the Kirrin police brought them home. As for Timothy, he'll have to stay chained up in his kennel until the end of the holidays. And it's no good trying to argue with me!'

By the time two days had passed, George and her cousins were beginning to think they'd never spent such miserable holidays before! They were kicking their heels at Kirrin Cottage, without being able to go out for expeditions on their bikes. They were so bored they didn't even have the heart to play games. George absolutely refused to leave Timmy's side, and Julian, Dick and Anne kept her company by his kennel.

'It just isn't fair!' sighed Dick. 'It's all thanks to us that the gang's behind bars, and the stately homes have their treasures back – Sir Donald Riddington's got his gold watches back too!'

'Speaking of Sir Donald,' said Anne, looking at the front gate, 'here he is at this very moment!'

And it *was* Sir Donald, looking happy and ten years younger! He had heard, from the inspector who arrested the gang, that his 'young heroes', as he called them, were in trouble, and so he had come to try and pay his debt of gratitude.

How did he manage to soften Uncle Quentin's heart and persuade him to let the children off their punishments? Well, no one knew for certain! But after talking to George's parents, he appeared out in the garden again, smiling broadly and carrying the key of the shed where Uncle Quentin had locked up the new bikes.

He showed it to the children. 'There – now you can take that dog off his chain, and off you all go for a nice ride!' he said.

They were delighted! George jumped up and kissed him. 'Thank you – oh, thank you!' she cried happily.

'Well, well, my dear,' he said, smiling, 'it seems to me that if anyone should be saying "thank you", it's me! So I *will* say "thank you", with all my heart,

my dear young friends. And thank *you*, too, Timmy
– what a fine dog you are!'

And very gravely, Sir Donald shook paws with
Timmy.

If you liked this book by Claude Voilier, you are certain to enjoy the original Famous Five stories by Enid Blyton. These are published by Hodder Children's Books: